When Things are Alive They Hum

HANNAH BENT

ultimo press

Author's note: *Marlowe's 'discovery' relating to the conservation of the* Phengaris arion *butterfly* (Maculinea arion) *is based on the work of J.A. Thomas and D.J. Simcox.*

Published in 2021 by Ultimo Press,
an imprint of Hardie Grant Publishing

Ultimo Press	Ultimo Press (London)
Gadigal Country	5th & 6th Floors
7, 45 Jones Street	52–54 Southwark Street
Ultimo, NSW 2007	London SE1 1UN
ultimopress.com.au	

 A catalogue record for this work is available from the National Library of Australia

NATIONAL LIBRARY OF AUSTRALIA

When Things are Alive They Hum
ISBN 978 1 76115 008 1 (paperback)

10 9 8 7 6 5 4 3 2

Cover and text design
Alissa Dinallo | Typeset in 11.5/17 pt Fairfield LT Std Light
Typesetting
Kirby Jones
Copyeditor
Ali Lavau
Proofreader
Pamela Dunne

Printed in Australia by Griffin Press, part of Ovato, an Accredited ISO AS/NZS 14001 Environmental Management System printer.

 The paper this book is printed on is certified against the Forest Stewardship Council® Standards. Griffin Press holds FSC® chain of custody certification SGS-COC-005088. FSC® promotes environmentally responsible, socially beneficial and economically viable management of the world's forests.

Ultimo Press acknowledges the Traditional Owners of the country on which we work, the Gadigal people of the Eora nation and the Wurundjeri people of the Kulin nation, and recognises their continuing connection to the land, waters and culture. We pay our respects to their Elders past, present and emerging.

For Camilla

Part One

Harper

When things are alive, they hum. You can hear it if you put your ear to the chest of an animal or if you lean close close close to a plant. My own hum goes dum dum da da dum da dum. This is the sound of my heart talking to me. I hear it best when I am in my favourite place: on the landing at the top of the stairs, where it is quiet and the wood feels smooth under my feet. My toenails sparkle with glitter nail polish, the same colour that my Marlowe used to paint on for me.

I look up and out, through the windows and over my dad's garden, which is on top of a cliff that touches the wide sea. The water is black from the night and the moon is orange and furry and full. In the glow of its strange light, I see birds flying low and slow.

The birds are fighting the wind.

Marlowe

We were naked in bed, breath still hot and fluttering, when the doorbell rang. It was only eight in the morning – no one ever rang at this hour. Before Olly even stirred, I rose, slipped on my robe and hurried down the stairs.

'Morning, love.' At the front door of our Battersea home, a courier was holding a bright yellow DHL package marked *Urgent*. Inside the waterproof wrapping was an all-too-familiar homemade envelope, addressed:

> For my sister Marlowe明月Míng Yuè Eve from your sister
> Harper明华Míng Huà Eve
> Number 23 Battersea Brije Road, SW11
> In the United Kingdom. My dad is from the United Kingdom.

Usually the letters arrived by standard post; why had this one been sent by courier? Shivering in the chill morning air, I tore open the envelope.

> This is the 24th January in the year 2000
> To Marlowe,
> It has been 11 months and 2 days sinse you visited us at home and 3 hole years sinse you left home for your bugs university.

How are you? I am not fine.

To tell you the truth I am upset rite now. Yesterday I went back to the hospital with a sore chest again. My hart is brocken. Not like in Romeo and Juliet becos I have my boyfrend Louis, do you remember him? My hart wont work properley even tho I am in love. I am not scared becos I know the doctors will fix me. They always fix me. The only thing that is strange in my hart and mind is that I do not understand why the doctors sent me home at the end of the day. Before wen I was sick I stayed overnite in the hospital until I was better. Remember?

This time, the hospital was a bit boring. I herd the nurses at the foot of my bed taking about the Down syndrome thing. Their words were stranje in my hed so I said HEY IT IS CALLED UP SYNDROME and that they were not as lucky as me to have the up syndrome but sometimes life is not fare. Then they looked at me and did not say anything so I asked them to get me a coke.

Marlowe I would like you to come home now pleese. 外婆Wài Pó and Dad said to wate before I call you becos we are going to speek to another doctor tomorow and he will sort me out. 外婆Wài Pó said it is good not to bother you rite now becos you are at the bugs university and that is very important. But I desided by myself to tell you to come home becos you fix things. You are very clever.

Yesterday Louis said he cod make this leter reech your hands like a speedy gonzaleez using the DHL sistem of posting mail.

If you come home to Hong Kong I promis to share my speshel things with you like my 3 mars bars and my personel packet of malteezers given to me by Louis with love. But pleese do not tell stepmonster about this becos it is personel private information between you and me.

Shakespere knows all about the love and I love you.

From your sister Harper明华Míng Huà Eve.

I reread it once, twice, the skin on my back prickling, then I shut the front door and climbed the stairs.

Inhale, exhale.

Dad had called a few days earlier to let me know Harper was sick, that her heart was playing up again, but I didn't think much of it; he called even when she had a minor cold.

Don't worry, Dad, she'll be okay. She's had this her whole life and she always pulls through.

In calming his fears, I'd reassure myself. I found his calls irritating because they tended to stoke my own anxiety. After Mum died I'd assumed the role of Harper's carer, but I had to remind myself that I *wasn't* her mother. For the first time, I had my own life.

'My own life.' I said it aloud, but with a twinge of guilt, aware that I had a healthy body and opportunities that my sister didn't have. How was it fair that things came easily to me and not to her? How was it fair that I had a strong, healthy, beating heart when hers was fragile and flawed? 'My own life,' I repeated, cringing at how selfish that sounded. And I was selfish. It had been almost a year since I'd visited home. I hadn't even returned for Christmas. But only one more month to go and my PhD would be complete. I could visit Harper then. And she would be fine in the interim. Despite her frequent trips to hospital to treat the myriad problems associated with her congenital heart disorder, she always recovered. And, I reminded myself, Harper wasn't alone – she had Dad, Wài Pó and, of course, Louis.

I folded the letter, slipped it into the pocket of my robe and headed back to bed. There was nothing to worry about.

Blood – it tasted rusty and sweet on the tip of my tongue. Damn, I must have been biting my lip again. I detoured into the bathroom and checked it in the mirror. Sure enough, it had begun to bleed. I applied pressure to it with my sleeve and I stared at myself for a moment. Strands of hair the colour of wet soil brushed my forehead. Mum's large eyes were lit with Dad's blue irises. I ran my fingertips over my pale skin, following the angular lines of my cheekbones – also just like my mother's. Now, more than ever, I longed for her. I briefly touched the gold locket at my neck, then made my way back to the warmth of our bedroom.

Olly was standing by the window, sandy curls tumbling over his forehead as he spoke tenderly to his cupped palms. Peering over his shoulder, I saw he was holding a seven-spotted ladybird.

'What are you doing here, little one?' I asked. At this time of year, the insect should be hibernating somewhere warm, somewhere safe.

'There's an old matchbox in my bedside table,' Olly murmured.

I poked several holes in the lid of the box with the nib of an old pen, then using one of my fine make-up brushes, I watched as Olly coaxed the creature from his palm.

'Let's put him over there.' I pointed to a dark corner of my dressing table, next to a photo of Harper and me when we were small. Dressed in matching light blue dresses, we stood under a banyan tree in Dad's garden.

'Who was at the door?' Olly asked. He put the matchbox down and looked at me.

'DHL. A letter from Harper.'

He frowned. 'DHL? What's the urgency?'

My stomach did a somersault. *Urgency.*

'She's sick again.' Why was I denying it? Something wasn't right.

I made for the phone in the hallway. Using my international calling card, I dialled home. Wài Pó answered.

'Míng Yuè!' I loved my grandmother's voice; although it seemed somewhat tired, she always sounded so elegant, regal even. Her words floated in the air for a second or two after they had been spoken. '*Nǐ hǎo ma?* Keeping warm in London, I hope?' Although she was born and raised in Shanghai, traces of her early British boarding school years had left their mark.

'I'm fine, Wài Pó.' As always, I replied in English. In the sixteen years since Mum died, I had refused to speak in her mother tongue. 'You okay?'

She described the weather in Hong Kong and then began to recount the latest dish she'd cooked for her mahjong ladies. In the background, I could hear sounds of the kitchen; dishes clanging in the sink, the steady drone of the exhaust fan and Wài Pó's Chinese opera on low. I pictured her sitting on a stool by the kitchen phone, the front window open allowing fresh sea air to waft in. Suddenly, I felt an unusual longing for our Clearwater Bay home.

'How's Harper *mèi mei?*'

There was a pause. Wài Pó cleared her throat. 'There's no need to worry.' I could hear the crinkle of a candy wrapper, followed by the smack of her lips as she sucked hard. 'You have an exam soon, yes?' She was trying to change the subject.

'It's not really an exam; it's called a thesis defence and it'll take place in a month. I just received a letter from Harper. She said she went to hospital.'

The sound of Wài Pó's hand smacking against what I presumed was her thigh.

Long exhale. 'She told you.'

'Dad called a few days ago to tell me she wasn't well.'

'There's no need to worry. She's just had a few issues with her heart. But she's okay.'

'Is she in the hospital again?'

The sound of hard candy cracking into pieces against a gold filling.

'Wài Pó?'

'Míng Huà is back home. She's sleeping now. No need to worry. *Jiā jiā yǒu běn nán niàn de jīng.' Each family has its own difficult scripture to recite.* 'You must study hard now. Your *mèi mei* has Louis by her side, looking after her.'

She was right. It was largely thanks to Louis that I felt I could leave Harper to come study in London. She was happy, and with that came a stretch of reasonably good health.

'How is Oliver?' Wài Pó asked. 'When can we meet him?'

'Soon,' I lied.

'You'll bring him to Hong Kong when you next visit?'

'Sure.' I had no intention of taking Olly to Hong Kong yet. Although I wanted to introduce him to Harper and Wài Pó, I also liked the fact that he was separate from them all, untouched by my family and their many needs.

'I'll call again soon,' I told her.

'Look after yourself. Study hard for your exam.'

Just one month to go, I reminded myself. Just one month.

'Yes, Wài Pó, I'll study hard.' I heard the crinkle of another candy wrapper. 'I promise.'

◆

'Hey,' Olly said, 'come back.' He was staring intently at me across the kitchen table. I had been replaying the conversation with Wài Pó in my mind, unable to shake the creeping sense of unease that tightened the muscles in my neck.

'You okay?' He reached over to take my hand. Despite the cold, his hand was always warm. 'How about I make you some eggs?'

There was still time. Olly didn't have to be in the lab until 10 am and my meeting with Professor Lipin was an hour after that. I nodded.

Olly sang when he cooked and it was the same song every time he made eggs: Van Morrison's 'Into the Mystic'. Hand in pocket, I touched the letter again, reminding myself yet again that Harper was hospitalised every few months. This time was no different.

I was distracted by a tickle on my leg. One of our little phasmids had escaped from its cage by the pantry. I leaned down, picked it up by the thorax and placed it back in its manmade home. I vowed not to think about Harper for the rest of the morning and instead focused on Olly, who was snipping leaves of basil, parsley and thyme from the pots under the kitchen windows. He was better at caring for nature than me. Everything he touched seemed to bloom.

He transferred the herbs to the chopping board, guiding his knife over them with the same precision he applied to his work in the lab, where he was studying the reproductive cycle of the large blue butterfly, *Maculinea arion*.

Crack, whisk, the splatter of eggs in an oiled pan, and then, with a kiss on my forehead, the omelette was on the table in front of me.

As I picked up my fork, he said, 'I have something for you.' He went to his backpack by the door.

My heart raced, scared he was going to remove a ring box. In the three years we had been together, he'd told me many times he wanted to marry me. When he produced a piece of paper instead of a ring, I felt relief wash over me.

'Read this.' He handed me an information sheet about the Royal Zoological Award. 'You'd make an excellent candidate.'

I swallowed a large mouthful of egg in one go, trying to quell the shiver in my belly. No. No. No. I could feel heat rise to my cheeks, my breath uneven. I resisted the urge to spring from my seat.

'Why are you showing me this?' I asked.

'A while back, a few of us decided to recommend you. The application has been sent.'

'What?' I clenched my sweaty palms into fists. How could he do this behind my back? 'Why didn't you ask me first?' I slid the paper back across the table.

He sighed and shook his head. Even when I knew he was irritated, he looked calm. If he were a tree, he would be an old pine, with a tall, sturdy trunk and roots that reached deep into the ground.

'Marls, you're one of the most promising PhD candidates the university has. Your research on the symbiotic relationship between the *arion* larvae and the populations of the *sabuleti* will significantly aid the conservation practices of the butterfly.' He gripped the side of the table and took a breath. 'You've got everything you need to win. You've done the hard work, your research is solid. You've got the brains, the dedication. You know as well as I do what winning this award could do for your career. Think of all the doors it could open for you.'

'You're right.' Still, I could feel heat intensifying in my cheeks at the thought of it. Attention made me uncomfortable, whether it was my supervisor praising me or socialising with a room full of people. I felt most at ease alone in the lab, looking down the lens of a microscope, observing rather than being observed.

My fidgeting hands refused to still. 'I know.'

'You know?'

I hadn't meant to sound arrogant. 'I didn't mean –'

'It's okay,' he interrupted. 'I just realised…' He rubbed his face with his hands. 'I've had this all wrong,' he said, more to himself than to me. 'You're not scared you won't win, are you? You're scared that you will.'

I wanted to crawl out of my skin.

'You don't want the attention, do you?'

To avoid answering, I swallowed the last of the omelette. 'Don't you have to leave soon?'

'I'm sorry.' He squeezed my arm as I brushed past him, carrying my plate to the sink. 'Forget I said anything. I'll go get ready.'

Suddenly I was alone in the kitchen, listening to the sound of water shuddering through the creaky pipes in our walls. For a rare moment, there were no eyes on me, no demands, no expectations. It was just me and a few dirty dishes in a warm room that smelled like basil. I washed our plates, put the eggshells into the compost, watered the plants and refilled the bird feeder outside the window. Then I looked around for another task, something to occupy my mind, dispel the unease that lingered in me.

I wandered over to peer into the phasmids' leafy cage. Anxiety was such a useless emotion. The fight-and-flight response had value if one was facing danger, but in that moment there was no danger. Everything was under control. Yet still I had this craving to be held, soothed. I wanted to run upstairs and fling myself into Olly's arms. How pathetic, I scolded myself. I wasn't the dependent type. I could handle things alone, just as I had been doing since Mum died. And then I saw our oldest *Carausius morosus*, affectionately named Lesley when we'd brought her home two years ago. She was on a twig on the right-hand side of the cage. I moved closer and gasped. Half her skin had shed but the rest was stuck, abdomen fixed to a branch. Her tarsi were dry and shrivelled. How could I have let this happen? With a toothpick, I gently tried to pry her free, but it was too late. She was limp, lifeless. I stroked her thorax to make sure she wasn't playing dead. She remained motionless. Those damn heaters; it must have been too dry for her. A careless, careless mistake.

Dropping the toothpick to the ground, I ran up the stairs, calling Olly's name. He was in the bathroom, towelling himself. Lacing my arms around his bare chest, I breathed him in. His scent reminded me of grass and fresh air. And, for a moment, I was at peace.

Harper

Today is a Tuesday, which means it is 'popcorn and romantic movie night', but my dad says I cannot go because I am too sick. To be honest, I'm a little upset about this. I am in a new hospital, and the doctors are very friendly, but I don't really feel okay about missing tonight. I don't like skipping things that are written in my diary. But I am practising some deep breathing skills that Wài Pó has taught me. This is helping my mind to relax. Another thing helping me to relax is that I have Louis, the love of my heart, by my side.

He is always so smartly dressed. Today he is wearing a navy suit with a pink shirt. He has a few watches on his arm because he loves telling the time, and when he looks down at them, his syrupy hair falls over his face. Even though he needs a haircut, he is one of the most handsome men I have ever met.

He brought me a gift today: a packet of coloured glass beads which he is helping me make into a necklace. As we do this, we are half listening to Dad and Wài Pó, who are talking in hushed voices to the doctors outside my bed curtain.

'You have a beautiful neck,' Louis says, 'and these beads will make you look like a princess.'

He tries so hard to put the thread into the hole of each bead, but keeps missing.

In – out – miss, in – out – miss. In – almost in – miss.

I wish I could help him but I can't because I have too many wires and drips and things stuck to me. Louis frowns as he threads, then sighs loudly and dumps his hands onto his lap, shaking his head. He missed another bead. Poor Louis. He is not enjoying this. I will ask Wài Pó to finish the necklace for him.

I can hear the hard sound of Irene's high heels against the floor as she comes into the room. She's always late.

'Hello, I'm Irene. It's a pleasure to meet you.' Her accent is always so posh when she is talking to new people. I hear the doctor say hello back. He doesn't know yet that she's a stepmonster.

They start talking again for a while at a low mumble, mumble, mumble, then Dad's voice becomes louder.

'We've already been to another hospital!'

Louis, fingering the beads on his lap, moves his head to the side and listens. He is frowning.

'Why can't you help us?' Dad asks.

Louis looks at me. 'Why do you have to keep changing hospitals?'

That is a good question and I try to think in my mind for a good answer.

'Dad said the doctors at the last hospital were useless and something called dis-crim-in-a-tory. That's why.'

'What does dis-crim-in-a-tory mean?'

Last night, I had used a dictionary to look this word up. *Discrimination: Showing an unfair or prejudicial distinction between different categories of people or things, especially on the grounds of race, age or sex.* That was a lot of new information in my head that I didn't understand. I needed more time to figure it out with the help of an internet search engine and my speech therapist, Mrs Green. But I didn't tell Louis this. I told him it meant anger towards doctors.

I knew this because when Dad spoke, I could tell he was growing a fire in his heart. He spat his words out and I knew there would be red in his cheeks. I thought he was being a bit unfair. Doctors always try to do their best. They always have with me, ever since I was small.

Suddenly, Dad's voice grew even louder. 'I don't understand why you won't put her on the transplant list.'

Transplant. I have not looked up this word in the dictionary yet but they said it in the last hospital too.

I cannot hear what the doctors are saying back to my dad; their voices are too small and quiet.

'If my daughter didn't have Down syndrome, I'm sure you would be giving her the chance she needs to survive.'

'Um, excuse me, it's called *Up* syndrome.' I speak in a loud way but no one pays attention.

'This is utter discrimination.'

That word again. I can feel Dad's heat. It is all over the room, making me feel breathless.

'James, please calm down.' My stepmonster's voice is cool, so cool.

Why does she get to speak and be listened to, but I don't? They are always talking about me, but I am never included.

'Hello!' I call from my side of the curtain. 'Hello!'

Louis joins in. 'Hello, everyone, Harper is calling you.'

'Keep your voice down,' I hear Stepmonster say to my dad. 'She'll only get sicker if she's distressed.'

Wài Pó slides through the gap in the curtain. She takes my hand and pats it. 'No need to worry, Míng Huà. The doctors are trying to make you better.' She looks sideways with her eyes at the gap in the curtain. Everyone's voices are quiet again.

'I don't like this talking behind my back one bit,' I tell Wài Pó. She takes a hawthorn candy from her pocket and offers it to me.

'Not hungry.'

She goes to Louis and takes the beads from his lap. 'So beautiful!' She sits beside him and starts threading. In and out, Wài Pó's quick fingers move between each bead. And then she starts singing; it is a Chinese song my mum used to sing for me. In my heart and in my mind I say, 'Hello, Mum.' I feel her with me.

We stay like this together – invisible Mum, me, Louis and Wài Pó – until the necklace is finished. Wài Pó holds it up to the light in the ceiling. It shines in the colours yellow, red, orange, green, purple and blue. This is a beautiful thing.

Dad pulls open the curtain so hard it makes a sharp scratching noise against the railings. His face is red, just like I knew it would be. Irene is behind him, searching for something in her bag. Her face isn't red like Dad's, but her red lips, red nails and red dress pop against the white walls of the hospital. She pulls out her car keys.

'I'll meet you in the car park,' she tells Dad, then goes clip clop clip clop down the corridor.

Dad faces me. 'Darling, we need to get another opinion from a different doctor again.'

I don't understand what this means.

'We just need to find you a doctor who will help. Don't worry – I'm sure there is one out there.'

I thought the doctors *were* helping me. But before I can say this, he is already talking to Wài Pó, telling her to pack up my things.

'Irene is getting the car. I'm going to settle the bill.'

He's off in a flash, stamping his feet as he goes.

A nurse enters. She walks over to me and takes off all the coloured wires on my chest. These wires measure my hum in a way that doctors can understand. I ask her why she is removing the wires. She says I am going home. This is confusing, because my chest is still sore, I am still out of breath, I have a terrible cough and my body is cold and puffy.

'Don't the doctors need to wait until I am better?' I ask. That is what usually happens. The doctors don't send me home until I am better and can walk without feeling like I am losing air.

The nurse looks away and tells me not to worry. Then Wài Pó talks to me in Chinese and tells me not to worry. But instead, I start to feel the panic in my chest.

'Don't worry,' she repeats. 'We will find a doctor to help you.' She is speaking in the English language now so Louis can understand and be calm in his heart too. But I think that is what Dad said, too, and it still doesn't make sense. I study her face for more clues but she won't look me in the eye.

'Louis.' I reach my hand out to have him hold it. 'I don't understand.'

Louis hops from side to side, which means he is nervous. I don't like it when he is nervous. It is not good if both of us feel bad, though, so I take a deep breath and say, 'Will you put my beautiful necklace on me?'

He stops moving and smiles. 'Of course, my beauty. Of course I will.'

—✦—

To be honest, I like it better at home than in the hospital, because even though my Marlowe is not with us in our big white house, I still feel her here.

Every day, when I walk past her room, I say, 'Hello to you, my Marlowe.' I wonder if she can hear me from far away. I think in my mind about the letter I wrote her, and all the other ones I have written since she has been gone.

'Writing a message to someone by hand is a special thing.' That's what Dad says and I agree. He also writes letters, though I don't think he sends them. But that's okay.

I think to myself that when you open a letter that has been made by hand with a pen and paper, you can feel and touch the mark of another person. You can see their moods in the shape of their words, and sometimes you can find their smell caught between the ink and the paper.

Oh, I do wish my Marlowe would come home soon.

I am back in my bedroom with its happy yellow walls. I am not thinking about missing popcorn and romantic movie night, or that Louis went without me. I know he didn't mean to make me feel sad, it's just that he finds it even harder than I do not to stick to the schedules that are written in our diaries. And anyway, I feel okay because I am doing something special. I am sitting with all my things that are in the in-between. I am trying to help them find their way again. But you can't force them; all you can do is try your best. This is something Marlowe did in her room when we were small. She was good at saving things.

By my window, I have the calamansi plant that forgot how to give fruit. It became sick and black in the roots. There is also the gecko that lost its tail by accident of the French doors closing on it. Last of all is the little duckling. I found her by the Silverstrand Mart in Clearwater Bay. The duckling must have lost her mother, so I put her in my pocket and gave warm love. Then I made a shoebox bed with some dried flowers. The first day this little duckling did not move much because I forgot to feed her and also because I think she may have missed her mum. But now this little duckling has a good, strong hum and is quack quack quacking away.

Today I give the duckling a name. It is Méi Lì. This is the same name my Wài Pó has. I sing to Méi Lì, just like when I was in the hospital and Wài Pó sang for me.

Marlowe

My grandpa was forty something in the photograph, standing on a rock, holding a butterfly net. His gaze rested beyond the frame. He had probably seen a *Papilio machaon* hovering by a purple coneflower. The photo was clipped from an obituary in the 1994 issue of the Lepidopterists' Society journal, stuck with blu-tack to the inside cover of my notebook. The caption read: *Arthur Marlow Eve, 1969. Norfolk Broads, United Kingdom.*

'I miss you, Grandpa,' I said to the photo.

The house was quiet. Olly had left, and I was sitting in the living room, reviewing my notes before heading into uni for a meeting with Professor Lipin, rereading the words I knew so well, trying to formulate a compelling way to eventually present this to my thesis panel.

The Conservation and Natural History of the *Maculinea arion*, Britain's Previously Extinct Species.

Factors involved in the decline of the *Maculinea arion...*
Since the 1979 United Kingdom extinction of *M. arion.*
Thomas. J.A. and Simcox. D.J.'s research on the symbiotic relationship between the *M. arion* caterpillar and the *Myrmica sabuleti* brought the species back from the dead and changed

conservation practices forever. *M. arion*'s social parasitisation of *M. sabuleti* occurs through a complex system of chemical mimicry and olfactory deception. Once the adult *M. sabuleti* has been deceived into caring for the *M. arion* grub, it will feed off the ant larvae...

I paused at a photo I had taken of a specimen, pinned. The small, blue butterfly was stunning. The insides of its dusty, metallic wings refracted the light in different shades of blue and silver. I thought of aspects of the *arion* grub's cannibalistic and predatory behaviour. How could something so beautiful be born from such a violent process? I looked at the image next to it. With a zoom lens, I had captured a cluster of hardened scales on the insect's left wing. They looked like a collection of iridescent blue snowflakes.

The sound of the phone ringing startled me. I uncurled myself from our armchair and went to the side table to answer it.

'Hello?'

'Darling?' Dad again. He never called just to chat.

'How's –'

'Not good.'

I felt his words sink to the pit of my stomach.

'I'm afraid Harper's condition is worse than we had thought...' He cleared his throat. 'I didn't want to have to tell you over the phone.' His voice started to tremble. 'I don't quite know how to say this...' Adrenaline snaked through my body. *I don't quite know how to say this...* He had used these exact words when Mum –

'Harper is dying.'

Dying.

That word.

That word that I had heard so many times before.

I hated that word.

His voice sounded fuzzy now, as if he were speaking in slow motion. 'Her heart and lung functions have deteriorated significantly. We've been told that medication and corrective surgery will no longer help. She needs a heart and lung transplant.'

The world both inside and outside my body went silent.

'Well, get her those transplants then!' I was shouting. Why was I shouting?

'It's not as simple as that. We've been to several hospitals. The doctors have told us there are not enough organs available to meet the demand, and because of Harper's disability they are refusing even to put her on a transplant list.'

It took me a while to make sense of what he was saying, and when I did, I sank to the floor.

'This can't be happening. Refusing to put her on a transplant list – isn't that discrimination? Surely something can be done!'

'Before we go down that road, there's one more hospital we can try. We have a meeting with the doctors from the Queen Victoria Heart Hospital on Saturday afternoon. I would like you to be there.'

'But Wài Pó said not to worry.' Words started flowing from my mouth as if of their own accord. 'Wài Pó said to focus on my PhD. I have my thesis defence in a month...' Why was I telling him this? Dad had never approved of my decision to leave Hong Kong to study overseas. My thesis defence meant nothing to him.

I paused for breath, suddenly realising what I was saying. Harper's life was at stake – of course my thesis defence didn't matter now.

'Sorry,' I said, ashamed.

'Harper's most recent test results came in last night. It's much worse than we had anticipated. You know Wài Pó... she couldn't bear to be the one to tell you.' He sighed into the phone. 'I think you should come home, Marlowe. This time is different. Harper needs you now.'

I felt like I was going to be sick. This couldn't be happening. I wouldn't allow it. I would fix things, just like I always did.

'I'll book my flight home today.'

I hung up the phone. Although it was warm in the house, I was shivering. I swallowed a deep sound that wanted to escape from my throat. I knew if I let myself cry, I wouldn't be able to stop. So, I counted: *One Mississippi, two Mississippi, three…* focusing on the numbers, their shape, their sound, until I hit my tenth Mississippi and felt my body go numb.

I was late. I stood up and reached for my shoulder bag by the front door; it smelled like the fresh thyme that grew abundantly in our lab. I thought of my research, of all the hard work I had done. And then I thought of Olly. It was like being hit by a tonne of lead. How was I supposed to say goodbye to Olly?

Don't think, just walk.

I opened the front door. Cold air pricked the skin at my neck and I readjusted my scarf so that no skin was exposed. My boots squelched against the wet pavement as I raced to the bus stop.

There was a queue for the 19. I joined the end of the line, trying to steady my breathing by watching a discarded Tesco sandwich being consumed by a ravenous black cat. I boarded the bus and fought my way through the press of damp, cold bodies to the upper deck.

There was an empty seat beside a foggy window. I sat down and exhaled deeply. In front of me, a middle-aged couple conversed in Hindi. The woman didn't pause for breath, her voice growing louder by the second. To her left, a teenage girl with Down syndrome sang.

Dad's words played over and over in my mind.

Harper needs you now. He had said those words so many times before. Damn it, he hadn't even asked me how I was. *Breathe,* I reminded myself. From my bag, I took a book on the conservation practices of the butterflies I had come to love and flicked through the pages.

Harper.

My gaze lingered over the close-up image of the *arion*'s wing, and I was mesmerised by the beauty of each hardened chitinous scale.

Harper.

What was I doing reading this book? I shut it and put it back in my bag. I thought instead of how to tell Professor Lipin that I would be leaving, and slowly the significance of what I was about to do sank in.

Don't think about it, I told myself. *One Mississippi, two Mississippi, three…*

The teenage girl was singing louder now. Passengers turned their heads, giving her steely looks. I suppressed the urge to tell her to be quiet and focused instead on the view outside the window. The bare limbs of trees reached towards the sky. People marched along the streets below, wrapped in black coats.

'Shut up, ya retard,' a bearded man shouted from the front of the bus. I turned towards the man, my body filled with heat. The teenager had her headphones in. She didn't seem aware of him approaching until he was towering over her. She looked up at him and removed the headphones from her ears.

'I said shut up, retard.'

Suddenly I was on my feet, fists clenched, ready to come to the girl's defence. But she had it covered.

'My name is Poppy, like the flower. Not Retard.' The bus stopped at Green Park station. 'I'm sorry. My mum also says I am too loud sometimes. I will be quiet now.' Poppy resumed singing, softly this time.

The man did not move. He just stood there, staring at Poppy, until the influx of new passengers forced him back to his seat. I unclenched my fists and exhaled. Sounds of chatter on the bus resumed, more animated than before, and I was alone with my uncomfortable thoughts once more.

———

The corridor outside Professor Lipin's office was quiet, but for a faint humming that emanated from the drinks machine close by. There was an empty chair by the door. I chose the floor instead.

I think you should come home… This time is different.

The urgency I had felt to return to my sister had dulled, to be replaced by dread. I needed to pull myself together. I would ask for an extension on my thesis defence and come back next term after the situation with Harper was sorted.

Professor Lipin emerged from his office. 'Marlowe, come in.'

He tied his shoulder-length hair back into a ponytail as he took a seat at his desk under the large crescent window.

'I've got some good news for you. I'm sure Olly has already mentioned that we recommended you for the Royal Zoological Award? Well I've just been notified you're on the shortlist. Congratulations!' He was beaming.

I gaped at him.

'Marlowe?' Professor Lipin was looking at me, his brow creased.

I'd been shortlisted? For a brief moment, I felt proud. But then reality hit me and I felt the life I had worked so hard to build for myself slipping out of my grasp.

26

'I'm sorry.' The words tumbled out of my mouth. 'I need to take a leave of absence.' My voice sounded high-pitched and small.

He was looking at me, bewildered.

'My sister is very sick…' A dove flew onto the landing outside the window. It turned, beady eyes latched onto mine. 'I need to go home to Hong Kong.'

Cold trickled into my bones. I thought of my recent application to take part in the *arion* conservation program in Devon, thought of the larvae I had painstakingly reared and the endless observational studies I had done. The disappointment dawning on Professor Lipin's face registered in my body.

'I'll be back next term,' I assured him.

Yes, I told myself, *that's right*. All would be well and I would be back.

At my locker, I fumbled with the key.

'Hey.' Olly walked down the corridor towards me. He was dressed in a smart blue shirt and chinos, with a nerdy *I love bugs* badge pinned to his breast pocket.

He really was my perfect match. It was the kind of ridiculous, romantic sentiment that belonged to Harper, not me, but I couldn't stop the thought springing to my mind. My eyes welled, knowing I'd have to say goodbye to him in a few days. I had never been able to deal with goodbyes. At least this one wouldn't be for too long, I reminded myself. I turned away to stare into my open locker.

'I was waiting for you in the lab but you never showed. You okay, Marls?' He brushed the hair out of my eyes. Despite myself, I leaned my head onto his shoulder. His arms went around me, his hand stroking my back. I wished we could stay like this forever.

My cheeks were wet. I quickly pulled away from him and picked up the empty cardboard box on the floor.

'What's that?'

'A box.'

'I know it's a box. What's it for?'

'I have to leave.' I grabbed the heavy lepidoptera and entomology hardbacks from my locker, trying to ignore my urge to hurl them to the ground, breaking the spines, sending pages fluttering through the air, creating a messy pile of words. For once in my life, things had been going well – and now I had to walk away.

'Talk to me, Marls. What's going on?'

I sat on the ground beside the box, my face in my hands.

Olly crouched down beside me.

'You'll have to look after the *arion* larvae for me.' My voice started to crack. *Hold it together.* My mind raced through all the things I would need to impart to Olly before I left. 'For the adults, I keep a jar of extra sugar water in the cupboard above the specimen containers. There's also –'

'It's Harper, isn't it?'

Breathe.

I nodded. 'She's dying.' Startled by the bluntness of my statement, I searched for something else to say. 'I won't be able to go on the field trip to the Cotswolds next week.' I cringed inwardly. Who cared about that? 'I mean…'

'It's okay.' Olly looked at me steadily. I couldn't read his expression. He was very still. 'I thought she'd be okay… I'm so sorry.' He spoke softly; it was the same voice he used to speak to our butterflies. 'When do you leave?'

My scarf felt too tight around my throat. I loosened it.

'I'll try and get the Friday morning flight. There's a meeting with the doctors on Saturday.' The words sank in the air next to us.

He took my hand. 'Marlowe, you know you're not alone in this, right? You have me. Why don't I come with you?'

'No.' I wouldn't let this affect his life too.

There was a long silence before he spoke again. 'I'll cook dinner tonight, okay?'

I nodded. 'See you at home.'

Harper

It is a Wednesday night and that means it is disco night – it is written in my diary with purple ink – but I am missing it. I am in the emergency part of the hospital again, this time because of a fever. To be honest, I don't like missing disco night, and I am finding it hard not to think about all my friends having fun without me.

It is strange to be back in hospital again so soon, but I am here with Dad and Wài Pó. Dad is on his mobile phone a lot and Wài Pó is asleep in her chair. Louis tried to stay with me for a while instead of going to disco night, but it was making him anxious because things were different in his routine. He was looking at his watches a lot and jumping about on his toes. He finds it harder than me to stay calm when there is change. I am not upset he is gone, because I have ways of cheering myself up.

Every time I go to hospital, I take my small, yellow photo album with me. In the first photo, my mum and dad are in the garden, looking at each other with a spark of romance in their eyes. Next there is Wài Pó and me cooking in the kitchen. I was only fifteen years old and Wài Pó had more black hairs than grey. Then there is a photo of Marlowe and me holding hands when we were small. We were wearing matching blue dresses that my dad got us for Marlowe's birthday. On the very last page, there is a new photo of me and the love of my heart, Louis. We are sitting in the garden, holding hands with matching smiles on our faces.

When I am feeling sad or scared, I think of the day when Louis and I first met. It is a day when something really good happened in my life.

I was shopping with Wài Pó for spring roll filling – minced chicken, carrots, chives, cabbage, and spring roll wrappers. Then I heard with my ears someone shouting. The voice said: 'I just need to find one more dollar.' He had an American accent. I know all about this kind of accent because my speech therapist, Mrs Green, is American.

Me and Wài Pó were making our way to the check-out counter but in front of us was a long line of people with moody faces. They were shaking their heads and making 'tut tut' noises at the man who was holding up the queue.

'Please, sir, step aside and let the other customers come through,' the check-out lady said.

'No, I cannot do that,' said the man, 'because I know I have one dollar somewhere in one of my pockets and it is three thirty-three pm and I have to be home at three thirty-five pm. There is only two minutes left.'

I walked closer to the man and saw from behind that he had hair the same colour as gingerbread. He was wearing a very nice suit and I thought to myself, *This man looks very smart.*

The lady at the counter called for help in Chinese, and two men in blue clothes walked towards the smart man and grabbed his shoulders. He turned and I saw on his face that he had freckles, a small, friendly-looking nose and the Up syndrome, like me.

'Wait,' I said importantly, in my loudest voice. I put my hand into my purse and took out one dollar and gave it to the smart man. He

31

looked at me and a bit of ginger hair fell over his eyes. I wanted to brush it away with my fingers.

'You should give her the money before she calls the police and puts you in prison,' I said.

So, he did. Then he took his bags and one of his watches rang with an alarm. He had two watches on his arm. As he was switching off the sound, I saw the time 3.35 pm flashing. But the man did not move. He just stared at me again, and then I got a swirly jumpy feeling in my belly, right near my buttonhole.

'Míng Huà!' Wài Pó was calling from the queue of waiting customers who were looking with their eyes. 'Míng Huà, come back.'

'My name is Louis.' The man gave me his hand and I took it. The soft parts of our skin inside our palms were warm together as they touched. I felt a smile on my face.

'My name is Harper,' I said. 'How come I've never seen you around here before?'

'I am new. I am from the United States of America, New York, Manhattan. I moved here three months ago, and I am Jewish. In New York, I was a waiter at the Honeybee Cafe, but here in Hong Kong I am unemployed. I cannot get a job here.' He looked at his watch. 'It is three forty pm. Now I am late.' Louis jumped from side to side like he needed to pee. 'I've got to go now.'

I felt sad in my heart, so I looked at the floor.

'Do you have a home or mobile phone?' he asked, and then the swirling started again.

He took out a shiny pen from his pocket.

'Yes.' My cheeks were a bit hot. 'Yes I do.'

'I would like to call you tomorrow night at seven pm just before my dinner at seven thirty and then the news at eight. We could chat. If you would like to chat with me, I would like that very much.'

'I would like that very much too.'

I told him my phone number and I saw that he wrote his number two backwards and in a funny shape, but that was okay with me.

'Goodbye, Harper. Thank you for your help with the money. I was never very good with money, ever since I was a baby.'

'Well I am very good with money. I always have a lot of money in my purse.'

Louis brushed his gingerbread hair from his face and waved at me. I waved back.

—

A yellow flower on my pillow.

Louis was here.

He is always with me, even when I am dreaming.

This is love.

Marlowe

Cousin Bì Yù's phone call came like clockwork. She always called on Wednesday morning my time, which was Wednesday night Shanghai time. We hadn't seen each other in nearly a year, not since my last trip back to Hong Kong. Whenever I went home, I always visited Shanghai for a few days with Harper and Wài Pó to see Mum's side of the family. Bì Yù had pink hair then. I wondered what colour it would be now.

'*Mèi mei!* Did you see the latest episode of *90210*?'

Mèi mei… Whenever cousin Bì Yù called me that, it felt like a weight was lifted from my shoulders. Although I wasn't officially her younger sister, it was good to know that someone had my back, even if she was halfway across the world.

'You're still watching that trash?' I asked.

She giggled. 'You know me. It helps me to sleep at night.'

She brought me up to date, taking great pleasure in the characters' juicy romances. Although she was older than me, Bì Yù had never had a serious boyfriend. There was something about her that was so wise and so naive at the same time.

Suddenly she stopped her recount to ask, 'Why are you so quiet? Is something wrong?'

She had no idea about Harper, I realised. Dad and Wài Pó must not have told the family in Shanghai yet. I wasn't surprised that Dad hadn't contacted them; Irene didn't like him to be in touch with Mum's side of the family. But why hadn't Wài Pó said something? Perhaps she didn't want to worry them until we knew for sure what was going on, I speculated. Or perhaps it was too hard for her to talk about.

Haltingly, I filled Bì Yù in.

Immediately, she said, 'I'm coming. I'll come to Hong Kong to be with you.'

'No,' I found myself saying. When Mum was sick, the family came when it was time to say goodbye to her. We weren't saying goodbye to Harper. 'I'll be okay. We'll be okay. Besides, you've just started working for your favourite designer – we both know how hard it was to land that job. You stay where you are; there's no need for you to come now.'

'I'm worried about you all.'

'There's no need to be, honestly. We're seeing a doctor on Saturday and I'll let you know how it goes. I'm sure everything will work out.' It had to.

I could hear her anxiously tapping the phone with her finger.

'If you're sure.' She sounded doubtful. 'But if you need anything, anything at all, please call me.'

I promised her I would.

⎯⎯⎯⎯

That night it began to snow. From the warmth of our bed I watched talc-like clusters collect on our window ledge. The purr of Olly's breath landed at the base of my neck as he slept, his arm slung over my waist. I was comforted by Olly, his touch, the stillness of the night, the silence.

Yellow light from a streetlamp outside illuminated the powdery sky. Although the view outside my window was pleasing, I knew that this was something Harper was more likely to notice than me. I was seeing through her eyes again; we would be together soon and she was becoming more alive to me, her presence more vivid, as if she was in me, with me, until her gaze and mine were one. If she were seated next to me I wouldn't know where she began and where I ended. As a child, I experienced that sensation so often that I thought it was normal, but this was the first time I'd felt it since moving to London. I wasn't sure I liked it.

I placed my hand on top of Olly's, which was lightly pressed against my belly, and listened to his slow, stable breath. Predictable. Safe. Outside our window, snow fell in thicker clumps, blown sideways by a strengthening wind. The glass rattled. The air howled. I felt small when nature displayed its strength. I tried to understand it in my work, tried to outwit it by finding ways to conserve its most delicate creatures. At times like these, though, I wondered if one could ever really outsmart nature, or grasp the phenomena of the physical world in its entirety. And if not, did that mean my work was fruitless? No. I stopped myself. That train of thought wouldn't lead me anywhere worth going. And so I forced myself to return to a simple appreciation of the thickly falling snow.

—

I had just turned eight and was sitting on a couch watching snow gather on the window ledge. A fire was hissing nearby and I could feel its heat on my cheeks. My mother was giving Bì Yù a piano lesson on my uncle's piano. My parents had decided to spend Chinese New Year at Uncle Bǐng Wén and Aunt Lǐ Nà's townhouse at the edge of Zhōngshān Park, in Shanghai. Bì Yù's sound was loud and clunky as she struggled with Beethoven's Moonlight Sonata. Dad had told me I must always be quiet when Mum was at the piano. I turned to look. Bì Yù's pigtails bobbed up and down with the movements of her hands. I wanted to laugh at her mistakes and had to bite my lower lip to stop myself. Even though Bì Yù was three years older than I was and much better at maths, she would never play piano as well as my mother.

'Lucky girl.' Uncle Bǐng Wén spoke with a British accent he had acquired from his years studying at the University of London. He patted his daughter on the head. 'Getting lessons from your talented aunt. One day you might be like her, eh! Up on a big stage.' He removed several glasses from his wood-and-paktong cabinet and turned to look at me.

'What about you?'

Suddenly, I felt small, aware of how my feet dangled over the edge of his couch, a long way from the floor.

'Still don't like the piano?'

'No.' Although Mum was reluctant to admit it, I hadn't inherited her gift for music.

'I've been trying to get her to play more,' Mum sighed. 'My beautiful, smart girl is also very stubborn.'

My beautiful, smart girl. In her eyes, I was the one with the potential, the one who could make something of herself. 'Your *mèi mei* can't do the things you can, Míng Yuè,' Mum would say when I refused to practise the piano. 'She won't have the opportunities you will.' This was usually enough to persuade me to sit at the keyboard and thump out a clumsy tune, but today she didn't mention Harper's shortcomings. Maybe Bì Yù's interest in the piano was enough for the moment.

I could hear Harper's frustrated cries coming from the kitchen. She probably wanted to be near the music. Sure enough, seconds later, there was a patter of footsteps. Harper, who was only three, plodded into the living room, pulling Dad behind her. I noticed her lips and fingertips were tinged blue, yet it didn't seem to affect her cheery disposition. She gave Dad's arm another forceful tug and gestured to the piano. I would never pull him like that! A tall man, he had to bend down to hold her hand. When she let go he straightened, wiping light hair from his brow and adjusting the bow tie he always wore. He looked, as Mum would tease, 'so British'.

Harper clapped her hands, then climbed onto Mum's lap. I waited for Dad to tell her off, but he didn't say anything. He just smiled and took a drink from Uncle Bǐng Wén. I crossed my arms. It wasn't fair.

Wài Pó entered the room, followed by Aunt Lǐ Nà. My aunt, a psychologist, had an unobtrusive manner. She tended to remain on the periphery, and I was often aware of her watching us. The two women took seats near the piano and listened attentively.

Harper continued clapping along with the music, pausing every so often to push her small, round spectacles further up the bridge of her nose. I found myself wishing that I had spectacles too.

'Hello, blossom.' Finally, Dad lowered himself onto the couch next to me. Immediately, I crawled onto his lap. He smelled of coffee and cologne – bitter and fresh. He kissed the top of my head and I burrowed deeper into his chest. All the heaviness I had felt while watching my mother and cousin play disappeared.

'All done,' Bì Yù announced. The music stopped abruptly. She jumped off the piano stool and took a bow. Harper followed, bowing also. Mum shook her head and laughed. She then wiped an unusual amount of sweat from her brow.

'Is that it? I don't think Beethoven would have finished a lesson halfway through.'

Bì Yù blushed. She took a step back from the piano and made space for Mum to play. Harper leaned her ear against the instrument. The room became quiet as the pianist made herself comfortable on the stool and loosened the clasp that held her long, dark hair in place. She played Chopin's Nocturne. The music was both quick and slow, light and heavy, filled with an energy that made the room seem large and all of its inhabitants small. I snuggled into my father's chest and listened to his breath relax and soften.

'Love.' Harper began to twirl, moving like a ballerina on her tiptoes. She raised her chubby little hands high and her fingertips skimmed the air. Her shirt gaped as she bent forward, revealing a thin scar across her chest. The scar that showed her heart was weak, the scar that made her so special in Dad's eyes. Her eyes were lit with a kind of wildness; the same wildness that ran through Mum's fingertips as they flew across the black and white keys. Harper laughed. Her eyes were closed and her body moved faster to the rhythm of the music. I couldn't take my eyes off her; it was like she had been transported somewhere I could never go.

What could she hear that I couldn't?

The room was hot. I closed my eyes and listened to the steady beat inside Dad's chest. It was a sound that I could understand, a sound that made me feel safe.

There was a loud crack, followed by the boom of thunder. I sat upright, my body heavy and sweaty with sleep. Dad was gone, and there was a pillow in the place of his knee. I turned. The front door was ajar, and through the window I saw my family standing outside on the street, staring at the sky.

'No bang!' Harper, hands over her ears, shouted. 'No bang!' She didn't like loud noises.

The living room was empty. I had been forgotten. There was another explosion, and then a shower of glittering gold. As I ran out the front door, the cold air bit at my bare throat. I grabbed hold of Mum's leg.

'Hello, darling.' She lifted me up, grunting with effort, and held me to her chest. 'Look how beautiful the night is. Let the noise frighten away all the bad spirits. This year will be a good year.'

Dad placed a hand on Mum's shoulder. 'Maybe we should go inside. These homemade fireworks are so bloody dangerous.'

'*Aī yā*,' Wài Pó interrupted. She said he was being silly.

'What did she say?' Dad asked. Instead of translating what my grandmother had actually said, I told him she thought he was handsome.

'*Hú shuō!*' She smacked her thigh and told him that even though he'd married her daughter years ago, he was still a foreigner in this city.

'Don't worry so much,' Wài Pó told him. She launched into the old story about Wài Gōng, my grandfather, who'd had a stroke and gone to heaven. 'His mind was far too active and his body responded to the stress,' she explained.

It began to snow heavily. Mum took the scarf from around her neck and wrapped it around me. I noticed a cluster of small bruises just above her collarbone and thought that was a funny place to have knocked herself.

'Photo time!' Uncle Bǐng Wén made us huddle together while, in the background, bright colours burst in the sky. I grabbed my mother's hand and directed my best smile at the camera.

'One… two…' He lowered the camera, frowning. 'Where's Míng Huà?'

Everyone looked around.

My mother put me down abruptly and started running through the snow, breathlessly calling Harper's Chinese name: 'Míng Huà!' Her voice was as sharp as the icicles on Uncle Bǐng Wén's roof.

'I'll get the torches,' Aunt Lǐ Nà said, and she ran into the house.

'Harper!' Dad shouted. He sprinted down the dark street. I tried to follow, but a hand grabbed my arm. It was Wài Pó.

'You go back inside,' she told me. 'You are too young to be roaming the streets.'

'But I can help,' I insisted. I knew where Harper had gone; I always knew.

Bì Yù pulled me by the hand towards the house. 'It's not safe,' she told me. 'There are monsters in the night that eat little girls like us.'

'Kuài diǎn, kuài diǎn.' Wài Pó gave me a forceful shove through the front door and quickly shut it behind us.

As soon as Wài Pó was out of sight, I told my cousin that I was going to get Harper. I hurried into the kitchen, where I knew Aunt Lǐ Nà usually kept the window ajar, and climbed out. Bì Yù dashed after me. 'Bú yào zǒu,' she shouted. Don't go.

There was a plum tree that Harper loved in Zhōngshān Park. Its long branches reached into the air, filling the space between its neighbouring trees with the rich colour of its magenta blossoms. By the light from nearby streetlamps, the fallen petals looked like drops of blood in the snow. The air was thick with smoke from the fireworks; it clung to the back of my throat as I walked towards my sister.

As if she could still hear Mum's music, Harper was twirling under the tree. Her lips were tinged blue again. She had stuck out her tongue to catch the falling snow and wore a blossom in her wet hair. She looked like something from another world.

My footsteps crunched in the snow as I ran towards her.

'Harper!' I grabbed her hand, which was as cold as the snow on the ground beneath us. I felt my own body go cold. Rubbing her fingers hard, I tried to give her all the warmth I had left.

Her body became still and she blinked, then giggled. 'Ma-ma,' she said, unable to pronounce my name. She pointed to the plum tree and smiled.

'Harper, we have to go. Your heart doesn't like to get cold, remember?' The fireworks had started again, a storm of light and noise in the sky. She quickly put her hands over her ears and lay flat on the ground, like she always did when she heard a loud noise.

Using all my strength, I heaved my sister up and lifted her onto my back. She put her cool cheek flat against the base of my neck, sending a wave of goosebumps down my spine. I stumbled back to the house as fast as I could while the fireworks cracked loudly above us – much louder than the sound of my sister's breath.

Harper

The doctors say they want to keep me in the hospital a bit longer, until my fever has gone. This is a good thing for two reasons:

1. They are making me well again, like they always do.
2. Tonight I got to make a new friend.

I was in my hospital bed, resting. Over the beeps of all my machines, I could hear the sound of voices arguing. I pressed the 'up' button on my bed so that I was sitting, tidied up the colourful wires on my chest and reached over to pull open the curtain around my bed.

A young woman with a sweet apple face was standing in the doorway of my room, talking to my nurse. She was holding the handles of a wheelchair, which pushed an old lady. This old lady had no teeth and her dark eyes were empty.

'I do not want my mother in this room,' the young woman said.

'I'm sorry,' the nurse said, 'but this is the only bed we have left. The ward is full.'

The old lady was making chomp chomp eating movements with her mouth. I know all about this bodily movement because my friend Tam does this when he is nervous. I wanted the old lady to stop worrying, so I tried to be friendly by waving at her and smiling. It took a while, and my hand was a bit sore because I had a needle stuck in it, but after a few waves, the old lady looked up at me. When the light went into her eyes, I saw that they were the very same colour as mine: chocolate brown.

'We have the same eyes, you and me,' I said.

The young woman started talking faster to the nurse, her voice louder. 'I'm willing to pay for an upgrade to a private room.'

'It's not about payment. We simply don't have the beds.'

'I do not want my mother in a shared room with her.' She pointed at my bed and I looked around, wondering what was upsetting her. After all, this was a very nice hospital.

'There's nothing wrong with my bed or the room,' I told her. 'This is a very nice hospital and the sheets are comfy and soft.'

The young woman stopped talking. Her mother laughed, her mouth wide and happy. She had lines like the whiskers of a cat spreading out from her eyes. I thought she was beautiful.

'It would be so nice if you could stay here with me.' I was careful not to tell her that I would be going home in the morning. I didn't want her to be disappointed.

Marlowe

My stomach lurched as I turned the corner from the departures hall into immigration.

Don'tlookbackdon'tlookback, a voice inside me repeated. As I watched the queue of slow-moving bodies in front of me, I kept picturing Olly as I had seen him only moments ago. His solid hands were sunk deep into his pockets and his shoulders were hunched. There was a hole in the sleeve of his thick maroon sweater. His wide green eyes were gazing at me intently. I could feel myself blush. I was sure he must be seeing the ugly emotions I wanted to keep hidden – the shame, guilt and grief I felt whenever I had to leave someone I loved.

Olly took off his jumper and pulled it over my head. It was still warm from his body. I held the sleeve to my nose, catching traces of his peppermint shampoo. It was comforting to know my olfactory perception could bring me closer to him, even when we were miles apart. From that point on, I vowed to avoid exposing his jumper to strong smells, to preserve the scent of him.

It'snotgoodbyeit'snotgoodbyeit'snotgoodbye. A mantra to suppress the sadness that was making my limbs turn cold.

As I walked through the body scanner near the on-board baggage check, a security officer asked me to remove the sweater and put it through the X-ray machine, then pass through the scanner again.

Reluctantly, I did as I was told. When I was finally cleared, I quickly pulled Olly's jumper back over my head, gathered my things and strode past the duty-free shops and cafes, searching for somewhere quiet to sit. A baby was howling in his mother's arms. An urgent voice sounded over the PA: '*Mr and Mrs Williams, travelling on CX flight 161 to Sydney, please make your way to the departure gate.*' A group of Chinese tourists were shouting at one another, competing with the sound of canned music, also much too loud. The noise threatened to overwhelm me. I placed my palms over my ears, much like Harper would, but quickly lowered them when I realised what I had done.

I'm not my sister. I'm not my sister.

Noise was never something I paid attention to until Harper was born. When Mum used to turn on the hairdryer, Harper would scream, place her hands over her ears and lie flat on the ground. 'Sensory overload,' was how Dad described it. Very quickly, I began to develop a heightened sensitivity to her triggers.

Breathe, Míng Yuè. Mum's voice felt like a whisper over my skin.

I stopped trying to outrun the noise and found a seat beside an oversized fake pot plant.

Breathe, my mother said again, and I did, inhaling and exhaling until I began to feel calmer. Then I opened the locket I wore on a chain around my neck. Inside was a photo of Mum and a lock of her hair. The image had faded, but I could still make out the dimples on her cheeks as she smiled. If only she could have stayed like this in my mind forever. But my last sight of her always intruded.

━━

Yellow satin sheets were twisted around my mother's emaciated body.

'Ma!' I climbed onto the master bed. I was nine, with legs long enough to earn me a new nickname: *xiǎo zhà měng*, Wài Pó called me.

I took Mum's hand in mine and stroked her damp, marked skin. 'Ma!'

She did not respond. All I could see was the slow rise and fall of her chest. A faint rattle followed as she took a breath in and let it go. No longer afraid of the ugly, bleeding marks that scarred her body, I kissed the spots that I was sure were hurting her the most. Skin to skin, I searched for her smell, which was like sweet milk and lavender. Instead I found the sour odour of decay, musty and thick.

I turned on the radio. Tchaikovsky's Piano Concerto No. 1 was playing; I recognised it from one of her concerts. How beautiful she had looked that night, her gown decorated with gold and blue flowers that twinkled under the lights. On stage, she was no longer my mother but 'Wáng Hùi Fāng, the award-winning pianist with hands of gold'.

My fingertips danced over her thin wrist. Her left eye opened first, and then her right. She looked at me, but it felt like she was looking at a stranger. I kissed her again on the forehead and she relaxed. A smile formed. Dimples pricked her sunken cheeks.

'Mā ma, the music.'

She nodded slowly, her jaw chattered feverishly as she stared into the distance, then her eyes closed again. The music drifted through the air. I snuggled closer, and my arm wrapped itself around her waist.

'I'm glad you're home,' I said. 'Soon you'll be all better and we can pick roses in Daddy's garden again.'

I lay next to her, watching her chest rise and fall – a slow and dependable rhythm – until the light faded and the air became cold. Suddenly, she opened her eyes and, with an unexpected burst of energy, slowly pulled herself upright in the bed. The orange bandana that was wrapped tightly around her head unfurled and trailed down her back, just like her long hair used to. Startled, I sat up to meet her gaze.

'Míng Yuè! I have something to ask of you.' The effort of moving had made her breathless. 'I need you to make me a promise.'

I bit my lip. I was never very good at promises.

'Darling.' She stroked my forehead, palm soft and clammy. 'You will always look after your sister, won't you?' Her eyes were red. Switching to Chinese she said, '*Tā xiàn zài gèng xū yào nǐ.*' *She needs you more now.* Her voice was softer, sweeter, when she spoke in her mother tongue. It reminded me of when I was small and she used to sing to me in Chinese. It made me feel safe; the language lulled me to sleep.

'Yes, of course. We will all look after Harper.'

'Here.' She pulled open the drawer of her bedside table. Inside was a box, wrapped in pink.

I tore away the paper and lifted out a necklace with a small gold pendant.

'Open it,' she said.

Inside was a photo of her, dressed in yellow.

'I'm always with you now.' She fastened the locket around my neck, then subsided against the pillows.

The necklace was uncomfortable and I wanted to take it off. I waited until her eyes were heavy and her breathing was rough, then I climbed off the bed. Standing, I wrestled with the clasp, wondering about the promise she had asked me to make.

After a long struggle, I gave up. I couldn't undo the necklace. It felt heavy around my neck.

My mother died that night. We never got to pick roses together again in my father's garden.

Harper

It is a Friday morning and I am home again. It feels good to be back with all my things and to be with my family (although Marlowe is not here). Most importantly, I can see Louis more. He is about to go on a special holiday to Thailand with his family, and today I get to spend the whole day with him before he leaves. I am so excited that I feel a swirling and skipping in my belly.

This will be the first time Louis is travelling in an independent way in Hong Kong all by himself. He is carrying his mobile phone and I have told him how many coins to use to pay for the bus. I know all about money skills because my kind of Up syndrome is different from his. Mrs Green at my vocational centre said I was called 'high functioning', which means I can count better than Louis, and I can play the piano, and sometimes I can find the right words to say how I feel in English and also Chinese. But I know that Louis is better at other things. He is better at making our friends laugh with his jokes and pretending to be Mr Bean or Basil from *Fawlty Towers*. Louis is also better at remembering important facts about things and people he meets. My Louis knows how to make everyone feel special, like when he notices things about Wài Pó that I don't. One day he told her she was beautiful when she tied her hair in a lovely way so that her pearl earrings were showing, and another time he told her that her custard tarts were very yummy – she had added extra butter and it was the perfect taste on our tongues and the most clever thing to do.

Wài Pó pushes me in my chair to our front gate. This is the second time that she has had to do this today, because Louis got the wrong bus in the morning and we had to go back inside and wait one hour. I don't mind about having to come outside again. It is always nice to be in the air that is fresh and salty from the sea, not like hospitals that have a smell like sour bodies.

I shiver a little because it is cold out here, but there is no need to worry. Wài Pó has put a beautiful blanket on my knees. She made it for me with wool in the colours of blue, yellow and white around the edges.

A minibus pulls in at the stop across the road. A few people get off, but I do not see Louis. My heart does a little hop inside my chest. I look at Wài Pó, who takes out her mobile phone and calls him. Her voice is small against the roar of the bus engine as it leaves our street.

'He'll be on the next one,' she says, patting my shoulder.

We wait. Buses come and buses go. Every time one of them stops, I notice at least one pair of eyes staring at me without blinking. It is a funny feeling when someone stares, but I am quite used to it because I am a beautiful woman and I always try to look my best. Today, I think these people must also be admiring my beautiful blanket because Wài Pó put a lot of effort into her crochet stitching for me. This is a blanket that carries love.

There is a line forming at the bus stop now. A lot of people are waiting. A lot of people are staring with their eyes. I wave at some of them, but no one waves back. Wài Pó tells me not to do that, but I don't understand why, so I explain to her that she is being very unfriendly.

'He's here!' she shouts. A green-and-white minibus pulls up and I see behind the window that my Louis is sitting, waving. Oh! I lose the air in my lungs. I haven't seen him in two days and I am feeling very, very happy. But then I realise Louis is not moving. He's just waving at me with a big smile on his face and is blowing me kisses.

'Get up!' I shout, but having to make my voice come out in a loud way gives me a coughing fit. Louis is still sitting, waving.

'Up!' I say 'Up!'

Wài Pó puts the brakes on my wheelchair and runs to him. She is a bit slow, because she is skinny and old, but that is personal private information that I will never say to her face.

Now everyone on the seats next to the windows have their eyes on me. I try to use my hands to tell them to help get Louis off the bus, but they just stare. Then I see Wài Pó get on the bus. She says something to Louis that I cannot hear. He smacks his hands on his head. He does this when he wants to say something like 'stupid me'. As he walks off the bus I see that the lady next to him takes out a tissue. She bends over and seems to be wiping his empty seat from top to bottom before she moves over to take his place by the window. I am looking at her face while she does this. She has big frown lines on her forehead and her nose is wrinkled up like she has smelled a bad smell. It makes my skin prickly and uncomfortable and my head feels confused. I push my glasses further up the hard part of my nose to make sure I am seeing things in a clear way. After all, she was a lady with a soft, nice-looking face. I had been planning to give her a friendly wave to say thank you for sitting next to my Louis and keeping him company, but I am not so sure I want to now.

'My sweet and precious flower!' Louis runs across the road, faster than Wài Pó. 'I did it! I did it!' He kisses me, a big fat one, on the lips.

'Yes! You did it. You are a clever man.' I am so happy in my heart to see him.

But as he pulls away, I see so many eyes on us at the bus stop. I decide that I do not like these eyes; they are sharp and unfriendly.

As Wài Pó wheels me back to the house, I ask, 'Louis, were you eating Doritos on the bus? You know you can't eat on the bus or you might make crumbs.'

'I was not eating Doritos on the bus. This is the truth because I ate three packets all in one go last night, at nine pm, when I was watching *Friends*. Now there are no more Doritos left in my house for me to eat.'

'*Aī yā*, don't worry about other people, Míng Huà. Other people *shén me dōu bù dǒng.*'

Normally, I would tell my Wài Pó not to speak badly of others, but today I didn't want to. Today, something inside of me has become different and knowing. I think of the time I was craving one of Wài Pó's egg tarts so bad, but she was too tired to bake, so I went to a shop and bought one with my money. It looked so happy and friendly sitting there in the cafe; so yellow, so buttery, so yummy. But then when I took one single bite, I had to spit it out. It was hard and too eggy and not enough sweet. Even though it looked very delightful, it was not.

Today I think that things are not always as they seem.

Marlowe

The eastern sun was rising chilli red over the South China Sea. I leaned my head against the aeroplane window. Heat prickled my lips, a sensation I didn't know I had missed until now.

'Would you like the omelette or the dim sum?' The flight attendant smiled, revealing a mouth of bleached teeth.

'Neither, thanks. I'm not hungry.'

My gaze drifted back to the window. The sky was already turning blue – a bright *arion* blue. I was reminded once more of my grandfather, who had first introduced me to the large blue butterfly on one of my summer visits to the UK. It had been over ten years since the delicate creature became extinct in Britain, but thanks to his long-standing connections in the lepidopterist world, Grandpa was taking me on a journey to a secret site where the butterfly was being reintroduced into the British countryside.

'Large blue's are of course known for their drunken flying,' he said. As we walked among the beeches, he told me about the two scientists, Thomas and Simcox, who had brought the species back from the dead.

'We all tried hard to understand why the butterfly had suddenly stopped thriving…' As he spoke, I watched his face light up with excitement. It had been so long since I had seen him this happy. 'And it all boiled down to the *Myrmica sabuleti*! Fancy that! The large blue caterpillar depends on the ant in order to survive. It produces a pheromone that makes the ant treat it as one of their own. Effectively, the caterpillar has deceived the ant. The *arion* larvae even eat the ant grubs until they transform into pupae and leave the underground.'

I pictured the carnivorous behaviour with a strange fascination, only able to utter one word in response.

'Wow.'

Suddenly, Grandpa stopped and, very slowly, crouched down. I followed his gaze to a thyme leaf near his feet. He was still. I couldn't hear the sound of his breath. The muscles in his face didn't move an inch, but I saw his eyes were brimming. Here she was – the *Maculinea arion*. She was tiny. Her outer wings were greyish blue and a shimmering aqua grew upwards from the base of her body. She fluttered and her wings blossomed to reveal a darker, more brilliant shade of blue inside. I blinked, and in an instant the butterfly was gone.

He had devoted his life to the study of the beautiful, rare butterfly, while I chose to study conservation through researching its carnivorous caterpillar.

The captain announced our descent into Hong Kong International Airport, Chek Lap Kok. I tightened the strap of my belt so that it was taut around my hips. The first of nine dragon backs came into view; long, luxuriant spines of mountains undulating into the waking day. I pressed my nose up against the glass. The glittering city caught the morning light. Different shades of metallic blue danced along the periphery of land like jewels on fire. The wheels hit the tarmac with a thud and I was home.

Harper

The sun rises fat and round like a tasty egg yolk. As I am watching it from my bed, I hear someone singing. It sounds like Mum. Has her spirit come to visit me?

Using all my strength, I get up and follow her sound. It takes me to Wài Pó's room. Her head is sticking out of the window. She is wearing a long, white nightgown and her hair is puffy from the sea salt wind. Her voice grows stronger and stronger. It is low and wild from her belly and heavy from her bones, high from in her nose and soft on her lips. I feel a shock to my breath. She is making a masterpiece – but I did not know Wài Pó was an artist. She has sung to me many times before, but never like this.

It is as if she is calling all those things that are humming around her and drawing them into the space between us.

She is singing in Chinese and in English. I do not understand it all but I know it is something like poetry because of the rhythm, sound and the pictures they make in my mind. Her story is about home: 'the home we find in country… the home we find in others… the home we find in ourselves'.

Listening, I feel like I am floating below the sun.

I do not know that Wài Pó is finished until she turns and a surprised sound comes out of her mouth.

'Míng Huà, what are you doing here?'

Even though she is old, I think she looks like a child.

'You normally knock before you come in,' she reminds me.

I don't know why she says this. I never knock, even though I know that is a polite thing to do.

'Why did you never tell me about your music?' I ask.

She takes my hand. We sit on her bed that smells like the minty oil she puts on her knees.

'You know, when I was young, I loved to write my own songs and sing them.'

She is smiling now. I like that.

'I would sing in the shower, in the car, on my way to school. My parents would fight and I would sing.'

Her smiling stops and her face becomes tight. All her wrinkles come out like the shell of a walnut.

'And then one day my mother stopped me. The back of her left hand landed on my cheek. "Singing is not for people of our class," she scolded me.'

I hold her hand as tight as I can. I do not understand what her mum meant by 'people of our class', but I know this is upsetting because of the way Wài Pó said it.

'My mother was hurting. You see, she found out my father was in love with someone else.'

My body feels jumpy.

'But, Wài Pó, when people marry, they do it because they love each other and no one else.'

'My dear Míng Huà, love is not always that simple.'

I have seen this kind of thing in movies but I always press the stop button when it happens, because that is not what love is. Love is loyal, kind and full of romance.

'After we fled Shanghai for Hong Kong, I found out my country had banned its people from singing these kinds of songs too.'

That is a strange thing, I think to myself. China is a fun place. It is where cousin Bì Yù lives, and Uncle Bǐng Wén and Aunt Lǐ Nà. I always eat good food and have a good time with family when we are there. China is the country of Mum's birth and therefore it is a special place. We all used to sing in the car when we went there on holidays and no one stopped us.

'Why did they stop the singing?' I ask.

But she doesn't reply. Her eyes seem like they are lost somewhere, and even when I squeeze her hand again she doesn't come back.

'Why?' I say it louder now and it lands in the air like a full stop.

She looks at me. 'It doesn't matter anymore.'

I think that she looks very tired indeed.

'At least your *mā ma* got to make her music. I made sure of it.'

'Yes. Yes she did,' I say.

'Music is in our blood.' Her voice is not soft and thin like it usually is; now it is young and full and reminds me of stamping feet.

I hear my own sound now, loud and clear. It goes: da dum da dum da dum.

I close my eyes and see red blood, swimming around my body.

Red blood, red music.

Marlowe

My family home – a two-storey, renovated village house – had deteriorated in the years I had been gone. Its crumbling white exterior was marked with thick strokes of browning magenta from a decaying bougainvillea vine. Mould speckled the wooden window frames. The water feature in the centre of the driveway was covered in moss and the statue of a Greek goddess was missing her left finger.

'Simply the Best' sounded from a nearby radio, interrupting the morning stillness. I stood on the gravel driveway, suitcases by my side as the taxi drove off in the distance. A wind chime sounded, interfering with the beat of Tina Turner's song. I looked up. A radio sat by Harper's open window.

I pressed the doorbell. No response. I tried a second time, then a third, until finally Irene, Dad's girlfriend, opened the door. The scent of Chanel No. 5 and Silk Cut cigarettes wafted out. Irene leaned in to kiss the air above my cheeks.

'Where's Dad?' I ask.

'At work.'

'On a Saturday?' Owning a successful business making leather shoes meant Dad could choose his own hours.

'There's something he needs to sort out. We thought you were getting the later flight.' Her shiny, expressionless face was framed by an immaculate bob. 'Your sister and grandmother don't know you're coming.' Her right hand rested on her hip, her curves snug in one of the red mini dresses she always had in stock at her boutique. 'We thought it would be best not to cause Harper any unnecessary emotional stress. Anticipation can take its toll on the body and we couldn't be sure you would actually come.' She turned her back and swanned into the house, her snakeskin stilettos loud on the marble tiles of the foyer.

My suitcases were heavy. Too heavy. I dumped them next to Wài Pó's antique table which, instead of a bouquet of fresh flowers and a tray of her assorted Chinese sweets, was now cluttered with Irene's ashtrays. Beneath it were a couple of pairs of Irene's designer shoes. *She lives here now?* My stomach did a somersault. Although Dad and Irene had been dating since I was a young teen, he had never let her move in. This was Mum's house. In the corner, next to the umbrella stand, was a wheelchair. It looked lonely and smelled of hospital disinfectant.

I removed my shoes. The floor was cool beneath my feet. I walked past the kitchen – it smelled sweetly of Wài Pó's egg tarts – to the living room. Following the sounds of the radio, I climbed the staircase. From above, I saw that Wài Pó's treasured display of Ming dynasty vases was missing from the living room. I stopped abruptly. Mum's grand piano was missing too. Panic quickened my breath.

'Irene?' I called.

She moved into my line of view from the foyer below.

'Where's Mum's piano?' I knew this had to be her doing.

Irene glanced at the vacant space where the piano used to be. 'We can talk about this when your father gets home.' She turned to walk away, then stopped and turned. 'I presume you'll want to come in the car with us to the hospital?'

What kind of question was that? Why else had I come?

Stay cool.

'Yes.'

Stay calm.

She looked at her watch. 'You won't have a luxurious amount of time to unpack and get ready. We're leaving at one thirty.'

I fantasised about releasing my frustration with a loud howl before running out of the house, hailing a taxi to take me to the airport and boarding the next plane back to London. Instead I continued up the stairs.

On the second floor, facing the hallway that led to our bedrooms, I saw that in the place of family photographs which had once adorned the magnolia-white walls was a selection of contemporary paintings in shades of purple, green and grey. It didn't matter how much she insinuated herself into Dad's life, Irene Gresham would never be Mrs Irene Eve, I reminded myself. Dad would never marry again. This wasn't a promise he had made aloud, but I saw him make it silently the moment Mum died. His fingertips had gently closed her eyes and his lips lightly brushed her forehead.

'Goodnight,' he whispered.

Goodnight – not goodbye.

Turning away, I saw that my sister's bedroom door was ajar. Wài Pó, dressed in smart navy pants and a chiffon blouse, sat with her back to the door, facing Harper's bed. Her body appeared smaller, yet she still looked good for a seventy-seven-year-old.

'I made your favourite. Eat, please, you're far too skinny.' She extended her hand and I saw she was holding a plate of egg tarts. I moved forward to get a closer look at my sister.

Harper was in bed, tucked beneath a thick golden quilt. Her long mane of cocoa hair had thinned dramatically and her cheekbones protruded beneath sallow skin. One leg stuck out from beneath the quilt, and I saw that it was swollen and discoloured. I gripped the doorframe tightly. This was not the sister I'd left a year ago.

'Not hungry.' Harper shook her head. 'No thank you, Wài Pó.'

My sister never refused food.

How had things got so bad? I never should have left.

'Do you want *siu mai?*' Wài Pó offered.

'No.'

'Fried rice?'

Silence.

Come on, Harper.

'Congee with scallops?'

My sister shook her head.

Seriously?

Wài Pó bowed her head. 'You must eat, Míng Huà.'

'I said I am not hungry, Wài Pó.' Harper coughed. It sounded deep and sticky, and her lips, I noticed, were tinged with purple. It was unbearable.

I strode into the room. 'Harper you have to eat!'

Wài Pó screamed and whipped around. Harper rolled over in her bed. They both looked at me wide-eyed, as if they were seeing a ghost.

I drew Wài Pó into my arms. She felt so light and small.

'Am I dreaming?' Harper asked.

Wài Pó pulled away. Her eyes were watery and pink. She took an embroidered handkerchief from her pocket and dabbed her cheeks.

'*Hěn piào liàng.*' She cupped my face in her palms. 'So beautiful, like your *mā ma.*'

Harper held out her hand and I took it. 'Is it really, really you, Marlowe?' Her skin was cold. 'I need to touch you.' She reached for my face, and like she used to do when she was small, closed her eyes and traced my features with her fingertips. 'You're home.'

My heart skipped a beat; the abnormal rhythm shuddered through my body. I listened to her rasping breath and felt my own lungs tighten. Was this my body I was feeling or hers? My top lip quivered. I began to count silently, until I felt the tide of emotion recede. I opened my eyes and gave my sister a kiss on the forehead.

'I'm home, Harper. I'm here to look after you.'

As her hand nestled into mine, I pictured myself in London. I hated myself for the longing I felt, but I couldn't help it. I closed my eyes and imagined riding on the bus in the morning, watching flakes of snow spiral to the ground – much like the white feathers of a dove in the mouth of a fox.

Harper

'Tell me a story.' I want to listen to Marlowe's voice and feel her close to me.

Her body becomes very stiff and still. Her long arms and legs do not move, not even a little bit. Her face is like an empty piece of paper with no writing on it.

'Maybe Wài Pó can tell you a story?' She sits on my bed. I think that Marlowe might be a little bit scared of telling stories. This could be because she reads the words with her eyes and her quick brain but does not want to feel them inside of her heart.

'The story about the flower spirits?' Wài Pó asks.

I love that one, I really do. My Wài Pó has been good at telling it ever since I was a young and sweet girl.

'Once there was a scholar who lived alone in a small house. He loved flowers very much and spent all his days in the garden...' Wài Pó touches the jade ring on her finger as she talks. I think that she gets her magic storytelling powers from this special green ring.

'One day, four beautiful ladies arrived on his doorstep. Their names were Salix, Prunophora, Persica and Punica. They came asking for help. "In your garden, please put up a scarlet flag with the sun, moon and all the planets painted on it so that when the evil east wind blows, we will be protected." The scholar obliged and that night, when there was a storm, he noticed that the flowers in his garden remained unaffected by the wind. He realised that Salix was the willow, Prunophora the plum, Punica the pomegranate and Persica the peach.'

My eyes are closed now so that I can see the words from the story come alive like the flower spirits in the scholar's garden.

'The next evening, the ladies arrived on his doorstep again, this time with a large bunch of flowers. They offered them to the scholar with gratitude and told him that if he were to eat the flowers he would become immortal. The scholar did as he was told. In time, he realised his new power and his eternal existence.'

I watch the scholar in my mind. He is immortal. I am sure this means his body can live forever.

Marlowe

My bedroom hadn't changed much since I had been gone; white walls, white bed, white desk, white wardrobe and apart from my mahogany dressing table, white everything. I liked white – it was tidy and clean. I dumped my cases and shut the door behind me. Dust tickled my nose. From the window, I could see Dad's garden below. The tangled green foliage looked like hair in desperate need of a trim. The jasmine bush was overgrown, the plants in the flowerbeds were dried and shrivelled and the fishpond was empty. The old banyan tree bowed low, its hairy vines skimming the uncut grass. It was unlike Dad to let his beloved garden get so wild.

Using the phone by my bed, I called Olly. Only after the phone had rung several times did I realise I had forgotten about the time difference. Just as I was about to hang up, he answered. The sound of his voice sent a wave of sadness flooding through me.

'It's me,' I said.

'How are you? How's Harper?'

'She's...' Suddenly I didn't have the words. 'She's...' The wave infiltrated the organs in my body. I closed my eyes and tried to focus on the memory of Olly's face. It was still fresh, I could see him clearly, but how long would it take before his image became fuzzy and started to fade?

'She's as good as can be expected… considering.' Considering what? That I had left her for nearly a year without visiting because I was too wrapped up in saving the *arion* instead of paying attention to her? Considering that, in my absence, she had become incredibly ill and I hadn't even –

'You're seeing the doctors soon, right?'

I imagined him taking my hand, pulling me close.

'Yes.'

'Good. Let me know what happens.'

He's stroking my hair.

'I will,' I say. 'I'm sure they'll have a solution. It's the best heart hospital in Hong Kong, after all.'

'And how about you, Marls?' His voice was soft. 'How are you doing?'

His question startled me. It was disconcerting to be asked that in this place; at home, no one ever asked how I was. The wave reached my throat, making it hard to breathe. I imagined my body filling with air in the same way a butterfly's would – not through lungs but through the many small spiracles that run down the sides of their thorax and abdomen.

'Fine,' I say.

'Are you sure about that? You know you can tell me anything, right? Remember: you're not alone.'

You're not alone. He had said this to me so many times before. *You're not alone.*

Why did I find this concept so hard to grasp? The answer was simple: Harper. From the day she was born, everyone in the family had discovered a new meaning for the word 'alone.'

It was spring and I was five. Hong Kong was covered in mist; it oozed down lush mountains. The air was dense and clung thickly to my skin. The plants in Dad's garden were a tropical, pulsating green. In the mornings, the wide banana leaves were lined with droplets of moisture that shone in the light like small fragments of clear quartz.

Aunt Lǐ Nà and Bì Yù were visiting, in preparation for the birth of my new sibling. The atmosphere in our house was charged with anticipation. Late one night, unable to sleep, Bì Yù and I sat at the top of the stairs watching as Mum paced the living room, padding back and forth across the wooden floorboards on swollen feet. Her belly was ripe, the shape of a whole jackfruit.

Bì Yù and I held hands as Mum groaned. Her pale brow was contorted and shiny with sweat. She looked like she was in pain. No one had warned us that she would suffer.

'Dà jiě, how will they get that baby out of her tummy?' Like a big sister, my older cousin always had the answers.

Her reply was certain. 'They'll pull it out of her belly button.'

In between Mum's groans, I watched moths outside the living room window fly into the glowing night lights on our patio. Occasionally, one or two would drop to the ground. I wanted to go outside and investigate why these creatures made such a dramatic descent but had to use all the willpower my little five-year-old self could muster to keep still. The adults couldn't know we were awake or we would be sent straight back to bed. It wasn't until I was a few years older that I would learn the moth – a phototaxic insect – had confused our garden lights for the moon.

Another groan, then Mum gasped.

Dad grabbed his car keys. 'Let's go.'

'What's going to happen next?' I asked my wise cousin.

She pointed to her belly button. Goosebumps rose to the surface of my skin.

'Will it hurt her?' I couldn't understand why my parents had seemed so excited in the months leading up to this day. This unborn baby seemed to be causing my mother a world of pain.

'No. It won't hurt her. Having a baby is a beautiful thing.'

No matter how confident Bì Yù sounded, I wasn't convinced.

'Can we give the baby back if we don't like it?'

Bì Yù gave me a stern look. 'Babies make people happy. You shouldn't ask questions like that.'

My aunt suddenly seemed aware of us watching. 'Aī yā, what are you two doing up so late?' And she ushered us back to bed.

When I woke the next morning, the sky was blood red. The sun rose with a temper that set the water into a frenzy. Waves chopped and crashed into the shore.

Bì Yù was still snoring in the bed beside me. I climbed over her and made my way downstairs.

Aunt Lǐ Nà was slumped in an armchair in the living room. Her face was the colour of the ivory blanket Wài Pó had been knitting for the baby. She had a tissue box in her lap and her nose was pink.

'Are you feeling sick?' I went to her and placed my hand on her forehead, just like Mum did with me when I was ill. She quickly put the tissue box away and scooped me onto her lap.

'No, Míng Yuè.' She hugged me tight. 'I'm feeling sad, that's all.'

I placed my palm on her cheek. It was wet.

'Why? Do you miss *jiù jiu*?' My uncle was a very busy businessman and couldn't make it to Hong Kong this time. 'You will see him soon. Mum said we will all see him in the summer and show him the new baby then.'

'I'm not crying because I miss your *jiù jiu*.' She blew her nose.

I had to ask the question I had been dreading. 'Has the baby come yet?'

'Your sister was born early this morning.'

Sister! I was hoping for a brother. I had heard Mum say she wanted another daughter, that boys were too much work, but I wanted to be the only girl. Now she had got what she wanted and I somehow felt replaced.

Aunt Lǐ Nà was staring into the distance. Why wasn't she happy like she had been the night before?

'When's Mum coming home?'

'Not for a while. Míng Yuè, your little sister is... she is not very well.'

'Is she sick?'

'The doctors need to do some tests.'

'Tests?'

'Yes, but this is a secret. We don't need to tell anyone just yet okay? Your *mā ma* doesn't want people to talk. None of us do.'

I slid off my aunt's lap. The conversation had left me feeling unsettled. I didn't understand what was wrong with this new sister of mine. All I wanted was to see my mum again soon.

The next few days were spent waiting. Bì Yù and I weren't allowed to go to the hospital, and when Wài Pó and Dad returned home each night, they were silent, their faces drawn.

'Is the baby a monster?' I asked Bì Yù one night.

She looked at me, her eyes searching mine, and I realised that, for the first time, she didn't have an answer.

A week later, Mum returned home, but she wasn't carrying a baby in her arms. I was so happy to see her that I clung to her leg and wouldn't let go. I was expecting her to give me a big hug, like she always did when she came home, but instead she gently prised me off her then went straight to her room and shut the door.

'Where's the baby?' I asked.

'She had to have a small operation,' Dad replied. 'But she's getting better now.'

'What's an operation?' I asked.

'Something the doctors do in a hospital to make her better. She has a sore heart.'

'Do you need to leave her in the hospital for a long time?' I hoped his answer would be yes, but he said, 'We should be able to bring her home next week.' He ruffled my hair and said, 'Have hope, little one.'

It was raining the day my parents brought my sister home. Water fell in sheets outside our windows. I was sitting at the kitchen table with Bì Yù and Wài Pó trying to keep my colouring neat, just like my cousin's, but it was hard to concentrate. The sound of Wài Pó's jaw clicking every time she chewed hard on a White Rabbit candy was distracting. She had told us to be on our best behaviour when the new baby came, because Mum was very tired.

'Dà jiě,' I said, 'are you feeling a bit nervous?' I wanted her to tell me she felt fine and that there was no need to be scared of this new baby, but instead she pushed her crayon harder against the paper, scratching red into the outline of a tree trunk. She should have used brown.

We heard the front door open and Wài Pó rushed from the kitchen. Bì Yù and I followed. I tried to imagine what a monster baby would look like – green-skinned with black eyes, maybe, like the fat emerald caterpillars that ate the leaves in Dad's garden. But when I saw Dad holding the bundle of pink in his arms, he was smiling for the first time in a while.

'Welcome home, little one,' he cooed, looking down at my sister.

Mum was standing beside him, but her attention seemed to be elsewhere.

Bì Yù and I trailed them to the living room.

'Come on, girls – come meet Harper Míng Huà Eve.' He beckoned us close.

Harper? I hadn't heard that name before. It was a different kind of name, a bit like mine.

I gave Bì Yù a push. 'You go first.' When she reached the swaddled lump of pink, I could see her shoulders relax immediately. A few minutes later, she bent over and kissed the baby.

'It's okay,' she mouthed to me.

I looked at Mum for reassurance, but she was gazing out the living room window, watching the rain.

'This is your sister,' Dad told me. 'Harper, meet Marlowe.' He lifted her slightly to face me. Inside the soft wool was not a green monster, but a sleeping baby.

Her wide eyes were closed. She had long, dark eyelashes and a little button nose. One tiny hand was curled in a fist near her cheek. I could see the edges of a white bandage over her chest, I presumed from where she had had surgery for her sore heart.

Leaning in, I sniffed her little tufts of hair. She smelled like sweet chamomile and warm, freshly washed sheets.

In the days that followed, I realised Bì Yù had been wrong: babies didn't make everyone happy. Although Dad seemed to love Harper, there were no flowers and no gifts when she arrived home. The friends who'd visited Mum while she was pregnant, fussing over her and speaking excitedly about the new baby who would surely inherit her talent for music, were nowhere to be seen. Only one visitor came: the old lady who lived next door. She told my parents not to blame themselves; Harper was this way because she had done something bad in a past life and it was just karma. She suggested they send my sister to an orphanage in Fanling. 'It's an excellent home that knows how to care for mongoloids,' she said.

Dad slammed the door behind her when she left.

I asked Bì Yù to explain what a mongoloid was.

She told me it was a flower.

I asked her to explain what the lady meant by an 'orphanage'.

'It is where they send children who don't have parents.'

'But Harper has parents.'

Bì Yù just shrugged.

I didn't understand why all the adults around me were acting so strange. With her chubby cheeks and moon-shaped face, Harper was a beautiful baby. She only ever cried when she was hungry or needed her nappy changed. I just couldn't find much wrong with her.

After the lady next door's mention of an orphanage, I refused to leave Harper's side. At night, I slept on the floor by her crib. When she would cry for her feeds, Dad or Wài Pó would enter with her bottle and usher me back to my own bed. I'd lie awake until I heard them return to their rooms before creeping back to Harper's side. Sometimes I would gently place my palm over her bandage, wondering what it felt like to have a sore heart. Was she in a lot of pain? I felt sorry for this peaceful little baby. Then I would give her my finger and she would hold it, tight.

The night before Bì Yù and Aunt Lǐ Nà left to return to Shanghai, I overheard a conversation between Dad and Aunt Lǐ Nà. I had got up to go to the toilet when I heard tense voices in the living room below. I stopped and hid in the shadows on the landing to listen.

'I think you should consult a psychologist.' Aunt Lǐ Nà was sitting in an armchair with a glass in her hands, while Dad paced the floor in front of her.

'You've spent too much time in the US.' Dad's voice was stern. 'She just needs time to adjust. The doctor said her depression should lift in a few weeks, once the medication kicks in. Don't underestimate her; she's a tough woman.'

He took a seat and poured himself a drink.

'It's not just Hùi Fāng I'm worried about,' my aunt said. 'Having a sibling with a disability could impact Marlowe in ways we may not yet understand.'

They were talking about me now? I could feel my cheeks getting hot.

'What are you saying? That my daughter will be scarred by her sister's birth?' Dad took a large gulp of his drink. 'What's the big deal? Her sister is a little different, that's all. She has Down syndrome. I don't understand why everyone is overreacting.'

Down syndrome. I wasn't exactly sure what Dad meant, but I knew it had something to do with how upset the adults had been since the day Harper was born.

Aunt Lǐ Nà shook her head. Her voice was softer now. 'It's no one's fault. But how much has Marlowe seen of you since Harper was born?'

'You're out of line,' Dad said. 'We're adjusting to the new baby and that will take time, but it doesn't mean Marlowe will be ignored and she'll end up with a mental illness. Excuse me.' He stalked out of the room.

I ran back to my room and shut the door. I couldn't stop thinking about what my aunt had said. It was true I hadn't seen my parents much since Harper's birth, but that was because my sister had been sick. Now she was getting much better and things would go back to normal.

The next morning, when Aunt Lǐ Nà and Bì Yù had gone, the house felt empty. I no longer had a friend to distract me from my mum's absence. Her bedroom door was often shut and she seemed to sleep all day and night.

Eventually, Wài Pó and Dad stopped moving me back to my own room every night. They let me sit with them when they gave Harper her bottle and some nights I even got to give it to her myself.

Weeks went by and I hardly saw Mum, until early one morning I was woken by the sound of her voice. She was sitting in the nursery rocking chair holding Harper in her arms. Her tangled hair was loose over her shoulders.

'Ma?' I wanted to make sure I wasn't dreaming.

She looked at me. Her cheeks were pink. She stood up and put Harper back into her crib then took me in her arms. She smelled sour, like she hadn't had a bath for a while. As I held her tight, I could feel the bones beneath her skin.

'Why did you sleep for so long?' I asked.

She stroked my head. 'It's my fault your sister is this way,' she explained. 'I made her broken.'

Harper was broken?

'Don't worry,' I said. 'Her heart is okay now.' I went to the crib and gently tugged the blanket loose to reveal the small scar on Harper's chest. It was no longer inflamed and red.

Mum started to cry.

'I'm sorry I made you sad, Ma.'

'No.' She wiped her eyes with her sleeve. 'I'm not sad. I'm lucky, because I have you.'

'And you have Harper too.'

She sighed. 'I feel so alone,' she said. She pulled me close again. 'We only have each other now, no one else will understand about our little Míng Huà.'

'Marls?' Olly's voice brought me back to the present.

You're not alone. But however much I wanted to, I couldn't feel that.

'Let me help you, please,' he said.

You're not alone.

'I'll be fine.'

Harper

A post-it note is a bright and colourful square of paper, useful for saying things that are hard to say when someone is face to face with the person they love. In my desk I have a drawer full of post-it notes in lots of different colours: yellow, pink, orange, blue and green.

Even though I feel a bit breathless, I get out of bed because I have an important message to write. I decide to choose blue, because this is Marlowe's favourite colour. But when I go to take the square of paper out of the drawer, I have a messy feeling in my brain. My thoughts are tangled in knots.

Pink is the colour for love, orange is the colour for happiness and yellow is my favourite because it is the colour of Wài Pó's egg tarts – delicious and sweet. Blue and green are the sadder colours; blue like the clothes that Wài Pó has never stopped wearing since my mum died, and green like the velvet chair that my dad sits in when he has his serious face on and wants to be alone.

My fingers touch all the post-it notes. Making decisions is hard, especially when I have the nerves in my body. I practise deep breathing like Wài Pó taught me.

With my eyes closed, I see Marlowe the very first moment she arrived home from London in the United Kingdom. Her hair was messy and her face looked tired because of swollen eye bags. She took my hand inside hers and I noticed that her touch was empty and loose.

Sometimes the body can be present without the spirit. That's what Wài Pó says. I think this is true.

Eyes open, my thoughts are clear now and I choose a pink post-it note. I write my message:

> We are such stuf as dreems are made on and our litle life
> is rounded with a sleep by William Shakespeare from the
> Tempest. Said by Prospero the majican. First red to me by our
> dad James Eve who explaned these words are somthing to do
> with the dreem of life. Love from your sister: Harper明华Míng
> Huà Eve.

I wiggle all my toes and all my fingers. For the first time in a long time they feel warm. This is because I am getting better. I always knew in my heart that I would.

Marlowe

I unpacked, putting my clothes into the same drawers they would have gone into years ago. I put my hairbrushes on top of the mahogany dressing table, which had belonged to Mum. She had given it to me before she died. Whenever I sat in front of it, I imagined it was her face I saw in the mirror.

—

Mum rarely wore make-up or gave much thought to her physical appearance – unless she was performing in a concert – but she did take care of her hair. When she was at the piano she wore her hair loose and sometimes it would brush her fingertips as they flew across the keys.

I used to love sitting with her when she did her hair. Her secret, she said, was to wash her hair with rice water several times a week, 'as the Yáo women do in China'. She would comb morning and night with two different brushes: one made with goat hair and wood, the other was plastic and wide-bristled (to increase scalp circulation, she explained). Often, she would tilt her head back ever so slightly and let me do the brushing. When I touched her hair with my fingers it felt like water.

One day, when I was eight, I came home from school and found her seated at her dressing table. I ran to her but stopped as soon as

I saw her face reflected in the mirror. She was pale. Her eyes were puffy.

'Why are you crying?' I asked.

She was holding a pair of gold scissors. The sight of them caused a flutter in my belly.

'What are those for?'

She put them down on the table and I climbed onto her lap.

'Míng Yuè, there's something I need to tell you. I'm sick.'

I put my hand to her brow. It was covered in a light sheen of sweat. 'Yes, I think you have a fever,' I said.

She turned her head to look out of the window. 'It's not quite a fever, darling.'

'Do you have a sore throat?'

She shook her head but didn't speak.

'Mā ma? What is it?' Still she didn't say anything. Was this the reason she had strange marks on her skin? 'Even if you have a funny rash, don't worry, I still think you're very beautiful.'

Her gaze fell to the scissors.

'If you're sick,' I told her, 'then you should take medicine so that you can feel better.'

'Yes,' she said in a daze. 'You're right.' She kissed me and gave me a little nudge to get off her lap. 'Now go and help Wài Pó in the kitchen. I'll be down soon.'

I left the room, pulling the door closed behind me, but not all the way. I stood in the shadows watching her.

It all happened so quickly. She took the scissors and, with one quick snip, cut into the side of her long hair.

Aghast, I burst into the room.

'Stop, Mā ma! You can't!'

But she didn't stop. Like a robot, she kept cutting mechanically. Clumps of her hair fell to the floor.

I didn't realise I was screaming until Wài Pó came into the room and lifted me into her arms. All I remember was the feeling of her hand on my back, patting in a steady rhythm, and the feeling of wanting to be sick. Soon, I was lowered onto my bed. Wài Pó was talking to me, but I couldn't hear what she was saying. I realised that my hand was curled into a tight fist. Opening it, I saw that I'd been clutching a lock of my mother's hair.

Harper

When I stand at the door of Marlowe's room I can hear that the shower is on in her bathroom. I go to her dressing table and stick my post-it note onto her mirror.

'You shouldn't be walking around so much – you'll run out of breath.'

Stepmonster is standing by the door. I think in my mind about how I was keeping Stepmonster's move into our home a secret from Marlowe. A secret is a dishonest thing, and I feel guilty in my heart about it, but Stepmonster changed the air in our house the day she moved in, making it electric. Some parts of my mind were worried that if I told Marlowe while she was in England, she wouldn't ever come home.

'Do you need help getting ready?' Stepmonster asked. 'We'll have to leave for the hospital soon.'

'I'm much better. I don't need to go back to the hospital now, because I am fine.' I say it in a snappy way because I want her to leave me alone and stop bossing me around like I am still a child.

Stepmonster's eyes become small and tight, like she is about to have a bad mood. I know she wants to frown, but she can't because she has a stiff face. Marlowe says this is what happens when someone has plastic surgery. I think a lot of her face must be full of plastic now.

'We can't be late today, Harper. This meeting is very important.' She turns and walks back down the stairs.

Late. I hate that word. Everyone is always rushing me, even Louis. I don't like it when people always tell me to hurry hurry hurry.

Over her shoulder, Stepmonster shouts, 'Your sister will help you down the stairs and into the car. Please start getting ready.'

She always makes my body feel closed and tight, ever since the first day I met her. She was younger then, and her face wasn't so plastic. She had long brown hair that was in a shiny ponytail. She had a red dress that showed her long legs and when she spoke I could tell she was from a part of London that my grandpa hated, where they don't care about bugs and trees and flowers and they like to go to the shiny shops and kiss the air when they see each other. I remember thinking in my brain that she was nothing like my mother. Mum was the earth, the night and the moon. This woman is the city, with its sparkly buildings, and she looks like money. When she first met us, she smiled at me and Marlowe, which is a nice human action, but when she turned her back, her smile went away. I looked into her eyes and her heart was hard to find. Something about her reminded me of Snow White's evil stepmother, the wicked queen. Every good story has what is called a villain. This is a bad person. In my story Stepmonster is the villain.

I go back to my room and to my desk where I take out my brand-new book for writing stories. It is a little bit like Marlowe's notebook she keeps for her bugs, but mine has some magic in it. The front cover is full of my decorations in patterns, colour, shapes and glitter. This is something I am good at: writing and colour.

The Storybook of Miss Harper 明华 Míng Huà Eve

That is what it says on my very first page. I have to think about what to write next. I remember in a book that Dad gave me called *Storytelling 101* the author said to 'start by writing what you know'. Dad explained that this means I can use my life as inspiration. I can use what happens in my day as something to make a big spark in me, send a special electricity from my arms and fingers to my pen.

The Speshel Hart

Once there was a beutiful young lady.-

~~She had a problem with her hart but not in a romanse way~~
~~becos she was good at loving –~~

Her hart was sick but she still new how to love.

The beutiful yong lady had speshel doctors who always helped her get beter, a speshel family, a speshel sister and a speshel boyfriend.

This is the story about how they all made her hart well agane.

Now all I need is for something to happen so I can write it down. I pack up my notebook and put it in my bag ready for the hospital.

There is a lovely pink rose on my bedside table. I take it out of the vase and slide it into the top of my bun. Looking into the mirror, I arrange the flower in a nice and special way. My fingers tremble as I am fixing my hair, which is the colour of black bean paste. Louis tells me that I am the most beautiful woman in the whole wide world, but today my cheeks are pale and my lips have cracks in them. I used to feel proud of my brown eyes like the lady in the song 'Brown Eyed Girl', but now they look too dark and I think they have lost their sparkle.

The thoughts in my brain and the feelings in my heart are fast, so I hold my breath, which makes my thinking slow down. Time for some peach blush to go on my cheeks with the soft hairs of a make-up brush. I smile. A good smile deserves some lipstick, so I choose the colour 'plum blossom pink' and put it over the cracks on my lips. I am not as good at putting on make-up as Marlowe is, but that's okay. As my dad likes to say, practice makes perfect.

Dum hum da da dum hum. My hum feels strange in my chest, more like a whoosh than a thud. My head is light and giddy. I lie on my bed to catch my breath. It takes some time, but when the sounds in my body slow and my hum starts to sing, I sit up again.

Dum hum dum hum dum hum dum hum.

From inside my bedside table, I take my special beaded necklace and put it around my neck. These beads trap the light and spread it out to the world in different colours: yellow, red, orange, green, purple and blue.

Across the corridor, I can still hear the sound of Marlowe's shower. This makes me smile in a cheeky way because this is not hurrying like Stepmonster wants. Marlowe is moving to the time of her own clock.

I put my bag and pink coat on and walk to Marlowe's room. I sit on her bed and wait patiently. We will leave together, just like we used to.

Marlowe

Hot water trickled over my body, loosening my limbs. I inhaled steam, the moist air filling my lungs so that the world beneath my ribcage felt light and open. I imagined what breath might feel like inside Harper's chest. Immediately, an image came to mind of a Burmese python wrapping itself around her upper torso and squeezing. My blood felt hot. I grabbed a bar of soap and ran it over my body until I reached my chest.

Shit. I was still wearing the locket.

I stepped out of the shower and, fingers trembling, opened the gold case. Inside, the photograph was damp and wrinkled at the edges.

Mā ma. This was all I had left of her. Why hadn't I taken better care? *Mā ma. Mā ma what have I done?*

This happened every time I came home; something always unravelled in me.

Mā ma, come back.

The shower was still running. The splashing water reminded me of typhoon rain. So much water…

Mum loved the water. In summer she would rise early and walk down the steps at the end of the garden to the beach, and dive into the ocean. Often, she would take me with her, leaving Harper behind at home with Wài Pó. Although I cherished time alone with Mum, I hated the sea.

'Why don't you bring Harper? She loves the water.'

'It's not safe, the cold will get into her chest.'

Mum would try to coax me in, but I refused. I didn't understand the sea. It was like her music: abstract, hard to pin down, free and unruly. If I got too close, it might snatch me and swallow my body whole.

At seven years old, and much to Mum's disapproval, I still didn't know how to swim. With fluorescent yellow floats strapped to my arms, I would sit by the shore, building sandcastles. I kept a close eye on her as she dipped in and out of the water, her body mimicking the movement of the waves; fluid, as if her legs had become a long tail covered in scales.

On one particular day, the tide was high. Weighty clouds hung low. It looked like it was going to rain, yet Mum kept swimming, going further and further from the shore.

I stood and waved. 'Mā ma!'

She stopped and waved back.

Reassured, I returned to work, determined to construct a truly impressive sandcastle. I mightn't be able to swim, but I could do other things.

It was a while before I noticed rivulets of water snaking into the moat I had made. The tide was coming in. I looked up. Clouds rolled and smacked against each other.

'Mā ma!' I couldn't see her.

I ran up and down the beach, trying to catch sight of her between the cutting waves. 'Mā ma!' I screamed. 'Mā ma! Come back!' Rain began to fall, cold pinpricks against my skin. I still couldn't see her.

I had no choice.

Jaw clenched, I stepped into the sea. To my surprise the water was tepid and felt soft; it curled around my legs like a cat brushing up against its owner. Taking a deep breath, I summoned more courage and waded further in.

'Mā ma!'

Suddenly I felt two hands on my waist. Mum's head, birthed from the murky green-blue, looked shiny and new.

'Míng Yuè, why are you so scared? It's only water.' She was laughing!

I shook my head, fighting back tears. 'Where did you go?'

'I was always close by.'

The rain felt colder now; I started to shiver. Mum drew me to her and held me close. I rested my head at the nape of her neck. Salt washed over my lips. Before I knew it, we were drifting together, weightless. Gradually, I felt my fear wash away.

In time, the tips of our fingers began to wrinkle. The rain had stopped and Mum began to wade towards the shore. I felt the weight of my body once more. When we reached the sand, she lowered me to the ground.

'No!' I shouted. I didn't want to let go.

'You can walk on your own now.'

Harper was the baby, not me, and yet I wanted to stay in Mum's arms. She helped me to make sense of things I didn't understand. With her I felt safe.

❥

Someone was dabbing my cheeks with a pine-scented tissue. I opened my eyes. Harper was squatting beside me.

'It's okay, Marlowe,' she whispered. 'It's okay.' She pushed her round glasses up the bridge of her nose then stood up, grabbed a towel and wrapped it around me. I noticed the tap had been turned off.

She took the locket from my hands and peered at Mum's photo, then tentatively stroked the sodden lock of hair beside it. 'Is this Mum's hair?' she asked.

I nodded.

'You know that it is a bit gross.'

My sob turned into a laugh.

She looked at me, her gaze piercing.

'Blue suits you best.' She walked out of the bathroom into the adjoining bedroom. I heard a dresser drawer slide open. 'You need to get ready now, Marlowe,' she called. I could hear her rummaging through my clothes.

'There are no blue clothes here. Only black. Oh dear.' After a few minutes of silence, she squealed. 'You have a jumper that's not black!'

She returned to the bathroom carrying a pair of ripped black jeans and Olly's maroon jumper. I stood and took the clothes from her.

'Thanks, Harper. Why don't you sit down? I don't want you to get too tired.'

'I'm okay.' She handed me another tissue.

I gently pushed it away.

She sat next to me.

'Why is your heart sad?'

I swallowed hard. 'I'm fine, don't worry about me.' I looked at her and put my hand to her cheek. Her skin was softer than the tissue she had used to wipe my tears away.

'You know, when my heart feels sad, I think of all the good things in my life.' She paused to catch her breath. 'There's so many things…'

'So many things,' I echoed. My voice did not sound like my own.

She took my hand in hers and patted it gently. She opened her mouth to speak, then closed it. After a few seconds of observing me quite thoughtfully, she lowered her head and planted a little wet kiss on my left hand.

Harper

The hospital smells like mint leaves and roses. Even though I came here a while ago for my emergency fever, this is the fourth hospital I have been to this week and it is very different from the others. It has shiny floors, sesame bun–coloured walls and pink flowers that look like fluffy fairy floss.

I am in a wheelchair. I always get put in a wheelchair when I come to hospital. Even though I want to get out, I don't, because Marlowe told the nurse that she will push me. I like it when she takes care of me. She does it best. Good things always happen when she is home.

Stepmonster presses the elevator button to the fifth floor and looks at her watch.

'We're late,' she says, looking at Marlowe and me as if we are the villains of this story.

We enter the elevator and rise up up up through the building like we are in a spaceship. I feel a squeezing in my chest like I am sure all astronauts do when they lift off into the world of stars and the bursting light of souls gone from this earth.

The doors swing open and my tall and handsome dad is standing there. He wears shiny leather shoes which have been made with love and care in his factory. My dad used to always wear a bow tie but he doesn't anymore.

'There you are, Dad! How was your day?'

He does not reply because he is staring at Marlowe and his face goes a bit pale. This is a great time to make my second writing entry in my autobiography storybook. In *Storytelling 101* the author says that 'relationships and conflict are key to the success of a good story'. I had to ask my dad to explain the meaning of this to me and he did. Now I can feel the relationship and the conflict in the space between him and my sister.

'A Hospital Meeting'
A father sees his first dauter after a long long time of not seeing her. Insted of giving her one big hug, he puts his hand on her back. His eyes are full with things to say. Insted only 4 words come out of his mothe.
  Good to see you.
  The dauter smiles. She says the same thing back to her dad. Then her evil stepmonster says it is time to go. The stepmonster was happy she culd stop the father and the dauter from talking to each other. She had bad feelings in her hart and thout no one else could tell. But they could.

I have been to many hospital rooms before but this one is the nicest because it has pretty paintings of a garden and flowers in yellow and orange and blue. There is a doctor sitting at a big round table with lots of chairs around it. Enough for me and Marlowe and Wài Pó and Dad and Stepmonster. The doctor has tired moon eyes and a shiny bald head. He is flicking through a folder of papers. He wears a white coat, red glasses and I have never met him before. On his nametag I read the words *Prof. Julien Anderson*.

'Excuse me.' I wave my hand at the doctor and point at his nametag. 'What does Prof mean?'

He stares at me but does not speak.

'It means professor, darling,' Dad says.

I know what a professor is because Louis's dad is a professor and Louis says his dad is very, very smart.

'Well then, Professor Anderson, you have a good brain.' Because this doctor is also a professor it means that he will take very good care of me. I feel a relaxation in my body and it is like I am swimming in a warm sea.

Something is becoming clear in my mind now. Now I know why I have seen so many different doctors and had so many needles and scans. It is because my dad wants me to have the very best care. He always wants the very best for me.

The professor puts his hand to his mouth in a fist and clears his throat.

'I'm just waiting for our social worker, Maggie Lin.' He looks at his watch. 'She should be here any minute.' He takes a red pen out of a helpful pocket on his shirt and begins to write on one of his papers. I cannot read his writing and want to tell him it is very messy but that would be rude. He shuffles the papers on the table and knocks over something close to his arm. When he picks up the pieces and places them in the centre of the table, I can see that it is a plastic model of a heart. I have seen these models many times before. The doctors use them when they need to explain what is wrong with my heart and what needs to be fixed. I take out my notebook and write too:

A hospital is a plase where peopel get fixed and where you tak about the fixing. This hospital is full of smart branes.

I stop writing because I have noticed with my eyes that there is a skeleton in the corner of the room. I think it would be good to include this in my storybook. I try to find the words to describe what is wrong with the skeleton's leg, because the art of writing is all about what you see and what words you use to show this. Then Marlowe leans in and whispers:

'It's missing its left fibula.'

'What's a fibula?'

She touches the lower part of my leg. Her hands are warm.

'Are they going to fix it?'

'Sure.' She looks away and rubs her hands together. She does this sometimes when she is a bit nervous.

The doors swing open. A small woman dressed in a pink cardigan, blue jeans and a large shell necklace comes in.

'Hi.' She searches the room with her eyes. 'My name is Maggie Lin. I'm your appointed social worker and I'm here to support you.' Her chocolate eyes find mine and she gives me a big and friendly smile.

'Ah, you must be Harper.' She bends down next to me. She is very close so I need to lean back in my chair.

'Yes, I am Harper Míng Huà Eve. You have a very pretty necklace.'

She touches the shell on her chest.

'Well, aren't you such a dear?' She pats my shoulder. Her words are nice but they make me feel strange. I look to Marlowe for help, but my sister's face is tight and her eyes are hard.

The professor starts talking to my dad. Even though he speaks softly, I can still hear what he is saying.

'I think it is best that Harper leaves the room now. This could be quite emotional for her.' The skin under his chin is loose and it wobbles.

'That won't be necessary.' Dad fiddles with the collar on his shirt. I can feel all the invisible feelings between us all. They are running around the room, zigzagging between our hearts and our heads, filling all the empty spaces with something heavy.

'Very well.' The professor takes out a machine for catching his voice. He clears his throat again then presses a button. 'Patient number zero five one seven: Harper Míng Huà Eve, twenty years old.' The professor moves his voice catcher so that it is below his chin and he turns off a button. He looks at my dad.

'We have considered everything you and your family have been through.' He puts his voice catcher near his lips again and presses the button again. 'Harper was born with an atrioventricular septal defect which was treated with corrective surgery at St Peter's Hospital on the night of her birth. Because of the graft failure, at the age of three she had open-heart repair surgery at the National Hospital in Shanghai. Aged fifteen she went into heart failure. In the beginning it was noted that she went blue on crying. Cyanosis later became persistent, indicating a current problem with the previous repair.' He takes a big breath. 'Throughout childhood she frequently required hospitalisation for recurrent chest infections, bronchitis and pneumonia.'

My dad gives one of those looks to Stepmonster that says he is in a mood. The professor sees him.

'My apologies, this is hospital procedure.' He looks at his notes. 'After presenting at our hospital…' He goes on talking about how last week I came into this beautiful hospital with a fever and a very weak hum. The more he talks, the more his words become small and start to fade.

'This is boring,' I whisper into Marlowe's ear.

The lady with the shell smiles at me again. Her necklace catches the light and shines brightly from her chest.

I write some more in my notebook.

> She thught the doctors would fix her but in fact it was a
> woman in the hospital meeting room who would heel her.
> She was called the lady with the shell. She was kind and was
> born deep deep deep where storys are hiden in the water.
> A speshel lite came from her neckless and filled her chest,
> making it warm.

I would like to write more about the lady with the shell, but the professor's voice is louder now and this gets in the way of my creative thinking.

'We have since stabilised her and done our own investigations.' The professor looks through his papers again. 'Harper's tests have shown a marked deterioration in her heart's ability to function, which is in turn affecting her lung capacity.' He circles something on a piece of paper in red pen. 'As you will know, these results are not good. Both the echocardiogram and Swan-Ganz catheter show that she has developed pulmonary hypertension and that her pulmonary vasculature is irreversibly damaged.'

Irreversibly damaged. Suddenly it is noisy in my head. I can't remember exactly what irreversibly means but I know it is a very strong word and damaged is a very broken word. My thoughts blur together and I can't separate them.

'You're not the first doctor to tell us this.' My dad's voice is sharp. I think a fire is burning in his heart. Heat spreads through the room.

'Calm down, James,' Stepmonster says.

I feel like ants are crawling inside my stomach.

'We're here because we want to know if you can help where others refused to.' His heat hits the professor, making his cheeks pink.

I slide my hand into Marlowe's and quickly feel my mind go quiet.

Wài Pó twirls her jade necklace around her fingertips and chews. She is probably eating another hawthorn candy.

'Based on Harper's most recent results, it has become apparent that oral medication won't help her heart failure, and corrective surgery is not advised due to the onset of pulmonary hypertension.' The professor pushes air out of his mouth like it is thick smoke. He looks sideways at the lady with the shell. She nods at him and then looks at me, smiling with pinched eyes. The professor moves his voice catcher below his chin.

'In my professional opinion, Harper requires a heart and lung transplant.'

Transplant. Transplant. Transplant. A word I have heard at all the hospitals I went to. It is a word I don't understand. It is a word that all the doctors say quickly and quietly, a word that makes the professor's eyelids twitch. I think that I must write this word down so I can try to find its meaning later.

Marlowe's hand is floppy in mine so I squeeze it. I look at Wài Pó, who is shaking her head and is saying things as quietly as the grass when it whispers to the air.

'We are aware of this,' my dad says. 'This is the fourth hospital we have been to now.'

The professor clears his throat again. I think maybe Wài Pó should offer him a hawthorn candy.

'So are you going to put my daughter on the list for a heart and lung transplant or will you just give us the same line that the other hospitals did?' My dad rubs his forehead. 'Look, if it is about the money, we will find the cash. Just do whatever you need to do to make my daughter better.'

I clear my throat like the professor does, but no one looks at me. I think they have forgotten I am here.

'Excuse me,' I say. 'What does transplant mean?'

No one answers me.

'Hellooo?'

Marlowe stands up. 'Come on, Harper, I think maybe we should leave.'

'Sit down.' My dad talks in a loud way. 'Harper is not going anywhere.' He looks at me, and I see the skin around his eyes is red. 'Darling, you are very sick.'

I know all about that; I can feel it in my body.

'You need the doctors to give you a new heart and lungs so you can get better.'

New heart and lungs? This is a very strange thing to say. I have not seen these sold in the supermarket, or even at the pharmacy where we usually get things to make me feel better. I think that maybe my dad is a bit confused about what a transplant is.

With his large hand, the professor scratches his shiny bald head and begins to talk again. I can tell that all of his brain is focusing on my dad and all of his body is trying to get rid of the heat.

'We have very limited resources. The demand for organs is much greater than the supply,' says the professor. 'We have assessed Harper's case carefully, but having Down syndrome not only limits an individual's quality of life and life expectancy, their physical ability to cope with a transplant is compromised.'

I start to think that maybe the professor is not so clever. He doesn't know that it is the Up syndrome not the Down syndrome.

'Harper would have to follow a complex anti-rejection drug regimen which can have severe side effects, not to mention the round-the-clock support required to ensure she adheres to this.'

He clears his throat again. I give Wài Pó a look that means she should give him one of her candies.

'Hong Kong is a small place. It may take a long time to find a matched donor, by which stage Harper's condition will have significantly deteriorated. Sadly, she is not an appropriate candidate for a heart and lung transplant.' He slides a piece of paper towards my dad. 'Here is our preliminary report.'

I am getting a bit frustrated by all this talking, so I stand up.

'I have to say something. First of all, it is called the Up syndrome not the Down syndrome, and second of all, I don't know why everyone has to be so upset today. I would like to let you know that I am happy for you to fix my heart so that it is like that model.' I point to the plastic heart. 'But I will not be needing a new heart and new lungs, because I like my own. You have fixed me in the hospital before and you can do it again without giving me new parts.' There has been so much information in this hospital room today and it is giving me a sore head, but I don't tell them that. 'Last of all: Wài Pó, please share one of your sweets with the professor. He has a sore throat.'

'Thank you for sharing your thoughts with us, Harper,' the lady with the shell says. 'We understand that this must be –'

'Please sit down, Harper.' Marlowe interrupts the lady, which is rude, but her voice is very soft and gentle.

My bum goes back onto the wheelchair seat and I rest my head on Marlowe's shoulder. In my mind, there is an image of a heart. Hearts are supposed to be red or pink, like the professor's model, but the one I can see is black, wet and sticky. I must close my eyes and take a breath – this is something that Ms Amanda Li, my independent living teacher, says is 'a technique for coping with emotional stress'. I know that sometimes my mind can play tricks on me when I feel the stress.

'Surely there must be something you can do?' The sound of my dad's voice makes me open my eyes again. It is like his lonely words have fallen to the ground and no one saw them leave his lips. The fire in his heart is out.

'This is a complex matter, and Down syndrome complicates the situation further.'

'Um excuse me,' I clear my throat again, like the professor does because that is what smart people do. 'I said it was the Up syndrome,' but no one seems to hear.

'So,' Dad says slowly, 'what you're saying is that you won't help my daughter because she has Down syndrome.'

The professor wipes his forehead. Dad must have sparked flames again.

'It's not as simple as that, Mr Eve. We just don't have adequate supply to meet the demand. We have a long waiting list for all organs, and Harper needs both a heart and lungs. Her physical and mental ability to cope with the treatment that is necessary after the procedure is severely limited.'

'You won't even put my daughter's name on this waiting list, because she has Down syndrome.' My dad is growling now.

My stomach begins to ache and my mouth is dry. Why does everyone keep saying things that make me feel alone?

'Even though your daughter is considered high functioning for someone with a disability, when assessing suitability for an organ transplant we take into account a number of factors, including the stage of the disease, life expectancy, capacity to contribute to society –'

The fire cracks and sputters. Dad jumps out of his chair.

'How dare you.'

I hold my breath. The heat, the heat, the heat.

'Are you suggesting my daughter doesn't contribute to society? She has a job as a librarian's assistant, loves to cook, has a mature, devoted relationship with her boyfriend and, above all, she is one of the most loving, compassionate and caring young women I know.'

'Calm down, Mr Eve.' The lady with the shell reaches her hand across the table. 'I can understand you must be devastated by –'

'Come on, James.' Stepmonster stands and collects her things so quickly it hurts my eyes to watch her. 'Let's get out of here.'

'Where are we supposed to go?' Now I think my dad looks a bit old. His face is tired and his eyes are empty. He always puts out his flames before they reach Stepmonster.

'We can offer Harper pain relief. In-house care or a hospice is also something worth considering as her condition deteriorates.' The professor closes his folder with my name on it.

'The Sha Tin hospice has a great reputation.' The lady with the shell slides a few coloured papers in Dad's direction.

'My daughter is more than her disability. She deserves a chance to fight this, just like anyone else her age.'

Yes, I think to myself. This is the Up syndrome.

The professor looks at his watch. 'I'm very sorry...' He looks at the lady with the shell. 'Perhaps Maggie could provide further assistance.'

'James.' Stepmonster places her hand inside Dad's. 'Let's go.'

My dad makes his collar straight again. Everyone stands to leave. Stepmonster pushes me into the hall and I can tell she is in a hurry to leave by the quick sound her heels are making on the floor. I look back at the large room with the poor, broken skeleton and the garden painting.

'Mr Eve?' The lady with the shell runs up to Dad and hands him a card. 'If you ever need anything, here are my contact details.'

Dad doesn't take the card. He turns his back on the lady with the shell and presses the button for the elevator. I turn and see Marlowe behind me. She is very serious. I think she is like the water, and her waves are very still. I think that soon they might overflow.

As we are waiting for the elevator, I decide to write a final entry in my notebook.

> She was luky. She had the lady with the shell looking after her and a smart profesor who said she needed a tran-s-plant. A tran-s-plant is a way to fix things, done by a profesor. It can be a confuseing word, but it is not a scary word. There is no need to be upset about this word. She knew that soon the hole in her hart wuld be fixed so she did not understand why her family was so upset.

I shut my storybook, even though I want to leave it open on my lap for everyone to see; there is no need for everyone to be so upset in their hearts and minds. I know everything will work out, like it always does.

Marlowe

I feel light-headed. It must be the jet lag, I tell myself.

'Marlowe?' Dad was holding the door to the lift open.

'I'll meet you in the lobby in five.'

I needed coffee. On my way to the vending machine, I think back over the conversation with the cardiologist, dissecting it, trying to make sense of it. Already it seemed unreal, remote, like it hadn't actually happened. Was there really nothing more that could be done for Harper? She couldn't die. *Just breathe.* Then I thought of Harper and wondered how she had made sense of the day. What was she feeling? It must be so hard for her, not being in control of her body. Her life was going so well, and then she got sick again. Even though she didn't show it, I knew she was scared.

I shoved coins into the vending machine quickly, one after the other, until I realised I had rammed a two-dollar coin into the slot and it was stuck.

'Damn it.'

My crappy can of Nescafé was only a few inches from my grasp behind the glass screen. I kicked the metal base, and my eye caught sight of a sign in Chinese and English: *This machine does not accept $2 coins.* I let out a groan.

'Marlowe!'

I turned to see Maggie Lin walking towards me. She smiled, teeth marked with pink lipstick the same colour as her cardigan.

'Can I have a quick word?'

'Actually,' I said, 'I wanted to clarify something with you.'

Another stained smile. 'How can I help?'

'Surely there must be something more' – I swallowed – 'something more we can do to get Harper the treatment she needs.'

'This must be very difficult for you.' Maggie seemed to say that a lot. 'As I mentioned earlier, there's a hospice in Sha Tin that provides excellent care.'

I bit my tongue. If I spoke, I would say something I would regret.

'I'd be happy to help you with the paperwork.' She clasped her hands together. 'Let me assure you, I know how hard this must be. When I was young, I had a friend next door who had Down syndrome and he was just a ball of pure light and energy.'

Don't vomit.

'Surely the refusal to give my sister a heart transplant because of her disability is a violation of her basic human rights?'

'It is not as simple as that. As Professor Anderson said, this is primarily a medical decision.'

'But you were in the room when the doctor said –'

'You seem like a smart young lady. If you care about Harper, I'm sure you'll do what's best for her. The Sha Tin hospice offers wonderful palliative care. It's in an old house overlooking the sea. A beautiful place.'

My head was spinning. 'Our own home overlooks the sea.'

A light in the ceiling above us started to flicker.

'I've read Harper's file. Being the sibling of someone who has a disability can be a challenge. You may have felt deprived of attention growing up, with your parents focused on Harper's needs. And then there was your mother's death. I wonder if…'

I stopped paying attention to her words. *Deprived of attention*; it sounded like something straight out of a psychology textbook. My upbringing was more complex than that. While my mother was alive, I was the apple of her eye, and when she died, Harper and I were *both* deprived of attention.

'Marlowe?' Maggie Lin looked concerned.

'My childhood was fine, thank you.' *And even if at times it wasn't, I won't be telling you about it.*

'It can be devastating when a primary caregiver dies, especially when a child is so young.'

She didn't need to keep bringing Mum into this.

'You need to understand that you're not responsible for your sister. That's your parents' job, not yours. Have you ever had any counselling?'

Yep. I'm going to vomit.

'No.'

Truth be told, I did have counselling once, about six months after Mum died. I was losing focus at school. Dad sent me to a grief counsellor who made me draw how I felt using coloured pens. I drew a large house with a garden. The psychologist asked why my family weren't in the picture. There wasn't room to fit four stick figures inside the house, so I just shrugged. She asked me if my house felt empty. I shrugged again. With a raised brow, she made notes in my file. I didn't go back for another session after that.

'I suggest you seek professional help,' Maggie was saying as she fiddled with her ugly, lumpy shell necklace. 'It might be useful for you to revisit the thoughts and feelings you have surrounding your mother's passing so that you are better equipped to deal with Harper's.'

Who did she think she was? I had known her for about an hour at most and she was already convinced she had unlocked my innermost thoughts and feelings. Time to go. I gave the vending machine a final kick then strode away.

Harper

Riding home in the back of the car, sitting in the middle of Wài Pó and Marlowe, I am trying not to listen to the words that are coming out of Dad's and Stepmonster's mouths, but the more I try not to hear, the louder their words are.

'James, you have to be calm now.'

'I am calm.'

'There's nothing more we can do. You have to accept that.'

The car speeds faster and so does my dad's voice.

'You're asking me to accept that my daughter is going to die. Do you understand that?'

'Dad!' Marlowe says, but it is too late, that word has been said.

Die.

A word that feels like a sharp object, poking inside my chest.

'Die.' The word comes out of my mouth now. 'Die, die, die.'

My world is very quiet. I can see from the corner of my eyes that my dad has turned his head quickly to look at me. I can feel them all talking to me but I can't see them because I am concentrating on the window outside and the buildings and the trees and the traffic lights and that word.

Marlowe takes my hand. Wài Pó starts munching on candy, munch munch munch. I can see her teeth are sticking to the candy and the candy is sticking to her teeth.

We stop at the traffic lights. My dad pulls over by the side of the road.

'James, what are you doing? This is a bus stop!' Stepmonster says.

'Darling.' My dad reaches his hand back to touch my knee. 'I'm sorry, I didn't mean to say that. I'm very upset. Can we talk about this properly when we get home?'

I think in my brain about the hospital meeting, about the model heart, about the smart professor.

Die. This is a word that was used so many times when Mum *died*. Everyone was so sad in their hearts but I couldn't understand why. When Mum's body was given back to the soil in the earth, her humming went everywhere; in the wind, the trees, the sun, the stars. All around us she was helping things grow. It is not a secret that when things die they still hum; it just changes. After the dum da drumming of a heart, it becomes a feeling that floods the air, like music.

But I am not going to die. I love my body. Even when it's sick, I enjoy being in it because I get to do things like: hold hands with my Louis, write letters to my Marlowe, read with my dad, cook with my Wài Pó, and chat and laugh with my friends. I am not going to die until I am old and all my dreams have come true.

'No need to talk,' I say. 'I am not going to...' The word is stuck. 'I am not going to...' It is there at the back of my tongue. 'Not going to...' It is tight at the top of my throat. 'Not going to...' I am absolutely and very surely, one hundred and one per cent not going to: 'Die!' I shout. 'No way. Not me.'

'It's okay, Harper,' Marlowe says. 'It's okay.'

The car is very quiet again. I can't even hear the sound of Wài Pó chewing. The sharp object is out of my chest. My breath is slower, smoother.

'Dad,' I say, 'there is no need to use that word on me. The doctors will fix me. They always do.'

He looks away. I see Stepmonster bow her head in the seat in front of me. Wài Pó takes my hand in hers. After a while, Dad starts the car again and we drive home.

Marlowe

We had been home only an hour; the smell of hospital still lingered on our clothes. Once Harper was settled in bed, the sound of her stuffy breath signalling deep sleep, I made my way outside to the garden. It had begun to rain. As I lay on my back on the grass, I could see how quickly the world was spinning. Even when I finally felt still, I wasn't.

When we were small, Harper and I used to lie on our backs and she would narrate the shapes and stories that emerged from the clouds: flying horses, friendly dragons, whispering trees and wonderful castles. Without her, all I can see are blobs, floating monotonously through grey sky.

Harper

Everyone thinks I am sleeping in a sickly way in my bed, but I am not. I still have all the voices from our afternoon at the hospital swirling around in my head. I call Louis on his personal mobile phone. We talk twice a day, every day, while he is on holiday in Thailand with his family.

'Hello?'

'Hello,' I say.

'Oh, my sweet lady, how are you? How do you feel? How was the doctor's?'

I have to remind him to ask me one question at a time. Then I tell him everything is fine and I will be better soon. There is no need to repeat the word that Dad said in the car. He didn't mean it anyway. Sometimes we all say things we don't mean when we are upset. There is also no need to tell Louis about the other word: 'transplant'. It is too complicated and may just make him worried in his heart when, really, there is nothing to worry about.

'I have something I need to tell you,' he says.

'What?' I am smiling because I can hear sparks flying around in his voice.

'I was looking at the sunset on the beach at exactly six twenty pm and I thought of you.'

'That's nice. I think of you at sunset too.'

'Excuse me, I'm not finished yet.'

'Sorry.'

'Well, I was thinking that I would like to marry you at sunset…
sometime soon.'

My hum started to zing and hop and jump. I smiled so big and
wide that it hurt inside my eye and cheek muscles.

'Maybe we can live together after that and have a family, and we
could watch TV in our own home, and make popcorn together, and
no one can tell us not to eat Doritos and drink Coke.'

'Oh, Louis, I would love that with all my heart.'

'Uh, I'm still not finished speaking my speech.'

'Sorry.'

'Most of all, I would love to spend every sunrise and sunset with
you from now on until the day I die.'

Die.

Why did he have to say that word?

Suddenly my eyes are spilling water.

'Uh-oh, I'm sorry. What did I say? Did I say something wrong? I'm
sorry, I didn't mean to.'

'No, it's nothing.' I shake my head, but he can't see that. 'Nothing.
I just don't want you to d–i–e.'

He's very quiet.

'Louis?' I say.

'Yes?'

'Why are you quiet?'

'I dunno.'

Sometimes he needs my help.

'Well, this is the part where you say, "Don't worry, I'm fine."'

'Okay.'

'Okay what?'

'Oh, sorry. I mean, don't worry, I'm fine.'

But it didn't feel right and I was still crying and I didn't know why.

'Harper?'

'Yes?'

'Do you not want to marry me?'

This made me cry more. I was hurting him in his heart and I did not mean to.

'Of course I want to marry you. You are the love of my whole life.'

'Yes, I thought so,' he said. 'So why are you crying?'

I thought in my mind and in my heart about this for some time, but there were no words that came to my mouth for me to speak about how I felt. It made my forehead go tight.

'I don't know,' I said.

Marlowe

Mum, blindfolded, had said she was turning eighteen again, then giggled. She was standing by the French doors.

'Happy birthday!' I sang as Dad guided her into the garden.

Harper, who had just turned one, squealed and tugged the hem of Mum's floral dress. Wài Pó lifted my baby sister to her chest. My grandmother was smiling, and it made her face look years younger.

For the last few months, Dad had been busy in his garden, working on a surprise for Mum's birthday. A section of the lawn with the best view of the ocean had been cornered off and no one was allowed to enter. Even though I could see what was being built from my bedroom window, I kept it a secret.

Dad took Mum's hand and led her through the jungle of greenery. Wài Pó, Harper and I followed, walking across the warm grass, past the fishpond with the fat koi, past the banana, bauhinia and papaya trees, to the edge of the garden, where salt water infused the air.

There we saw an elegant red-and-green-tiled pagoda. Its upturned roof had a ceramic phoenix at each corner. Inside were two benches and a small table, all in matching red-and-green tiles. Citronella lamps stood in the grass by the arches of the temple. Flames snapped and crackled, their scent sour and sweet. It was the most beautiful thing I had ever seen, like something out of one of Harper's storybooks.

Wài Pó's eyes looked wide and dreamy. Harper clapped her hands together.

I desperately wanted to rush inside the temple, but knew I had to wait patiently for Dad to undo Mum's blindfold.

She was silent, staring at her gift, hand over her mouth.

'Ma,' I whispered, 'do you like it?'

She didn't speak. Her hands were trembling. She took Dad's arm, and they walked in together.

Wài Pó said we had to leave them be. As we walked back to the house, I turned to see them sitting side by side. They were watching the dotted lights of ships hover over the ocean like fireflies.

The pagoda became Mum's sanctuary, one that she had shared with Dad. Most days, when he returned home from work, she would meet him for a gin at sunset and they would sit together, holding hands. I wondered what they spoke about, or if they even needed to speak at all.

Now, as I watched the sun setting from my bedroom window, a movement in the garden below caught my eye. His shoulders were slumped as he walked towards the spot where Mum's pagoda used to be. He reached a square of sparse brown grass – the only remaining trace of her sanctuary – and bent down to place his hand on the spot. After Mum's passing, he'd had the pagoda taken down and the grass never grew back.

I pressed my nose against the window and held my breath, waiting for him to make his next move. Head bowed, his shoulders shook. I had only ever seen him cry once before, and that was a long time ago.

I was nine. Two months had passed since Mum was buried. There were no more funeral preparations to distract us. Flowers had stopped coming, along with the cards and hampers of food, and there were no more visitors. Before she left to go back to Shanghai with Uncle Bǐng Wén and Bì Yù, Aunt Lǐ Nà sat me down for a talk.

'When someone dies, it is normal to feel very sad,' she told me. 'Your dad, Wài Pó and Harper will feel it too. It is important to let yourself cry.'

I'd been expecting my family to cry, but they didn't, not even Harper.

After Mum's funeral, I was very busy. We were doing an exciting science project at school and I was preparing to submit my findings on the feeding habits of Indian cabbage white and great Mormon butterflies. This involved laying different-coloured circles of paper in a row in Dad's garden, some laced with honey and water, some not. For hours, I watched to see whether the butterflies searched for food based on colour or scent. There was no time to feel sad.

Wài Pó was also too busy to cry. Cooking elaborate dinners had become her latest obsession. She would spend every morning at the markets and then all day in the kitchen. I thought it was a strange obsession, since she never ate very much herself, but she had often said she liked the taste of other people's food more than her own.

Harper had seemed her normal, cheery self. She continued to dance and sing, eat as much of Wài Pó's cooking as she could, and was just as chatty as she was when Mum was around. In fact, she still spoke to Mum, as if she were still alive. The only time it became a nuisance was at night. Harper had refused to sleep, unless it was in bed with me, and her incessant jabbering would keep me up. She was still learning her words so I couldn't understand half of what she was saying.

Dad seemed to be coping the best out of all of us. He would rise early every morning, tend to his garden, go to work, eat three meals a day, and generally carried on as if nothing had happened. The only thing that seemed different about him was that he had stopped reading. When Mum was alive, he'd read three different newspapers in the mornings and had a new book in his hand every evening. Mum would always say: 'For your father, reading is like taking breath. It is something he will always need to survive.'

We continued like this for weeks. It was as if Mum had simply gone on holiday.

I don't remember feeling her absence until the day Harper came home from kindergarten with a bad cough and a fever. She was clammy and lethargic. All she wanted to do was curl on my lap on the sofa, sucking her thumb and twirling my hair with her free hand.

Wài Pó took her to the GP, who gave her antibiotics, but they must have been the wrong ones, because at two in the morning I woke to the sound of her crying in the bed beside me. She was white, sweating and delirious, and her lips were tinged blue. It all happened so quickly after that. We bundled her into a taxi and made straight for the closest emergency department. There she was diagnosed with pneumonia and immediately put into the intensive care unit. I watched from a corner of her room as medics stuck wires on her chest and put an oxygen mask over her face. When they prodded a needle into her vein, trying to thread a cannula in for a drip, I shuddered, but Harper never cried. The more stoic she was, the more powerless I felt. All I could do, it seemed, was watch from the sideline. She didn't even need me to comfort her.

Harper never seemed fully conscious. It was as if she was half with us and half somewhere else. A doctor told us she had become septic. I didn't understand what that meant, but I knew by the tone of voice that it wasn't good. Wài Pó sat in the corner of the room thumbing her beads in a daze. Dad paced the corridor outside the ICU, frantically calling other doctors he knew, trying to get Harper the best medical care possible. But as the days wore on, I noticed his demeanour change. He moved slower. His body seemed to shrink. His voice softened and his face looked long and tired.

One afternoon, I heard Dad talking to the doctors outside Harper's room and crept to the door to listen. 'Should I be signing a do-not-resuscitate order?' he asked.

Do not resuscitate. I knew what that was. Dad had been asked if he wanted to sign one of these when Mum was very sick. It was a form that meant they wouldn't help her heart start to beat again if it stopped. But he had refused to sign it then, so why was he asking about signing one now for Harper? How could he? He had always told me to have *hope*.

'No,' one of the doctors assured him. 'There's no need for that.'

'You don't understand,' Dad said. 'I've just watched my wife die. I can't do this again. She was in so much pain.'

The doctor tried again to reassure him. 'We've made Harper as comfortable as possible. A DNR isn't going to help the situation. Give her a chance to fight this.'

Dad shook his head. 'I can't do this again,' he repeated.

My head spun. Harper was in her hospital bed, still breathing. She was my sister and she was still young and she wasn't supposed to die. No, she *wouldn't* die. We wouldn't lose another member of our family.

And then I heard Dad begin to sob, a sound that was deep and raw. As his sobs intensified, so did the twist and rise of acid in my stomach.

While the doctor tried to soothe him with words, I attempted to count myself out of panic – *one Mississippi, two...* but it was hard, too hard. My mind was racing. Dad had always been the one to fix things. He had fought so hard for Mum, even flying in a doctor friend of his from London. Dad was the fighter. I could always trust him to do his best. But now...

I stepped out into the corridor. 'Why are you being like this?' I demanded. 'Harper will get well! Where's your hope gone?'

The doctors turned to look at me, startled. Dad met my gaze for a moment and then quickly looked away. I waited for him to answer me, but he didn't. Suddenly it felt as if the ground beneath me was no longer stable. Dad, who was supposed to make me feel safe, had turned everything upside down.

I vowed to take matters into my own hands. I could not call doctors from London, I could not administer Harper's medicine, but I could sit with her and guard her life with mine.

I sat with Harper night and day. I missed school, I missed the deadline for the science competition, I even missed my own birthday party. Wài Pó stayed with me during the day, and when I refused to leave at night she sent our domestic helper, Esmerelda, to stay with me. Dad didn't try to make me go home; I think a part of him was secretly pleased someone was watching over Harper constantly, even if it was his nine-year-old daughter.

Days went by and she did not stir. I was starting to feel worried, so I did something I hated doing: I read to her. I had never liked children's books – the world of the imagination scared me – but I knew Harper loved them.

Early one morning, as I was reading *The Wonderful Wizard of Oz*, she opened her eyes.

I dropped the book. 'Harper?'

She looked dazed, like she had just stepped off a very long flight and was trying to figure out which country she had landed in. Then she touched my arm.

I felt a rush, like a cool shower flowing through my body. I kissed her all over. She had pulled through.

The doctors arrived moments later. I took a step back and stood by the window as they fussed over her. Heat licked the side of my neck, I turned and saw the sun rising, as a perfect ball of gold light. The furniture in the hospital room, the doctors and Harper were glowing. It looked like a scene from one of her fairytales. I enjoyed this for a moment too long and then came to my senses; life was not a fairytale. Although Harper had woken from her sleep, I knew that from this point on, everything had changed.

Dad's study smelled of stale coffee and old books. I found this familiar mix strangely comforting as I rested briefly in his old green armchair. While I waited for him to join me, I scanned the room, looking for any sign of change in my absence. The floor-to-ceiling shelves lining the walls were filled with books arranged in alphabetical order, everything from the classics to the latest bestsellers. Anyone would assume he was a writer, or a librarian, perhaps, not a businessman who made and sold shoes. The surface of his oak desk, which sat underneath the arched windows that overlooked his garden, was immaculate; Dad was obsessively tidy.

A cool breeze blew through the open window, knocking something from the ledge. I got up to retrieve it and discovered it was a black-and-white photo of Grandpa as a young man. Dressed in an army uniform, he had one arm wrapped around a leggy woman who wore a smart hat clipped to a bob of shiny, curled hair. She was looking away from the camera, her eyes downcast, hands clasping a small purse.

'Your grandmother.'

Dad was standing in the doorway, hands in his pockets. The corners of his mouth lifted as he strained for a smile. He walked over and put an arm around my shoulders, giving me a quick squeeze – his idea of a hug.

'She's beautiful,' I said.

I'd never seen a picture of his mother before. She had always been a mystery to me. All I knew about her was that she had left him when he was very young.

I studied the photo. Something about her lowered gaze and her tight grip on her purse made her seem painfully unhappy.

'I'm really glad you're home,' Dad said.

Home.

'How've you been?'

I shrugged. 'Fine.'

'How's Olly? I'd like to meet him at some point.'

I shrugged again. As far as I was concerned, Olly belonged to my other life – a life separate from this one, with all its complications – and I wanted to preserve that.

'And your studies? How are they going?'

'My thesis project is devoted to the conservation of the *Maculinea arion* by studying its carnivorous caterpillar.' That ought to stifle conversation.

Dad frowned. 'You don't still trap and kill butterflies to study them, do you? I've always thought that was so cruel.'

He didn't need to tell me again. He'd always made that very clear.

'I wish I had never let your grandpa expose you to that at such a young age. It's far too morbid for a child.'

This again.

'I never saw his work as a lepidopterist as being morbid,' I said.

'You know, he only started capturing butterflies and killing them after my mother left.'

My body grew still. Grandpa had always refused to speak about my grandmother and all Dad had ever said was that he 'drove her away.'

He poured himself a glass of whisky before settling into the green chair I had so recently vacated. 'We've missed you around here.'

His words startled me. He'd missed me? Dad rarely expressed his emotions like this.

'Thank you.' I didn't know what else to say. We were in unfamiliar territory. I looked back at the photo.

'You look like her,' I observed.

He nodded. 'Thankfully, I don't look anything like him.'

'Why have you always hated him so much?'

He waved his hand in the air. 'Hate is such a strong word. I didn't hate Grandpa, Marlowe.' He sighed. 'Anyway, let's not talk about this now. We have much more pressing issues on our plate.'

'Yes we do,' I said. 'What are you thinking of doing about Harper?'

Dad shook his head. 'Those bastards,' he growled. 'It's blatant discrimination. Harper damn well deserves to have a heart, just like anyone else her age.'

'Yes,' I said, 'but what are you going to *do* about it?'

He looked up at me. His blue eyes were blank. 'What can I do? I've been to four different hospitals and they all say the same thing.'

I clenched my jaw. Was he really going to give up again?

'You can do something to help her instead of just getting angry.'

He took a big swig of his drink, swallowed, then said, 'I wish things were that simple. But the older I get, the more I realise how cruel life really is.'

My jaw was locked so tight, it started to cramp.

Carefully, I put the photograph down on Dad's desk and walked to the door. Opening it, I saw in front of me the empty space where Mum's grand piano used to be. My hands curled, nails digging into my palms. Then I registered all the missing pieces. The Ming dynasty vases, the bronze horses... My stomach did a somersault. All our family's most prized possessions were missing.

'Dad?'

'Yes?'

'Where's Mum's piano? And the vases? Where has everything gone?'

Dad turned his head so that I couldn't see his face. 'I can explain, but now's not the time.'

'But –'

'I said not now, Marlowe.'

I stared at him for a few minutes but he didn't turn around.

Finally, I said, 'Goodnight.'

As I walked out of his study, I was visited by an old sensation. I was nine years old again, realising that I could no longer rely on my father to keep me and Harper safe.

I was alone.

I felt too small for this very big world.

Harper

I am not good at keeping secrets but today I will try my best.

Even though I had watery eyes and a tight, hiding heart last night, all I am feeling this morning is excited about my very special engagement. I want to shout it out to my whole family (without losing my breath or coughing), but I can't because Louis wanted to make a very special event of it by inviting all our family and friends to an engagement party.

As I am lying in my bed, I think in my mind about how we will make this celebration a night to remember, with yummy food, good company, dancing music and maybe a few white doves to be set free in Dad's garden for the romance, just like they do in the movies.

I feel a zinging wave rising in me – up up up it goes until it reaches my heart.

Da da dum dum, da dum dum.

Too fast, too fast, too much for my heart.

I have to wipe my mind clean and catch my breath.

The beating in my chest is pounding all over my body like the sound of a chugging engine. Chug chug chug. I close my mind and try to make my body go calm in the way that Wài Pó taught me, but the more I try, the heavier my heart feels, the lighter my head feels and the more electric my body feels. My chin begins to shake and water runs from my eyes all the way down to my cheeks. This is happening a lot lately. Maybe because my heart does not feel like my friend anymore. It is stopping me from doing things that I love. It is stealing my happiness. It is making me tired.

No, please, don't let this be.

But I can't help it. My voice that I hear in my head is wondering if maybe I should let the doctors fix me with a heart that is not my own.

With a trans-plant.

Transplant.

Then I have to pinch myself for thinking such silly thoughts about my heart.

No, this is not love. Love is loyal, love is kind, especially even when it is for yourself.

'I'm sorry,' I say to my heart.

I look out of my window now and listen as the morning sky is talking to me. I see its words in the shape of the clouds. A horse gallops. It opens its mouth and a circle comes out. I watch the circle. It gets bigger and bigger and bigger until all the other clouds are inside it. I think to myself that this must be the circle of life.

Marlowe

Butterflies sleep hanging upside down, attached to the stem of a plant or flower, eyes open in peaceful quiescence. Sleep was something that came naturally to me in London, yet it seemed that I had forgotten how to do it back in Hong Kong. My mind would flutter from one thought to the next in a kind of half-consciousness. I found myself wishing I was a fat little caterpillar with not much else to worry about other than eating and the gentle act of metamorphosis. Not that it was so easy for the caterpillar, I reminded myself. Metamorphosis involved a huge transformation and caterpillars, like all things in the natural world, had to fight for survival.

And as long as Harper wasn't fit enough to fight, I would do it for her.

When Dad had left the house I went to his study, turned on his computer and began researching cases of adults with Down syndrome who had been denied transplants. The list was long, but one caught my eye: a 1995 report on the case of an American woman, Sandra Jensen. I read quickly:

> Born with Down syndrome and a congenital heart disorder,
> at age 34 Sandra Jensen needed a heart and lung transplant,
> but was told by medical professionals that heart and
> lung transplants were not given to adults who had Down

syndrome... Jensen fought for her rights, and on 23 January
1996 received her transplants from Stanford University
Medical Centre...

I felt a tumble in my ribs. *What if?* I pictured Harper's name instead
of Jensen's, imagined a public battle in Hong Kong that led to
reformed laws. At the end of it all, Harper was rosy-cheeked and
full of energy, having finally received a new, healthy heart. Then
I came to my senses. Sandra Jensen had fought for her rights in
America, not Hong Kong. Hong Kong had deeply entrenched views
about disability; the 'less-abled' members of our society were often
shamed and families preferred to conceal their 'imperfect' members
from the world. But how would Hong Kong ever change if no one
took a stand?

I closed my eyes. Harper's face appeared once more as a photograph
in the *South China Morning Post*. The headline trumpeted: *A victory
for Miss Eve!*

As a child I had sworn that I would fight for Harper, and perhaps
this was a way to do it. Dad and I agreed on one thing: Harper
deserved to have a heart as much as anyone.

Harper

Wài Pó is sitting by the window in her room. I can only see her back.

'Wài Pó,' I say, but she does not reply.

I walk into the room and call her name again.

Still, she does not move. I sit beside her on the bed and stroke her arm.

When I am with people who are sad, I can feel it, heavy, inside my bones. My Wài Pó has a lot of sadness in her. Like the ocean, it does not have a beginning, middle and an end. I think in my mind that this is why she holds her prayer beads so tight; they are her rope when she is sinking.

She gets like this a lot, when she remembers those who have died, like Wài Gōng and Mum. She used to say, 'I was supposed to go first.' But she has stopped saying this now. She just gets quiet, like she is today.

As I stroke her arm, back and forth, back and forth, she turns to me and takes my hands.

'So cold,' she says.

She asks me how I am feeling. Her eyes are small and she does not blink.

The fear.

'I will be fine,' I say.

I will be fine.

I will be fine.

I will be fine.

Yes, I will be fine.

We sit like this, staring at the grey sky, letting her heartbreak come and go.

Marlowe

Two long days went by before I could see Uncle Johnny, one of my parents' oldest friends in Hong Kong. According to his secretary, he had been at a conference in Beijing.

I was early. Too early. When I reached Sheung Wan, west of the CBD on Hong Kong Island, I asked the taxi to drop me off two blocks before Uncle Johnny's office. I stepped out of the cab near a trio of large bamboo baskets filled with dried fish, perfectly arranged like the petals on a daisy. Pungent, salty aromas lingered in the air as I passed tubs of fish maw, abalone, shrimp, oysters and sea snails. Weaving through throngs of local shoppers, I passed colourful market stalls that sold paper offerings for the afterlife – flimsy replicas of money, washing machines, air conditioners, jet planes and the occasional paper mansion. Turning the corner to Ko Shing Street, the air turned sweet and musty as I neared Chinese medicine stalls displaying jars of dried herbs, insects and various animal products. I was reminded of the many times Wài Pó had brought me shopping here for reishi mushrooms, ginseng and cordyceps and other smelly herbs to boost Harper's immune system; through my research I'd since come to know cordyceps as a fungus that infected and manipulated the brain of an insect. I used to hate coming here as a child, but on this particular morning I found it strangely soothing to revisit these familiar streets.

As I sat in the waiting room of the *Asia Daily* offices, all I could think about was Mum. If we were in the neighbourhood, Mum would bring me here to meet Uncle Johnny for lunch. He had a way of listening as if your every word was interesting and important. 'He is very present,' Dad used to say, 'and in today's world that's rare. It's what makes him such a good journalist.' I would often come and visit Uncle Johnny after Mum died; he was someone who seemed able to understand how I felt without my needing to say anything.

The reception area had changed in the years since I'd come here with my mother. The beige carpet had been replaced with marble and in the place of the old receptionist was a young woman with tortoiseshell glasses.

'Marlowe?' Uncle Johnny strode into the room. 'It's so great to see you.' I stood up to hug him and, for a brief moment, felt like everything would be okay.

As he pulled away, I noticed the changes in him. In the year since I had last seen him, his beard had thinned, and there was a little more salt than pepper in his hair.

He smiled at me sadly. 'You look so much like your mother.' He shook his head, as if to bring himself back to the present, and said, 'Come on through.'

As he led me to his office, he asked, 'Does your dad know you're here?'

'No.' I had wanted to set things in motion before I involved Dad. I was sure he'd have some reason why we shouldn't ask Uncle Johnny to help us.

'How is university?' Uncle Johnny asked as he moved to sit behind his desk and I took a seat facing him. Did I like London? I answered his questions as quickly as I could, then handed him the article on

Sandra Jensen that I'd printed out. 'This is why I'm here,' I said. 'You can help.'

He scanned the page then looked up at me, head cocked to one side.

'How?'

How? I would have thought it was obvious.

'You can write an article about Harper,' I said.

He frowned and sat up straighter in his chair. 'Harper? What do you mean? Is she okay?'

It was my turn to frown. 'You don't know?'

'Know what?'

'Dad hasn't said anything to you?'

Uncle Johnny grimaced slightly. 'I don't see that much of your father these days. Tell me, what's going on?'

I paused for a minute before speaking. 'Harper needs a heart and lung transplant.'

I heard Uncle Johnny catch his breath, but I wasn't done. 'And she has been denied one because of her disability.'

I listed the hospitals that had rejected Harper, finishing with a description of Saturday's meeting, at which we'd been urged to seek palliative care.

Uncle Johnny rubbed his face with his hands. 'Oh, Marlowe, I'm so, *so* sorry.'

'She doesn't have long,' I said quietly. 'So can you write a piece on her? Get her story out there? It worked for Sandra Jensen...'

But Uncle Johnny was shaking his head. 'Marlowe, it doesn't quite work like that. I'm a business journalist; I don't normally write feature articles. And even if I did, Hong Kong is not America – the law is different here.'

'I know the law is different.' I gripped the sides of my seat. 'Please, I don't know what else to do…' I hated the sound of my voice, the desperation in it. I hated begging for help.

Uncle Johnny sighed. 'Okay, okay… Let me see what I can do.'

I exhaled. 'Thank you.'

As he walked me back out to reception, he asked me how Dad was holding up.

I stared at him. 'You really don't know?'

'Like I said, we haven't seen each other in a while.' He glanced away.

Why was there such distance between them? It was as if Dad was slowly erasing all vestiges of the life he had lived with Mum. I swallowed. Soon there would be nothing left to hold our family together.

✦

It was dinner time. Wài Pó had placed an unusually bland looking omelette and plain rice on the kitchen table. Harper and I shared a look while Wài Pó prepared a tray for Dad and Irene to eat in their room.

'I'll take that to them.' I whisked the tray from her hands. This was the perfect opportunity for me to tell Dad my plan. I'd already spoken with Uncle Johnny so it was too late for him to object.

From outside Dad's bedroom, I heard an argument between him and Irene. The door was slightly ajar and their words travelled clearly out into the corridor.

'You have to control your temper with the doctors, James,' Irene was saying. 'It's embarrassing.'

'Is that seriously what you're thinking about right now?' Dad retorted.

There was a pause; I heard the click of a lighter and then Irene exhaled. 'You have to accept there's nothing more we can do,' she said.

I didn't wait to hear any more. I pushed the door open. Irene was by the window, cigarette in hand, while Dad was on the opposite side of the room, leaning against the cupboard.

'Actually,' I said, 'there is something we can do.' I placed the tray on their side table.

Irene looked at me. 'You didn't consider knocking?'

'What are you talking about, Marlowe?' Dad asked. His voice sounded weary.

'We can get a story about Harper's case in the media.' I handed him the Sandra Jensen article and told him about her case. He shook his head dismissively.

'Dad?'

'I already know about this story, darling, but this is Hong Kong. No one is interested in the rights of disabled people here.'

Irene exhaled smoke in a long, steady stream.

I squeezed my eyes tightly shut until I saw stars.

'Don't you want to help?' I asked in a small voice.

'Your father's right,' Irene cut in. 'The culture here is different. People just don't care.'

'No one is going to want to write about this anyway,' Dad said, his tone softer now.

'Uncle Johnny will. I went to see him and he said he'd see what he could do.'

'Uncle Johnny?' Dad paused, his gaze averted in recollection. 'How is he?'

When I didn't answer, he passed the article back in my direction.

I folded my arms, refusing, suddenly disgusted by his passivity.

'Why am I the only one who is trying to do something?' I demanded. Then, startled by my own anger, I fled the room.

Irene's voice followed me down the hall. 'You really should tell her that she can't talk to you like that, James. It's so disrespectful.'

—

From the back of my wardrobe, I retrieved the empty rearing cage that Grandpa had given me one Christmas. With a damp cloth, I cleaned away the dust from the netted walls and wiped the floral tubes for milkweed cuttings. Why was I setting up an empty home with nothing to inhabit it? I stared at the cage, trying not to think of a life that was slowly slipping away from me.

'Hello.' Harper was standing in the doorway to my bedroom. She held a book in her hands. Its front was covered in a thin sheet of silver glitter. 'I want to show you something.' She plonked herself onto my bed.

She held her notebook in the air and glitter rained onto the floor. 'This is my autobiography storybook. I want you to know that I have started my own great story.' She turned to the first page and, with her index finger following her loopy handwriting, began to read slowly. I sat down next to her and listened, marvelling at how her brain could turn our painful hospital meeting into a series of enchanted tales.

She asked me if I liked her writing and I told her it was wonderful.

'Do you think I can get this published soon? I would like an agent as well.'

Ever since she was a teenager and started writing seriously, she would send me her work and ask me to help her find a publisher. 'We can always keep trying.' I didn't want her to lose hope.

'Harper,' I said, 'are you sure you're okay? I know the meeting at the hospital a few days ago was really full-on.'

My sister pushed her spectacles further up her nose.

'Yes, yes. I am okay because I know the doctors will fix me.'

I bit my tongue to keep my rage in check.

'Also, the lady with the shell was nice,' Harper added.

That damn social worker.

'Do you understand what a transplant is, Harper?'

She nodded her head slowly. 'Yes. Yes, I do.'

I took her hand in mine. Her fingers were cold. I massaged them gently. 'Harper, a transplant is when they give you a new heart and lungs.'

'Yes, you told me already.' Then she tipped her head to the side and looked at me, puzzled. 'But I did have one question: where do these hearts and lungs come from?'

From someone who is brain dead.

'From someone who doesn't need theirs anymore.' I was a coward. I was treating her like a child. 'Sorry. I should have said from someone who has been in an accident and can't live anymore, but their organs can live on in another person.'

'I like my own heart. I don't need someone else's and you should know I am not going to die. I am quite happy in my body and with all the parts of my body, and I know the doctors will fix me.'

My head began to throb.

'I like my own heart,' Harper repeated in an urgent voice. 'I like my own. I want to keep my own.'

I drew her close.

'It's okay.' I rubbed her back like I used to when she was small, resting my cheek against the top of her head. She smelled like strawberry shampoo. We stayed like this for a while.

'It's okay,' Harper whispered back eventually. 'We'll be okay.' I listened to the certainty in her voice. All at once it was as if *she* were holding *me*. 'We will be okay because you are home.'

She stood and made her way to the door. 'I am going back to my room to write now.'

And then my sister was gone, leaving a trail of glitter behind her.

Harper

The feeling in our house has changed. This afternoon, the air in our home is calm and still because everyone has gone to their rooms and shut their doors. The quiet feels soft around me, like fur touching my skin.

Below my feet are wooden floorboards where my Mum's piano used to be. I close my eyes and hear her music like it was before. White and black keys sing to one another.

'Hello, Mum,' I say. 'I love you, Mum.'

I walk through the house to my second-most favourite place, which is Wài Pó's kitchen. There are so many colours and smells: Wài Pó's salty, dried fish that are hanging by the window and all her jars of pickled chillies and vegetables in orange, red and green. We have a little yellow chirping bird in a cage near the pantry. I call him Prince William after the very handsome prince in the United Kingdom.

I place my storybook flat on the kitchen table and prepare my special fountain pen. In front of me there is a bowl. It is full of fresh plums that Wài Pó bought from the market. My fingertips feel the smoothness, as soft as the skin behind my ears.

The silver tip of my pen is touching paper. Ink drops. A small spot of black water spreads. I write:

Plums are shiny and the colour of blood.

Being a writer is hard. I wonder if Shakespeare also had this thought in his brain. I bite into a plum and its skin cracks open. Plum juice covers my whole mouth and drips down all the tubes in my body to my stomach. I feel like I am standing under the air conditioner on a day when the sun is making fire.

I chew and the insides of my cheeks fizz. I know all about plums and how they are made because of the plum trees in Zhōngshān Park, Shanghai. Marlowe told me about the stages of a plum being born from its tree; first it is a bud, then a blossom, then a fruit to be picked and put into a mouth. Delicious!

A bit of plum blood swims down my chin and drops onto the paper next to the ink spot. It all becomes clear to me now. I see my body as if I am a tree. I have roots that reach all the way into the earth. And just like in the hospital, on the plastic model of the heart, I have veins that reach all over me like branches and my blood is like red juice. My heart is like a plum.

I pick up my pen. I must write quickly now because the story words are spilling out of me all in one go.

The Plum Hart

1 time there was a beutiful yung lady.

Her hart was sick but she still new how to love.

Her 外婆 wài pó told her a story with the word ~~death~~ imm-or-tal in it.

Imm-or-tal is a very speshel word.

She could get beter if she went to find a speshel plum on a tree – a speshel tree like in zhōngshān park, Shang-hi.

If she eats one bite of the plum she will be imm-or-tal.
Imm-or-tal meens her body will live. Her body will not die.

Now I understand more about what a transplant is. It is like taking a bite of the plum heart.

Marlowe

Evening light flooded my room in lavender. I had fallen asleep in the afternoon again. Was this jet lag or the beginning of despair?

I forced my eyes to stay open by staring at the white wall in front of me. I was helped by the high-pitched notes of Wài Pó's Chinese opera, which rang through the house like howling cats. She only ever played it when she was trying to get herself out of a funk.

My knuckles ached from gripping the bedsheets tightly. Had I had a nightmare? The hairs at the base of my neck prickled. I rolled over, and for the first time in my life I was prepared to see the face of a ghost. No matter how many times I told myself that *ghosts aren't real*, the fear remained. Suddenly, I found myself longing for Mum again – so intensely the feeling squeezed at the bones in my chest. Whenever I had a nightmare, she used to lie in bed next to me, stroking my back. I closed my eyes and imagined her with me until I felt my body relax and my rational mind was able to take control, returning me to myself.

I rose from my bed, turned off the purring dehumidifier and walked through the house.

Dad's office door was ajar. I saw him asleep in his armchair. A newspaper rested on his lap and he held an empty whisky glass in his hand. As I took the glass from his slack grip, his brows twitched, eyes moved rapidly under their lids. He looked like a child having a bad dream as his bottom lip quivered. It was hard to witness Dad turned into a boy in his sleep. I quickly left the room, shutting the door behind me.

The sound of Wài Pó's opera was replaced by the steadier drone of voices from a Chinese news channel. I passed the living room, note again the missing antique vases, and followed the sweet and sour aromas of Wài Pó's cooking to the kitchen.

Harper sat at the round table with a camellia in her hair. She was stringing beans. The small TV flickered in the background next to the microwave. Wài Pó was stirring a pot. I bent over the bubbling liquid and inhaled the familiar scent of homemade chicken broth. Beside her, two big woks were steaming away. Peeking under one steel lid I saw a large snapper garnished with ginger and spring onions. I asked her why she was preparing such a big meal.

'I'm making a welcome home dinner for you.' Wài Pó lifted her long cooking chopsticks in the air. 'Better late than never.'

Wài Pó usually had Esmerelda helping her in the kitchen. When I first arrived home, I had asked where she was; she had been working for the family since I was two and was a constant presence in my life. Irene told me she was on holiday and didn't respond when I asked when she would return.

'When is Esmerelda returning?' I asked my grandmother now.

Wài Pó, a master of selective deafness, pretended not to hear.

Harper sighed. 'That one is a sad story. Esmerelda is back in the Philippines for good, with her own family – her son, her husband and her pet dog called Locky. I miss her.' Her bottom lip trembled.

'What? Why did she leave?'

'Marlowe, I want to tell you something.' Harper patted the empty chair next to her for me to sit. Her glasses slid down the bridge of her nose. She pushed them back up again with her stubby finger.

Her nails were painted pink, purple and blue. 'I want to tell you something about my boyfriend, Louis.'

'But why did Esmerelda leave?' I asked, interrupting Harper. The missing vases, Esmerelda gone… There were too many unanswered questions.

'Wài Pó, please tell me what's going on,' I insisted.

My grandmother immediately dipped her spoon into the pot of broth, blew on it and shoved it in my mouth. Creamy, warm flavours of chicken flesh, rice wine and peppercorns slid down my throat. My stomach rumbled.

'Delicious.'

She then proceeded to lecture on the importance of preparing real broth, not the kind you get in a packet from the supermarket. 'All these dishes I am making tonight are from a collection of my mother's recipes.'

I swallowed my irritation. Pressing Wài Pó further was pointless. She had always been so stubborn, just like Harper. I would have to pick a time to question her carefully.

'Never mind then, Marlowe.' Harper had folded her arms across her chest.

'Sorry, Harper,' I said, returning my attention to her. 'What do you want to tell me?'

She cleared her throat. 'There will be a surprise guest tonight. A big surprise and excitement.'

'Who?'

Harper just shook her head and mimed zipping her lip. 'It's a secret.'

Our round dining table was neatly laid with bowls and chopsticks.
Harper had folded the napkins into the shape of swans.

Irene took the seat facing the window and Hong Kong's sparkling
harbour. Harper and I sat opposite, facing the wall.

'Where's James?' Irene asked.

'Asleep,' I said.

She got up. I could hear the sound of her heels clip-clopping
down the corridor to Dad's study.

Wài Pó placed a steaming bowl of rice onto the lazy Susan, before
returning to the kitchen. Although it was rude to start serving before
everyone was seated, I started dishing the rice into bowls.

Irene returned. 'I've decided to let your father sleep. There's no
use in waking him.' Her cheeks were flushed.

'He does this a lot,' Harper chimed in.

'He does?' It wasn't like Dad to miss dinner.

Irene told Harper to leave the subject alone.

The doorbell rang and I seized the chance to escape. I opened
the front door to find Louis standing there, wearing a crisp navy
suit.

'Twenty-two minutes and fifty seconds! Yessssssssss! I am speedy.'

He tapped his wrist. A bright yellow digital watch was strapped
alongside a black one.

'Oh, Marlowe!' He pulled me close and gave me a big hug.

I held on, tight. It was so good to see him. He felt like a breath of
fresh air in our stuffy home.

'I was wondering when I would see you, Louis!' I said.

'I've been away in Thailand for a beach holiday but I am home
now. I am so happy that you are back from the bugs university.
Harper has been missing you so very much and that means that I
have been missing you too.'

Before I had a chance to say anything, he ran into the house. Over his shoulder he shouted, 'I love your Wài Pó's cooking so much. I like her dumplings the best, then her fish, then her spring rolls, and of course her egg tarts...'

I followed him. When he entered the dining room, Harper sprang up from her chair.

'My Romeo has arrived! Oh, how I've missed you!' She flung her arms around his neck and they touched noses. They were so cute together. The sight of them made me long for Olly.

'Please. Not at the dinner table.' Irene stood.

I moved in front of Harper and Louis, blocking them from Irene's view.

'Irene, there's no need to stop them.' Heat bled into my cheeks.

'I'm not kissing him with my lips, you know,' Harper said. 'This kind of kissing is with the nose.'

Louis stroked her cheek and asked if she was okay. He was always so attentive and caring. I was reminded of the fact that it was because of Louis I'd felt I could leave Harper for London all those years ago. He made her happy. For that, I loved him.

Irene asked Harper to sit back down at the dinner table, but of course she took no notice. Who did Irene think she was? I'd struggled with her presence when I only saw her occasionally, but now that she lived here it was a whole new ballgame.

'They're not causing any harm,' I said. 'Can't you just leave them be?'

Irene turned to face the large windows overlooking the sea. In that moment, there seemed to be something tired about her expression and the way she placed her long, slender hand to her chest. Her fingers rubbed the pale skin at her collarbone until a little red mark formed.

Wài Pó emerged from the kitchen once more, carrying the last of her seven dishes: abalone and green beans.

'There she is! My second favourite lady.' Louis embraced Wài Pó. She quickly ushered him to his seat by Harper's side. He asked my grandmother if she had cut her hair. 'You look smart and precious.'

I laughed, and realised it was the first time I had done so in a while.

'Before I eat my *delicious* meal, I want to say something and give you these invitations.' He reached into his suit pocket and pulled out a wad of envelopes. 'You are all invited to come to my house for ice cream and some cake tomorrow because I am going to give my love a ring and make a proposal so she can be my wife. I made a letter for you all about this. Your names are on the front.'

I took the proffered envelope. It was decorated with sparkling love heart stickers.

A very loaded silence followed.

Wài Pó unwrapped a White Rabbit candy and put it in her mouth.

'Louis, there will be no proposal.' Irene handed back her invitation. 'Remember what they told you at the vocational centre? This is inappropriate behaviour.'

Was I actually hearing this? Just because she'd moved in now, she didn't have the right to dictate what Harper could and couldn't do.

I took a breath, trying to calm the surge of adrenaline that swept through my body. 'Excuse me, Irene, but it's not your place to tell them if they can be together or not.'

'Not my place?' She turned to face me.

Shedoesn'tscareme. Shedoesn'tscareme. Shedoesn'tscareme.

'It most certainly is my place. Harper is my responsibility now too. Since you've been gone a lot has changed. I have been looking after Harper.'

I could hear Wài Pó muttering something under her breath in Chinese.

Since you've been gone. I wanted to throw something at the woman. My hands were in fists and my voice came from my throat in a low growl. 'You aren't Harper's mother. You're not even married to my father.'

I took a step back, realising what I had done. I'd hit Irene where it hurt. It was no secret that she longed for Dad to propose, but we all knew it would never happen.

Irene looked me in the eye. 'You think *you're* her mother?'

'Stop!' Harper's voice broke and she began to cough, sticky and wet. 'Stop fighting!' She was struggling to breathe. 'All that matters is that I love Louis in my heart. Please don't fight.'

I felt small then, realising I could have dealt with this situation differently. I went to help Harper but Louis was already beside her, softly patting her on the back.

Irene held out her hand. 'Marlowe,' she whispered, 'give me your invitation.'

She wasn't going to let this go.

'No.'

'We can't encourage them.'

'They're adults,' I told her. 'It's not your place to tell them what they can and can't do.'

Her eyes narrowed. 'They don't understand what they are doing. Please don't complicate the matter.'

I didn't even know where to start. After all these years, had she not learned anything from Harper at all?

Louis stood and addressed Irene. He lifted his chin and stood tall, ready for battle, with ten times more courage than I could ever muster.

'I want to tell you something, Irene. I know Harper loves most of all to watch *Casablanca* on Friday nights and sit with me on the couch holding my hand. She also loves spaghetti and Wài Pó's egg tarts. Harper is very smart at writing stories. When she is mad, she gets red cheeks and it means I did something wrong, so I have to figure it all out in my head and not do it again. I love this lady and I want to marry her at sunset.'

I couldn't take my eyes off him. He had such soft features, such a graceful way of speaking. If he were a butterfly, he would be the same as Harper – a yellow *Pyrisitia nise*. I felt my body go still. If I breathed loudly, I might scare him away.

'Someone call his mother.' Irene looked at me, then at Wài Pó. Did she really think we would oblige? When neither of us responded, her heels stabbed the marble floor as she went to the hall.

'Oh no!' Harper wailed. 'Stepmonster has ruined everything!' She was looking drained and sallow.

Wài Pó rushed to her side and stroked her forehead while Louis spoke calmly to her.

I had to get Dad. As I made my way out of the dining room, I could hear Irene on the phone in the kitchen. Her voice, clipped and stern, was saying, 'This is totally inappropriate. Your son has disrupted our family dinner. I would expect you to keep a closer eye on him… He's much lower on the spectrum than Harper is. He needs more care.'

However much Louis's parents hated these calls, they were smart, educated people whom I was sure would have no problem putting Irene in her place.

'What do you mean you won't come to collect him?' She was shouting now. 'He's not an independent young man. He has the intellect of a child!'

I was standing outside the door of Dad's study now. I wondered if Irene's raised voice had woken him.

'Do you realise my stepdaughter is dying?'

I stopped dead in my tracks. That word. It hit me in the gut. I put my hand on the wall to steady myself.

The door to the study was flung open and Dad emerged, his face creased with sleep. 'What's happening?' Startled, confused, not quite alert.

'You're too late.' *Stay calm*, I told myself. If I said any more, I would surely regret it. I struggled to understand what Dad saw in a woman like Irene. After all these years, why was he still with her?

I followed him to the kitchen and watched as he took the phone from Irene and placed it on the receiver.

'Enough.'

I wasn't about to hang around for the ensuing argument. I hurried back to the dining room. Harper was still in her seat, breathing heavily. I took her hand. It was cold. She was sweating.

'You need to lie down,' I said.

'No.' She shook her head. 'I'm not leaving my Louis.'

'Louis can come with you,' I said. 'Please, come up to bed.'

She shook her head. Stubborn.

'I'm tired of people telling me I cannot be with my Louis. You have a boyfriend, Marlowe, and no one tells you that you cannot be with *him*, right?'

I swallowed hard. Did I deserve to be with Olly when Harper couldn't be with Louis?

'It's not fair,' Harper continued. 'Love is the same even if you are a person with Up syndrome or without Up syndrome. Why can't Stepmonster understand that?'

What could I possibly say to make things better? I would never really know what it was like to have to fight to be understood in this way.

Louis put his palm on her cheek. 'Don't worry about Stepmonster. You're right, she doesn't understand. But I do.'

I took a step back, realising all Harper was asking for was the right to live her life as any young woman does.

Harper

My heart is skipping and hopping. Flames are burning under my skin. My chest feels stuffy and blocked. Stepmonster's words are loud in my mind: 'inappropriate behaviour', 'unacceptable', 'don't encourage them'. I want to say, 'Why can you only see my Down syndrome and not my Up syndrome?'

The moon looks like a circle high in the night, watching me. I let its special light wipe my mind clean.

The doorbell rings. I hear footsteps climbing the stairs, up up up.

My body is lifted and put onto a floating orange bed and carried into an ambulance that is filled with fear and big eyes.

They put a needle into my skin and fill my body with healing water and potions from the ocean.

Marlowe

My neck was stiff from having spent the night in an armchair. My eyes felt swollen and heavy. I forced myself to sit up. I hadn't meant to sleep.

Harper's heart monitor beeped in a steady rhythm. I watched her chest move up and down with each ragged breath. I looked around the hospital room. I was alone. This was strange, I thought. Dad, Wài Pó and Irene always came to the hospital when Harper was sick.

The events of the night before played over and over again in my mind: the raging fever that had taken hold of Harper's body, how distant her eyes had looked, caught in delirium. As we waited for the ambulance, Dad had paced while Wài Pó thumbed her prayer beads and whispered healing mantras in a steady drone. Irene was silent, wide-eyed. It felt as if I were in a nightmare; as if I were standing on the edge of an abyss, about to fall.

Harper looked quiet in sleep, her body still. She seemed so small, as if her blankets might swallow her whole. I crawled into her bed and filled the empty space beside her. She smelled like the Kwan Loong oil Wài Pó had rubbed into her back and chest. Her skin felt soft; too soft.

'Don't leave me,' I whispered.

Enough. I was letting myself get carried away again.

I got out of the bed and returned to the chair.

Rain smacked against the window. I walked to it and watched the morning clouds settle over the city below.

'I'm awake.' Harper's voice was faint and croaky.

I rushed to her and took her hand in mine.

'How are you feeling?' I asked, adjusting the oxygen tube under her nose.

'Much better.' Her cheeks were pricked with colour. 'It's a new day and the doctors are fixing my body.' She smiled. I noticed her lips were chapped. I rummaged through my bag for lip balm but all I could find was a half-empty packet of Skittles and an old tissue.

'Well good morning, my beautiful lady.' Louis was standing in the doorway, holding a large bunch of red roses. He crossed the room to stand by Harper's bed. 'These are for you, to remind you about happiness and love, from my heart to yours.'

My chest ached. I couldn't watch them anymore without thinking about how this love might end too soon. I retreated to the window again. Outside a hawk was circling. I wondered what it would be like to be a hunting bird, observing the world from up high, only touching land briefly to feed.

A nurse entered carrying a kidney dish. 'Hello, Harper, it's time for your medication.'

'What are you giving her now?' I asked. So often doctors and nurses medicated Harper without bothering to explain what they were doing, as if Harper's disability meant she didn't require an explanation.

To my surprise, the nurse smiled and introduced herself. 'I'm Anita.'

'That's my big sister, Marlowe,' Harper told her. 'She looks after me.'

'Uh, excuse me, I look after you too,' Louis said.

'I always wanted a big sister.' Anita took a syringe from the dish and showed it to Harper. She said, 'These are your IV antibiotics, and you've also been given morphine for your cough and your breathlessness, and to help the pressure in your heart.'

Anita's movements were slow and careful as she injected the antibiotic into Harper's cannula. I felt the tension in my shoulders ease.

Louis ran his fingertips lightly over Harper's forehead. 'My brave, brave girl.'

In that moment, the hospital room seemed so large. It was as if some part of me had fled my body and was floating above.

Harper began to sing 'Hey Jude'. The sound of her voice was so gentle, it made something inside me want to break, so I focused on the illustrated instructions for hygienic handwashing above the nearby sink. It was a six-step process.

The momentary calm was broken by the sound of Irene's voice in the corridor outside declaring that she was here to see Harper Eve. She strode into the room and stood at the foot of Harper's bed. The scent of Chanel No. 5 was overpowering.

'Louis, what are you doing here?' she demanded. 'I asked your mother to call in advance next time you wanted to visit.'

I opened my mouth to argue, but Harper beat me to it.

'He's here because I want him here,' Harper said loudly. Then she began to cough.

Anita immediately reached for the oxygen.

'Where is my dad?' Harper asked through the plastic mask.

'He's got some urgent business to handle. He'll be here soon,' Irene replied.

'What could possibly be so urgent after what happened to Harper last night?'

'I'll explain later,' she whispered.

'What about Wài Pó?' I asked. 'Where's she?'

'She'll be here soon.'

Clearly, something was going on, but I decided not to press the matter in front of Harper.

'To be honest,' Harper said, her voice muffled under the mask, 'I am a little upset that you are here, Irene. You make my heart jumpy and sometimes you can be a bit rude.'

I found myself suppressing a smile. In the years that I had been in London, it seemed that my sister had found her voice.

I watched as Irene, her cheeks flushed, brushed the creases on her skirt as if she were trying to flick Harper's retort away like a speck of dust on one of her designer gowns.

She grabbed the bunch of roses from Harper's bed and ordered me to put them elsewhere. But Louis got to the flowers before I could and put them safely on her bedside table.

'Irene.' Louis moved into her line of sight. 'I want to tell you that I forgive you for last night after you made Harper and me upset. I would like you to know that I love her with all my heart and just want her to be my wife and –'

Irene held her hand in the air. 'Enough, Louis.'

Here we go again, I thought.

'But –'

'Do you know why I am not going to accept this engagement?'

My breath quickened. 'Irene, please, we don't need to go through this again,' I said quickly.

Ignoring me, she said, 'Harper is dying.'

I gasped. The baldness of the declaration was brutal.

The room was quiet, but for the faint ringing in my ears.

'Ex-ex-excuse me?' Louis's face was pale. He looked like he might be sick.

Even Anita had stopped what she was doing and looked up, aghast.

'Irene, you've gone too far.' I went to stand beside Louis. How stupid was she? After last night, could she not see how much she was hurting them? I noticed that my hands and feet were pulsing. It made me want to run.

Undeterred, Irene continued to address Louis. 'I know this is hard for you to hear, but it is time someone told you.' She took a lace handkerchief out of her bag and wiped a bead of sweat from the corner of her forehead. 'I didn't want to have to be the one to tell you, but you deserve to know.'

She wasn't about to... No, she wouldn't...

'Harper needs a new heart to get better. The doctors can't give her one, so now she only has a few months left to live.'

'Irene, that's enough!' I held a hand out as if to ward her off.

'You cannot marry Harper, Louis.'

Louis turned his back on Irene. Harper began to sob. Trying to keep my voice steady, I said, 'I think you should leave.'

She held my gaze until the muscles above her right eyebrow began to twitch. 'I only have Harper's best interests at heart,' she said before striding out of the room, chin held high.

Anita removed the last syringe from Harper's cannula and reattached her IV. She then asked Louis and me to leave. Numbers flashed on the screen above her head. I felt like I was falling again.

⊷

Louis gulped down a can of Diet Coke, then let out a hearty burp. He guzzled a second can before sitting beside me in the waiting room.

'That's a lot of Coke, Louis.'

He looked up at me, face sunken. 'I don't have a problem with sweet things. Sometimes my mum says I do, but I really don't.' He shook the empty can in the air. 'You see, this is a diet drink with less sugar. It is healthy.' He sighed and bowed his head.

I told him it was okay and put my arm around his shoulder. Together we watched the movements of the hospital ward and I found myself focusing on the patients fit enough to walk. They moved at a slow pace, pushing their IV drips ahead of them. A young woman with yellow slippers walked towards us. I tried to visualise Harper in her place, fit enough to walk, but all that came to mind was Mum when she was having chemo. She would shuffle around her hospital ward, orange bandana concealing her patchy scalp, eyes focused in a kind of deep concentration.

'Is Irene right?' Louis asked.

I didn't know how to answer that question. I was still struggling to find a way to describe Harper's condition when Louis sighed. 'It's okay,' he said. 'I can see the sadness in your eyes and on your mouth. Harper is...' His bottom lip quivered.

I told him not to lose hope. 'I'll find a way to help her,' I told him.

'Will you be able to get Harper a new heart?'

When I didn't reply, he stared at me for a few long seconds. I couldn't read his expression. Abruptly, he stood and looked at his watch.

'I am speedy,' he said, 'and I have an idea. See you soon.'

He pressed the start button on one of his digital watches and raced towards the elevator. When that didn't come in time, he headed for the stairs.

'Louis, wait!' I called.

'No time to wait!' came his voice from the stairwell.

I was too tired to follow, so I leaned my head back against the wall then exhaled heavily and closed my eyes.

I pounded the large oak door with my fists, calling for my mother.

The door opened and water surged out, sweeping me off my feet. My arms were flailing, legs kicking, as I tried desperately to swim to the surface for a breath.

I cried for help. Words emerged from my mouth in bubbles.

And then my head broke the surface, and warm air filled my lungs. I gasped and coughed.

In the distance, I could see a beach.

I called for my mother again, and then I saw her swimming towards me. She wore a yellow swimsuit and had an iris in her hair. I watched her gliding through the water, unaffected by the current.

I reached for her. Our hands touched. Mum's skin was warm.

She told me to go back, but I refused to leave her. I grasped her hands, but the tighter I squeezed, the more she began to fade, until I found I was clinging to nothing.

My body became heavy and I began to sink. The sea water filled my lungs. I dimly heard a voice calling from the surface.

'Marlowe! Marlowe!'

'Marlowe.' A hand was patting my back. 'Marlowe, are you okay?'

Anita's face was a blur before it came into focus. I felt sweat trickle down the side of my brow.

'Sorry, I fell asleep.' I sat up and wiped my face with the back of my sleeve. 'How's Harper? Is she okay?'

'The doctor is with her now. Your grandmother and father have also arrived. I thought you might like to be present.'

I got to my feet, blinking. Small flecks of light danced around the corners of my eyes.

'Do you need to lie down?' Anita asked.

I assured her I was fine, then, after thanking her for waking me, hurried back to Harper's room.

Harper was sitting up in bed, chatting to a young doctor. Underneath his white coat he wore a brown shirt the same colour as his hair. As soon as Harper saw me coming she smiled and waved. 'This is Dr Arora,' she told me.

The doctor turned. 'You must be Marlowe. I've heard a lot about you.'

Something about the way his eyes brightened when he smiled reminded me of Olly. Suddenly I found myself lost for words.

'Hello, darling.' Dad and Wài Pó were by Harper's side.

'Where have you been?' I asked them.

They looked at each other. Wài Pó stuck a jelly bean in her mouth.

'We had an urgent appointment at the bank,' he said quietly. 'I'll fill you in later.'

I made a mental note to ensure that he did.

Harper eyed the attractive doctor. 'You've got a nice face,' she said.

He placed a stethoscope on her chest and asked her how she was feeling. As he examined her, he listened to her chatter, occasionally laughing at her jokes. He stated his observations about her condition aloud so that Dad, Wài Pó and I could hear, reassuring us whenever he found something had improved or was stable.

'How were her recent bloods?' I asked. 'Previous results showed her CRP and white blood cell count were very high. But I guess that's to be expected with a bad infection.'

He raised his eyebrows and asked if I was a med student.

'Marlowe is very smart and studies bugs and butterflies in London,' Harper informed him.

In answer to my question, Dr Arora told us that although Harper's overall bloods had improved, her CRP and white blood cell count were still high. He wanted to keep her in for a few more days. I saw Dad and Wài Pó exchange an anxious look.

Harper said, 'You're a very friendly man, Dr Arora. If my Marlowe didn't have a boyfriend already I would suggest that you two go on a date so she could go out and have some fun for once.'

'Harper, stop,' I whispered. I could feel myself blushing.

Harper went on, 'Marlowe might seem like the ice queen in *The Lion, the Witch and the Wardrobe*, because she does not laugh or cry much, but she is not the ice queen, she is lovely in her heart... just so you know.'

The doctor placed his finger to his lips, suppressing laughter.

'Harper,' I hissed. I had forgotten how easily she could embarrass me.

Dad laughed. 'Darling, I think we ought to leave off psychoanalysing Marlowe for now, don't you?'

'It's okay, Harper, she doesn't seem like an ice queen,' Dr Arora assured her. He told her she was looking much better and promised he would come and visit again in the evening.

'Wait.' Harper held her hand in the air. 'How is my hum?'

'Your hum?'

She held her hand over her chest and he passed her his stethoscope.

She closed her eyes to listen. 'Da dum da dum da dum da dum da dum.' She smiled. 'It is beautiful.'

'That's the kind of rhythm we like to hear,' he said. 'How about you hold on to my stethoscope? When you hear that rhythm change, you call me.' He left the room quietly with a pen stuck behind his ear.

'The friendly doctor told me I was looking better, Marlowe,' Harper said. She pointed to my lips. 'But you should put on some lipstick because you are not looking so good.'

Lipstick? That was the last thing on my mind!

But I was aware, suddenly, of how gritty my eyes felt from lack of sleep and I couldn't remember when I'd last brushed my hair. 'I'm going to the bathroom to splash my face,' I said.

Gazing at my reflection in the mirror, I saw that Harper hadn't been exaggerating. My skin was pale, I had dark rings under my eyes and my hair looked greasy. A lack of lipstick was the least of my problems, I thought ruefully.

Needing a break from my family, I walked the hospital corridors for a while before, on impulse, taking the elevator to the fourth floor: the maternity ward.

It felt different up here. A bunch of pink lilies stood in a vase at the reception area and the atmosphere was quieter, less urgent; the people I passed as I walked down the corridor towards the nursery were smiling rather than stressed. A painting of an angel shrouded in light, hung on the main wall.

At the nursery, I stared through the glass at the little humans cocooned in blankets. The baby closest to me was asleep. A yellow bonnet covered his head. He looked like a pupa, glossy-skinned, very still and oblong-shaped.

It dawned on me that I would miss the day when the new batch of pupae I was rearing in London would hatch. My hands gripped the window ledge. At least Olly would be there to look after them.

Olly.

If he were here beside me, he would be telling me some fun fact about how babies operate, how important the connection between mother and child is for that child's development, how many similarities there are between us and mammals in the animal kingdom.

A newborn wrapped in white began to scream. Her mother picked her up and carried her from the nursery. I watched her walk slowly up and down the corridor, cooing at the bundle in her arms. I couldn't understand why she was so happy. Her life would never be her own again.

I turned back to the baby with the yellow bonnet. He was stirring now. His face tightened and relaxed. He made O shapes with his lips. He did not have almond eyes. His face was not swollen and round. He did not have Down syndrome.

I felt a hand on my back. It was Wài Pó.

'Where were you and Dad earlier?' I asked. My words came out sharp and clipped. 'Sorry, Wài Pó. I didn't mean to sound angry, but I don't understand why you would leave Harper when she's so sick.'

'It couldn't be helped, Míng Yuè. Your father and I will explain everything when we get home.'

'What's there to explain?'

She shook her head. 'Please, have patience and don't worry. You have enough on your plate.'

Don't worry. Usually when she said that, she was worried herself. Wài Pó didn't like to talk about difficult things; it wouldn't be fair to make her tell me what was going on.

'New life,' she said, gazing at the babies. I noticed how she had shrunk; her back had curved and shoulders hunched, as if she were trying to protect her heart.

'How did you know I was here?'

She smiled. 'You used to come here all the time when you were small and Harper was sick, to watch the babies. This is happy medicine.'

Happy medicine? I would never have put those two words together.

'Happy until one of those little babies gets sick,' I said.

Wài Pó took my hand. 'You gave up your studies to come home.'

Her words hit me in the chest. No one had acknowledged this. I had barely acknowledged it myself.

'Oliver misses you.'

I bit my lip. I didn't want to think about Olly. He wasn't here. I wasn't there. It was no use longing for him.

'He doesn't like to be called Oliver,' I said. 'It's so formal. I keep telling you to call him Olly.'

The baby in the yellow was wailing now, his face shrivelled and red. He looked like an old man.

'I hope I live to see your baby one day.'

My baby? I had decided long ago I would never have children, but she didn't need to know that. Why bring another life into a world already so full of suffering? And what if my child was born with a faulty heart? No, I wasn't going to risk that.

A nurse entered and picked up the crying baby. As soon as she started rubbing his back, his screaming softened.

'Ah.' Wài Pó squeezed my hand. 'This one just wanted to be held.'

'Let's go,' I said.

I laced my arm through hers. I could feel her frail bones under layers of clothing and skin. As we were waiting for the lift, a nurse wheeled an empty basinet into the corridor beside us. When she left, I touched the crumpled blanket. It was still warm.

—

I sat next to Harper, who was in her hospital bed, writing an entry in her storybook.

Dad was in a chair facing the window, seemingly lost in thought. I waited for my irritation at his passivity to seep in, but it didn't. Because I was too tired? Or was it Wài Pó's acknowledgment of what I had sacrificed to be here? Knowing someone was aware of what I was going through had made me feel less alone.

Wài Pó had taken out her crochet. She was making a blanket with white and blue wool.

Dad's mobile rang. He answered, gave Wài Pó a look, then walked out of the room. Wài Pó rose and followed, leaving her crocheting on the seat behind her. I was so tired of not knowing what was going on. I got up to go after them, intent on answers, but Dr Arora was standing in the doorway, holding a small stack of *National Geographic* magazines.

He handed them to me. 'These are for the bug lady. I know how boring hospitals can be, so I dropped by the library at the end of the corridor.'

Harper clapped her hands together. 'What a kind and sweet thing to do.'

I glared at her. *Don't forget I have a boyfriend.*

Dr Arora chuckled and turned to leave. Despite the heat in my cheeks, I followed him out.

'Can I have a word?' I asked, pulling the door closed behind us. 'I take it you know about my sister's prognosis. She has been given only a few months to live.'

He nodded. 'I'm sorry,' he murmured.

I was so tired of that word. Without bothering to hide the exasperation in my voice, I asked him if there was really nothing he or anyone else could do?

'Hong Kong doesn't have a large supply of organs. Even if Harper were to be placed on the recipient list, the likelihood of her getting a heart and a healthy set of lungs would be slim.'

He wasn't telling me anything I didn't already know, but that didn't make it any easier to hear.

'Coming through!' Louis raced past us carrying a white plastic bag. His suit jacket was tied around his waist and the back of his blue shirt was drenched in sweat.

We followed him into Harper's room.

'Thirty minutes and twenty seconds. YESSSSS!' He pressed a button on his digital watch. 'I am speedy.' He gave Harper a kiss on the forehead. 'How do you feel, my sweet lady?'

Harper smiled and gave Louis a long and passionate kiss.

'I'll leave you all in peace.' Dr Arora turned to leave.

'Wait!' Louis shouted. 'I need to talk to you, Doctor!' He gave Dr Arora the bag. 'I've got something in here to make Harper better.'

Harper leaned forward in bed. 'You do?'

'Yes. I've got you a new heart, my love. A special, brand-new one.'

Dr Arora and I peered into the bag. Inside was a large, bloody heart. It gave off a warm, meaty odour that made my insides turn.

'Where did you get this?' I stepped away, trying not to gag.

'From Wan Chai Market.' Louis puffed his chest out proudly. 'From the butcher.' Then his posture softened and his eyes glazed over. 'Actually, it is from a poor, sweet cow.' He bowed his head. 'I think that now I am feeling a bit sorry for the cow that is missing its heart.'

Harper sighed and leaned back on her pillows. 'I don't want another heart anyway. Mine is fine.'

Why did she keep saying that?

Dr Arora retied the plastic bag and asked Louis to take a seat. He explained that this was a very thoughtful thing to do, and even though animal to human transplants had been attempted in the very early stages of transplant research, unfortunately they didn't work.

Louis looked at the doctor blankly.

'Do you like cars?' Dr Arora asked.

'Oh yes.' Louis nodded fervently. 'Very much.'

'Well, giving Harper this heart would be like trying to give a Jaguar the engine of a Honda. The Jaguar wouldn't be able to run with that.' He paused and he put his hand on Louis's knee. 'I'm very sorry, but this cow's heart won't save Harper's life.'

'But –' Louis shook his head, his face tightening. 'But –' As I saw his eyes fill with tears, I turned away.

'Louis…' Harper reached for him.

My breathing became shallow. Their pain was unbearable. I had to leave the room.

I walked back to the entrance to the cardiac ward. It was buzzing with visitors. I saw Dad and Wài Pó standing with their backs to me, deep in conversation. I moved closer.

'How much do you think it will sell for?' Wài Pó was asking.

'One point two.'

'That's not enough.'

What were they planning to sell? I wasn't sure I wanted to know. I backed away before they saw me listening.

'Marlowe, wait!' someone called as I hurried down the corridor. I turned. It was Anita. This time, she wasn't smiling. 'Can we talk?'

Harper

Red flowers.
   Red lips.
   Red nails.
   Red heart.

Marlowe

I closed the front door and turned on the light in the hall. The rest of the house was dark. A pair of Irene's high heels, Hollywood red, sat in the entrance. The impression of her dainty toes marked the soles of her shoes in the shape of thimbles. When I was a child, our home was always full of visitors, music, chatter and beautiful things. Today it seemed that everywhere I looked, Irene had already made her mark.

I walked down the hall quietly, wanting to avoid a scene with her. She hadn't returned to the hospital after our argument that morning, and I had no idea where she had gone. I made it to Dad's study without encountering her and slipped inside, closing the door behind me. I sat at Dad's desk and switched on the computer. As I waited for it to boot up, I thought over the conversation I'd had with Anita.

She had led me into a stairwell and handed me a slip of paper on which was written a Hong Kong phone number and the name Mr Zhāng. Anita told me this was the number for someone who could help Harper get the heart and lungs that she needed. A hospital in Shanghai could perform the transplant surgery in a matter of weeks.

I gaped at her, unable to believe what I was hearing. 'I don't understand,' I said.

Anita explained that many lives were saved this way, including her brother's. The only problem was the expense. It cost US$30,000 for a heart and a similar amount for lungs, although prices varied depending on the brokers and the hospitals they worked with. Anita said she had already spoken to my stepmother, who had told her that our family didn't have that kind of cash. 'But I thought I would mention it to you, too,' she finished. 'This would save Harper's life.'

Irene had told Anita we couldn't afford to save Harper's life? How dare she! Yes, it was a lot of money, but if it meant saving Harper's life of course we would find a way. But then I paused. This all seemed too good to be true. Yes, China had a huge population, but were organs really so readily available? If they were, why was there such a shortage in the world?

'Why is it so easy to get organs quickly in China?' I asked.

Anita looked away. 'I've heard that they use the organs of executed prisoners.'

My body went cold.

'The way I see it,' she said, 'this is the one good deed they can do before they die, to redeem themselves.'

Pulling the computer keyboard towards me now, I typed the words 'executed prisoners organ transplants' into the search engine. Surely Anita had it all wrong. But the first search result was a newspaper article titled: *China's Organ Transplant Tourism*. In the accompanying image, a man kneeled on the ground, handcuffed, head bowed. Behind him was a wall marked with bullet holes. I felt like I was going to vomit.

So Anita was right.

I shut down the computer and stared at the blank screen. I had two competing voices in my head. Was I really prepared to save my sister in this way? the first asked. At the expense of another life? But would I really turn down the chance to save Harper? asked the other. Surely nothing mattered more than that. Surely our family had suffered enough loss already.

I rose from the chair and left the study, walking into the living room to stand in the empty space where Mum's grand piano used to be. I tried to recall the sound of her playing, but the memory refused to come. My body felt heavy, weighed down by her absence. What if I could have saved Mum? Wouldn't I have done anything? Standing there, it was as if I was that scared little girl again, woken by the sound of my parents arguing.

⊶

'You can't give up,' my father thundered. 'I won't allow it.'

It was the first time I had ever heard Dad raise his voice.

I crawled out of bed, still wrapped in my feather duvet, and tiptoed along the corridor to my parents' room. The door was ajar, and I could see Dad pacing back and forth.

'Why won't you just give the chemo another shot, damn it?'

'James, it's too late,' Mum replied, her voice soft. 'You heard the doctor – almost all my marrow has been replaced by abnormal –'

'We need to get another opinion,' Dad interrupted.

'I can't put myself through it again,' she said.

For a moment, there was silence. I moved closer to the door. I could see Mum sitting on their four-poster bed. Her orange bandana was wrapped around her head, long sleeves hid the red and purple marks that had spread across her skin.

'My darling, you need to accept there is nothing more that can be done.' She reached out her hand and Dad came into view. He sat on the bed beside her and buried his head in her chest. His back shook as he wept. It made me feel wobbly, as if the ground beneath me could give way at any moment. I turned and shuffled back to my room.

I was in bed when I heard the creak of my door opening. Mum. I could sense her watching me, something she had started to do most nights since she came home from hospital. I sat up in bed and turned on the bedside light.

She blinked. 'I didn't mean to wake you.' She approached my bed. Her skin was so thin, I could see the movement of her bones beneath it. 'Go back to sleep, my darling.' Her hand felt cool against my forehead.

'Why have you given up? Why won't you have more chemo?' I asked.

She went still. Then, recovering herself, she whispered, 'Don't worry about me, darling. You're too young to worry.' She switched off my light and walked to the door, pausing once, a silhouette in the doorway, to look back at me.

As the days passed, Mum got worse. All she did was sleep. She barely ate. She no longer had the strength to stand in my bedroom doorway at night.

Dad rarely left her side.

I continued to go to school as usual and was waiting at the gate one afternoon for Wài Pó to collect me when the mother of my friend Pearl Wong came over to talk to me.

'Marlowe, dear,' Mrs Wong said, 'how is your poor mother?'

'She's very sick,' I told her, adding, 'She told my dad she won't do chemo anymore.'

To my surprise, Mrs Wong nodded her approval. 'Your mother has made an excellent decision,' she said. 'The western way is not as good as the eastern way in cases like this.'

'Really?' I said.

'Chemo works by treating toxins with more toxins. What use is that?' She threw her hands into the air. 'Chinese medicine, on the other hand, does not attack the body's qì. Tomorrow I will give Pearl a packet of herbs for your mother.'

'But Wài Pó has already given my mum Chinese herbs and they haven't done anything,' I said.

'Ah,' said Mrs Wong, 'but they were probably just herbs from the market. My herbs come from Dr Leung, and he is Hong Kong's top Chinese medicine doctor.'

Hong Kong's top doctor! I paid close attention as Mrs Wong rattled off the instructions.

As promised, the next day at school Pearl gave me a small parcel from her mother.

That afternoon, with Esmerelda's help, I prepared the concoction then carefully carried the jug of warm brown liquid to my mother's room. It smelled like faeces, dried flowers and mould; I was secretly glad that I wouldn't have to drink it myself. *Your mother must drink a cup of this every half-hour on an empty stomach*, Mrs Wong had said. *Even if she vomits, she must continue to drink. Have faith, dear. I've seen Dr Leung's herbs cure many sick people. His medicine is better than chemotherapy.*

I found Mum asleep. I put the jug on her bedside table and patted her back.

'Ma, wake up, I have something for you.' But Mum did not stir. 'Ma,' I tried again, this time, blowing on her eyelids. 'Ma wake up.' My breath became shallow. 'Ma?' *Was she dead?* 'Ma? Please?!'

She stirred slightly, then, with what seemed like an enormous effort, opened her eyes.

'Darling.' Her voice was croaky. 'I've been so tired.'

I poured her a cup of the brown liquid, resisting the urge to gag, and held it out to her.

She looked quizzically then shook her head. 'No.'

'But, Ma…'

Her eyes were closing. 'What a beautiful girl you have become,' she whispered. Then, as I watched, she drifted off.

＊

In the unoccupied space where Mum's piano used to be, I knelt. The memory of her last song came to me. She had played a slow melody, not one of the classics. It was something I hadn't heard before, something raw, abstract, something I didn't like. My eyes were starting to feel heavy. I curled into a foetal position. My body was uncomfortable against the hard, wooden floor.

Harper

It is easier to hear my heart with the kind doctor's listening tube over my chest. I close my eyes: da da dum dum da dum. Its rhythm is a bit mixed up, but I am not upset about it, because it is a part of me, made with love by Mum and Dad. I have had this heart of mine ever since I was in Mum's tummy. We have grown together, loved together, cried together. I do not understand why I am sick. I have been sick since I first opened my eyes to this world. Sometimes I wish I wasn't this way, that I could do all the things I love without going to hospital, but no matter what anyone says, I haven't given up hope that my heart and me will get better soon.

'How are you doing, darling?' Dad sits in a blue hospital seat next to me. Even though Marlowe has gone home to take a nap, I feel grateful my family is with me. Stepmonster has come back, and she and Wài Pó are sitting in the chairs by the window. Wài Pó is asleep and Stepmonster is sitting very still, watching my dad. Her face is soft now. Her hair is a little bit fluffy and messy at the top, and her make-up has worn off from a long day. I can see the real colour of her lips; they are peachy and pink – much nicer than her red lipstick. I think to myself that now she might even look a little bit pretty.

I lean over to my bedside table and take out my autobiographical storybook.

'What's this?' Dad opens it and then he smiles a big smile.

I tell him that it is only the start, but I am proud of myself for doing this and proud of him because he has been my best writing teacher. He showed me how to read and write, and he is the one who told me that with our words we can make stories live forever.

Dad turns the pages and it is like everything that I have written swims up into his eyes, moves through his brain and drops down, cosy and warm, into his chest.

'You're turning all our chaos into something meaningful with your words.' Dad takes my hand. 'My girl...'

I wait for him to finish speaking but he doesn't. He looks away for a moment and then he reaches for a book. 'How about we read?' he suggests.

He opens a classic book called *Jane Eyre* by a wonderful woman named Charlotte Brontë. He has read this story to me many times before because he knows I like the romance in it. His voice is steady and quiet.

As my dad is reading, I look at Stepmonster. Her eyes are smiling as she watches him. Her hands are on her lap, and her face is open and listening, free from her talking, talking mind. It is as if she is sinking into Charlotte Brontë's words, made brand-new by Dad's voice. In this moment, I feel bad for calling her a stepmonster.

'Dad,' I say.

He stops reading and looks up at me with his blue, blue eyes, the same colour as Marlowe's.

'I don't want a new heart,' I say. 'I don't want a transplant thing.' I have told them this before but I need them to hear it again – really hear it.

He bends over to stroke my cheek and some of his grey, wavy hair falls over his forehead.

'What *do* you want, darling?'

My stepmother takes off her noisy shoes and walks softly to Dad's side. I can hear her listening, listening with Dad for what I am about to say.

'I want to keep my own heart. I want to get well with my own heart.'

Dad takes my hand and kisses it. His cheeks are wet. And for the first time in a very long while, my stepmother touches her fingertips to my forehead in a gentle way.

I look at Wài Pó and see that she is not snoring anymore. Her eyes are open and she is watching me while muttering a prayer with her beads.

'And I want no more fighting, please. Not with the doctors, not with anyone.'

Then I tell my dad to start reading again and, slowly, my heart and me fall asleep.

Marlowe

I sat on the living room couch, my mind buzzing. Thanks to Anita, I had found a way to save Harper. All I needed to do was act on it. I would have to come up with enough money, of course, and that would involve talking to Dad and Wài Pó. I doubted Irene would have told them about her conversation with Anita; she'd never spent a dime on anyone but herself.

Despite my unease at the source of the donor organs, I reminded myself that this was the only way. And I was sure that, once I'd explained, Dad and Wài Pó would be as excited as I was that Harper would have a chance at life. I allowed myself to imagine her with a new heart. She could get married, play sports, dance, work…

The sound of the front door opening roused me from my thoughts.

Wài Pó, Dad and Irene entered the house, deep in conversation.

'Hello,' I called.

Irene let out a small scream. 'Why are you sitting in the dark like that?'

She switched on the light; I hadn't even realised that night had fallen.

'I've been waiting for all of you. There's something I want to talk to you about.' My pulse quickened. This had to work. Surely it would work.

Wài Pó sat next to me on the couch, while Dad and Irene sat in armchairs facing us. The scent of Harper's hospital room; a mixture of muggy dampness and bitter disinfectant, lingered on their clothes.

'I've found a way to save Harper,' I announced. 'She can get a set of lungs and a heart – we just need to come up with the money to pay for it.'

Irene let out a long sigh. I had expected an argument, but instead she seemed to slump.

'I need a smoke,' she said quietly. She stood and crossed to the French doors, then stepped out onto the patio.

I looked from Dad to Wài Pó, waiting for one of them to speak, to ask questions, to express some surprise or excitement, but neither of them said a word.

Wài Pó took a hawthorn candy from her pocket, quickly unwrapped it and shoved it into her mouth. Dad wiped a bead of sweat from his upper lip and forehead with his handkerchief.

Come on, say something, I urged silently.

Finally I said, 'Don't you want to know what I'm talking about?'

Dad and Wài Pó exchanged a look, then Dad said, 'Go ahead. Tell us.'

I recounted what Anita had told me about the organs from China, and the cost, though I left out the detail about the executed prisoners. 'So you see,' I concluded, 'all we need to do is come up with sixty-five thousand dollars. I know that's a lot of money – but if it means saving Harper's life, there's no question we should do it.'

The room was so quiet. I could hear the sound of banana leaves in the garden brushing against the window. Wài Pó looked at Dad and whispered something inaudible under her breath. Dad rubbed his forehead.

'I don't understand.' I was standing now. 'What's the problem? I thought you would be happy!'

Wài Pó's face hardened. She was the first to speak and said only one word: 'No.'

Hope draining from my body, I subsided onto the couch again.

'Marlowe…' Dad moved to the edge of his seat. 'I don't think this is what Harper would want. You should know, we've called Uncle Bǐng Wén, Aunt Lǐ Nà and Bì Yù. They will come as soon as we give them the word. Our job now is to make Harper comfortable.'

I stared at him. 'What are you saying?' I had the urge to shake him until he saw sense. 'How can you just give up like this?'

'Míng Yuè,' my grandmother said, 'it's really not good to give Harper organs from another body. A person must die with their own organs in their body for –'

'For the afterlife? Do you really believe that?' I was tired of Wài Pó's mumbo jumbo.

'Darling, even if I thought this was a good idea, we just don't have the money.' Dad bowed his head. 'We've been struggling a little with all the hospital bills.'

Struggling? My blood felt hot. 'What do you mean?'

'Business hasn't been doing so well. Harper's hospital bills have been adding up and her insurance premiums are skyrocketing.'

I heard his words but they weren't quite sinking in. We'd had many problems, but money was never one of them. Wài Pó came from a wealthy Shanghai tea merchant family and there was Dad's successful business. We'd always been well off. When had that changed? It occurred to me then that the Ming dynasty vases and my mother's piano had been sold.

Irene stepped back into the room and my focus turned to her. She wore Jimmy Choo heels and a smart Armani dress. She crossed the room to the drinks cabinet, and as she walked towards us carrying a tray with a whisky bottle and glasses, the diamond rings on her fingers glinted. I had a pretty good idea where most of the money had gone.

'Maybe if *she* spent less of *our* money on botox, you would be in a better position to help,' I burst out.

Dad's mouth dropped open and his eyes widened. I waited for an explosion, but it never came. Irene poured whisky into a glass then, holding my gaze, downed the drink in one go. Then she turned and left the room without a word.

'I know you're upset, Marlowe, but you can't talk to Irene like that.' Dad stood. I thought he looked tall, unusually tall. 'And quite aside from that, I won't allow Harper to undergo a transplant. It's not her wish.'

It began to rain heavily outside, droplets pounded the French doors like the call of hungry ghosts. I didn't understand. Dad said, 'I want Harper to live as much as you do, but it's not your place – or mine – to make decisions without involving her.' And then he too left the room.

Wài Pó shifted closer to me on the couch and laced her fingers through mine.

'You must listen to your *mèi mei* now. Please think about what she wants. I know she doesn't want this.'

I knew Harper had said she didn't want a transplant, but how could she make that call? Did she really understand what the consequences of her decision would be?

I needed Harper to live. She had to.

I pulled my hand away from Wài Pó and ran up the stairs to my bedroom.

Harper

In my brain there is a new word: in-vis-ible. I write it in my autobiography storybook again and again and again: *Invisible. Invisible. Invisible.*

This word got into my brain on Thursday night at 7 pm, just after Louis left my hospital room. I was alone with Wài Pó while Dad and Irene went to get dinner. Together we were watching the Chinese news with careful eyes and ears. A lady's voice from inside the TV was telling us a sad story about an old man who lived in Kowloon, Hong Kong, in his own apartment all by himself. I saw the old man's photo from inside the TV; he had big ears, grey hair, a long beard and age all over his face. He looked like a cute, sweet man with a bit of the magic in his beard, like a wizard. Then the lady from the TV said the man had died and no one knew about this because he was alone, all by himself.

No single body, like his friends or family, knew in their hearts and minds about his death because this old man did not have any friends or family.

The only reason he was found dead was because there was water dripping and flooding from a broken pipe in his house and someone had to fix it. This fixing person had to break into his home like a thief, and that is when they saw him. I am sure that he was a bit stiff, and probably he was purple and blue because there was cold under his skin. Like Mum, when her heart stopped, and she was put in a box in the ground and part of her soul went to live on a bright star.

At night, I watch Mum glow.

Marlowe

In the darkness, I wandered through the house: past Harper's empty bedroom, past Wài Pó's room and the sound of her snoring, to Dad's study.

As I turned on the computer again and waited for it to boot up, I spotted a newspaper clipping on top of a pile of bills. The headline read: *Man Charged With Killing Endangered Butterfly, England*. I read on. The butterfly was the *Maculinea arion*. I looked at the photo of the man, caught mid-stride on a busy street outside the courthouse. He had a star tattooed on his neck and he did not look remorseful.

I put the clipping down, unable to read any more. In a way, the man and I were the same and Dad knew it.

➤

I was eight, nearly nine, and had started wetting the bed again. Dad told me it was time I grew out of it but I couldn't seem to help it. I kept having the same nightmare in which I couldn't stop growing until I was larger than our house. I had become an eight-year-old monster.

I woke one morning and noticed that the sheets were damp. I stripped the bed, changed out of my flannel nightie and lugged the soiled linen to the laundry room. The nightmare still lingered in my body, making my shoulders tight. I told myself that dreams weren't real. I was not a monster, I did not need to run to Mum for comfort. Dad had told me I should not disturb her while she was sick and, anyway, I'd had a silly dream, that was all.

I wandered into the kitchen to ask Wài Pó for breakfast but she wasn't there. Opening the fridge, I saw a jug of freshly squeezed orange juice. This gave me an idea. I dabbed the juice onto my arms – an old trick Grandpa had taught me to lure butterflies – and made my way to the garden. I wanted to become the youngest lepidopterist to find a rare subspecies of the *Actinote*, one that Grandpa had shown me in his lepidopterists' encyclopedia.

As I passed the koi pond and old banyan tree, I heard the sound of clipping. I found Dad pruning the jasmine bush that ran along the left border of our garden. He wore a wide-brimmed hat and his face was streaked with sweat.

'Good morning, darling,' Dad said, and I ran to him, instantly forgetting about my search for the *Actinote*. Dad told me it was too hot out and that I should go back inside, but I didn't want to. The smell of Mum's sickness lingered in the house like sour milk.

Dad continued to work, moving from the jasmine bush to nearby plants, and I followed. Banana leaf, bauhinia, hibiscus, coral plant – he named them all and I listened, concentrating as hard as I could. In that moment, he reminded me of Grandpa. They both loved their gardens but for different reasons.

Eventually, though, the heat got too much for me, and I went to rest under the shade of the old banyan tree.

'Pretty tree, tree pretty.'

Harper.

I got up and followed the sound of her voice. On the other side of the trunk, she was spinning under drooping branches. She wore a pink floral skirt which puffed out as she twirled. She lost her balance and fell in a heap, laughing. Her hands ran over the roots beside her as she whispered to the tree. I couldn't hear what she was saying, but watching her, it was as if she had become a part of the tree. Banyan branches, vines and roots looked like they had curled around her protectively, and were whispering back to her. I frowned. I was the one who worked so hard to make sense of nature, I was the one who loved to study it, yet it was as if she was a part of it in a way I could never be.

In a huff, I stomped back to the other side of the banyan. As I rested my head against the rough trunk, something furry swiped against my ear. In a fright, I swatted it away with the back of my hand.

'Careful,' Dad warned. I hadn't noticed his approach. His body was as still as a deer when it hears the crackling of leaves. I followed his gaze to a butterfly. It fluttered and swooped in pockets of warm air, showing off flecks of black and lemon yellow.

'Looks like a golden birdwing,' he said. 'They're rare in Hong Kong.'

I was surprised that Dad could identify butterflies; he rarely showed any interest when I related what Grandpa had taught me. Yet now he was smiling, something he seldom did since Mum had become sick.

I jumped up and raced into the kitchen. Rummaging in the cupboard under the sink where Wài Pó kept her jars to pickle chillies, I chose the biggest one I could find. Although I didn't have a butterfly net like Grandpa used in Cornwall, I thought it might still work.

Moving as quietly as I could, I walked barefoot through the garden. I searched and searched and finally saw the birdwing hovering by an orange tree. I moved slowly towards the insect but the butterfly seemed to sense my presence and it spiralled upwards and away. My hand held high, I moved in circles after it, but the golden birdwing was too quick for me. In a second, it was gone.

The back of my shirt was soaked with sweat. I swallowed hard, trying to push down the rising lump of tears in my throat. I thought of Mum, Dad and Wài Pó, and how they had changed. It was as if they were all sick now, with a kind of tiredness that made them move about the house like they were carrying mountains on their backs. I hated the fact that there was nothing I could do to make them feel better.

I was marching back towards the house when I saw Harper sitting on one of the small stones that led to Mum's pagoda, eating an orange. On her nose was the birdwing. Its wings breathed slowly in and out. It wasn't fair – Harper wasn't even trying to catch the butterfly!

She was laughing and babbling as I moved slowly towards her, jar in hand, ready.

'Shh,' I whispered and she obediently fell silent. Gently scooping the creature into the jar, I slammed the lid shut. The butterfly tumbled against the glass walls. I closed my eyes tightly and counted to ten. When I opened them, the birdwing was still. Harper began to sob.

'No, no, no,' she cried. 'Poor fairy-fly. Poor fairy-fly.'

'Stop crying,' I scolded, then I ran back across the garden screaming, 'Daddy, Daddy, look what I have for you.'

Dad was sitting on the porch, sipping a glass of iced water. He put down the glass and took the jar from me, his lips tight.

He unscrewed the lid and gently rattled the jar, urging the butterfly out. Its wings began to flutter in short bursts but instead of flying away it moved in drunken circles and then went still.

Dad rose. He picked up his pruning shears and, without a word, walked away from me to the other side of the garden. I saw him lift Harper into his arms, his hand rubbing her back in soothing circles until she was calm.

⚊

I stared at the computer screen, at the photo of the prisoner about to be executed. *Did he have a family? A wife? Children? Was his mother still alive? His father?* I recoiled from the thought but I couldn't stop staring at the picture. I needed to remind myself that he was real.

'What are you doing?'

I looked up. Irene was standing in the open doorway. In her hand, she held a suitcase.

'I'm leaving now,' she said. 'I know you think I don't care, but please, Marlowe, for Harper's sake, for your father's… for all of your sakes, do not go down this path.'

She walked away. I heard the front door open and close.

The house felt lighter with her gone.

Harper

At night-time, when the world is sleeping and it is past midnight, the spark of writing often visits me. But tonight, even though I want to write, I can't.

In *Storytelling 101* they say this is called 'writer's block' and some things that will help this are:

1) Going for a walk
2) Reading your favourite novel
3) Something called 'free writing', where you write everything that is in your brain so that it spills onto the paper like emptying a rubbish bin.

But I can't do any of these things. My eyes are sleepy. My body is tired and sore and my mind feels like a cloud about to burst with bluey blue rain. All I can hear is the sound of beeping machines around me, louder than the sound of my writing sparks at night.

Marlowe

I couldn't sleep.

Again.

The sun would rise in an hour or two anyway.

Irene had unsettled me.

Had I driven her away?

Dad would wake up soon. How would he feel when he realised she'd gone?

But I wanted her gone.

Even though I knew that made me a horrid person.

For all of your sakes, do not go down this path.

There was that too. If I pursued the transplant, knowing what I did, how would I sleep at night?

But how would I ever forgive myself if I didn't do everything I could to save Harper's life? Dad and Wài Pó had said that Harper didn't want a transplant – but Harper thought her heart would heal on its own, and that she would live happily ever after with Louis. Besides, I had promised Mum that I would look after my sister, and I intended to keep that promise. As for the money, well, I had an answer for that too. I would use the money Mum had left me to pay for Harper's heart and lung transplant in China. She had told me that I was to use it to follow my own dreams, but if it meant the difference between Harper surviving or not, I was sure I knew what she would want me to do.

I rose from my bed and went to the wardrobe. From the top shelf, I removed a shoebox. Inside were letters from Mum – one for every birthday she missed until I turned eighteen. Opening the box, I lifted the bundle of papers to my nose and inhaled. Nothing of her sweet fragrance was left.

Even though she had died years ago, I still felt like I was losing pieces of her every day.

I read the last letter, written in blue ink, wanting to be sure I was about to make the right decision.

> I have left you some money that will be made available to you now, as you turn eighteen. I want you to use it to follow your dreams, as I was able to follow mine. Physical possessions, health and relationships can come and go, but an education, a fulfilling career, can never be taken from you...

I had already used some of the money to support myself while I pursued my PhD in London. I had been planning to save the rest to use as I continued my research, but there was just enough to use for Harper's transplant instead.

I swallowed. I would have to let Professor Lipin know.

I walked through the silent house to Dad's study, and settled myself in front of the computer once more. When I signed into my email account, a series of unread messages from Olly came up:

> Have been trying to call.
> What's going on?
> Are you okay?
> Please tell me you're okay.

My chest ached. I found it hard to keep things from Olly, but how could I tell him what I was about to do, pursuing the transplant in China? Would he think less of me? I didn't want to risk it, not with him. More importantly, I was scared he might talk me out of it. I wrote him a brief message, telling him I was fine and would call tomorrow. I didn't want to have to lie to him but that was probably what I would end up doing.

I started composing a letter to Professor Lipin, explaining that, due to personal and financial reasons, I would not be returning to the university to finish my PhD. With a sick feeling in my stomach, I hovered the cursor over the send button.

Help.

I picked up the phone and dialled Shanghai. It wasn't quite 6 am, but Bì Yù was an early riser, and I was sure she wouldn't mind…

Her voice sounded groggy on the other end of the line.

'*Dà jiě.*' It was the first time I had spoken in Chinese since Mum died.

'*Mèi mei*! I've been trying to call you but you haven't been answering your phone. Is everything okay? How's Harper?'

'Harper's stable for now.' I apologised for not calling sooner then said, 'Remember how you said if I ever needed anything I should call? Well, I've found a way to help Harper…'

I told her how Anita had suggested we go to China, how quickly Harper could get a heart in Shanghai. I asked her to be my translator.

To my surprise, instead of trying to dissuade me she said, 'Sure! I'd be happy to. The medical system is very good in China.'

I was relieved that she didn't ask about the source of the organs, and I didn't volunteer the information.

'So, is it okay if I transfer you the money? Then I can take out the renminbi when I get there.'

'Can't Uncle James pay by card? Why go to all the trouble of transferring cash?'

I hadn't thought this through. How was I supposed to convince her to help me with only half the truth?

'Here's the thing,' I said. 'Dad and Wài Pó aren't exactly on board with this, so it would be best if we kept it between us for now.'

She didn't say anything.

'Bì Yù?'

'What's going on, Marlowe? Why can't they know?'

Think fast.

'Dad doesn't have enough money, so I'm using my inheritance. Please don't tell Uncle Bǐng Wén and Aunt Lǐ Nà. I know they'll want to help and Dad won't be okay with that.'

It was only half a lie, I told myself.

'But, Marlowe, Mum and Dad would be happy to help. We're family, remember? And we have the money.'

'No, please, they can't know,' I said desperately. 'You know Dad – he can be quite proud.'

Losing face. Whether she liked what I was doing or not, losing face was something Bì Yù would understand. Pride was something her father took seriously.

'Okay.'

Phew.

'*Mèi mei*, I'm so sorry to hear about Uncle James and the family situation. I can understand he might be ashamed, but please give this some thought. That money is your inheritance. Your *mā ma* would have wanted that to be kept just for you.'

'All right, I'll think about it,' I lied.

'Just let me know when you book your flights. You can stay with me.'

'Thanks,' I said. 'And you won't tell your parents we're coming, right?'

There was a long pause.

'*Dà jiě*, please.'

'Okay, okay. But you know Mum – she can always tell when I'm hiding something.'

She was right; Aunt Lǐ Nà was incredibly perceptive.

'Don't worry, it won't be for long,' I said, trying to reassure myself as much as her.

When we'd hung up, I returned to the letter I'd written Professor Lipin. *This has to be done.* I took a breath, closed my eyes and clicked send.

I had one more call to make. I needed a translator in Hong Kong I could trust to speak with the broker, Mr Zhāng, and Uncle Johnny was the only person I could think of. I checked the time: 6.15 am. Way too early for him.

I went back upstairs and crawled into bed although I wasn't expecting to sleep. I was lying to my family and making Bì Yù do the same, and that didn't sit easily with me. And more than that, there was the ethical dilemma. Was I really right to go against Harper's wishes and save her life, possibly at the expense of another life?

But then I thought of Mum and the promise I'd made. I thought of Harper building a happy life with Louis.

My body was heavy and I felt as if I were falling again, but this time I closed my eyes and let myself go.

⚬

When I next opened my eyes it was 10.30 am. I'd overslept.

I reached for my phone on the bedside table and dialled Uncle Johnny's mobile.

'I need your help,' I said without preamble.

'Good morning to you too, Marlowe. How's Harper?'

I explained that she was back in hospital, but stable for the moment. 'How's the article coming along?'

'To be honest, I haven't made much headway yet. I've had a colleague look into it but it is not being treated with much urgency.'

I let his words sink in for a moment before speaking again. 'It doesn't matter so much anymore.' I told him about Anita and the broker who could arrange for a transplant to be performed in Shanghai. 'Drop the article, this is something that could actually work… I would just need you to translate for me.' Unlike Bì Yù, though, Uncle Johnny seemed wary.

'Marlowe, do you realise what you're getting yourself into?'

'Yes, of course I do. It makes me feel sick; it keeps me up at night.'

But what choice did I have? It was either this or another funeral in a few months.

'I don't want to bury my sister.' I blinked, hard.

'I don't want that for Harper either.' Uncle Johnny's words sounded softer, quieter. He seemed less anxious, more thoughtful. 'I just want to make sure you've really thought this through. I don't know much about how this works in China, but I can tell you that you would need to be very careful. It's not a regulated industry.'

'I know.' Did I? Maybe not everything, but surely I knew enough.

'You know I can't come to China with you,' he said.

'That's okay. Bì Yù will be helping me in Shanghai.'

A long pause. *Come on, Uncle Johnny.* 'I made one promise to Mum before she passed, and that was to look after Harper. Everyone else has given up. Please, I can't let her down…' I couldn't keep the desperation from my voice.

Uncle Johnny sighed. 'Your mother would be so disappointed if she knew you weren't able to speak Chinese anymore... Okay.'

Did he just say okay?

'Really? You'll do it?'

'Let me know when and I'll be there.'

I hung up feeling jubilant. And for the first time since the family dinner that had gone so horribly wrong, I felt hungry.

As I emerged from my bedroom, I could hear Dad on the phone.

'Just come home, Irene, and we can talk about this in person,' he was saying.

The pain in his voice startled me.

'Well at least tell me where you are. Please, Irene...'

Had I done this?

I quickly retreated into my room and shut the door behind me.

Harper

Louis is sitting on my hospital bed with me, holding my hand. He is very quiet today, so I have to ask him what's wrong.

He looks out the window. 'We are putting on a play at the vocational centre. It's *Romeo and Juliet*, and they wanted me to be Romeo and you to be Juliet because we are in love.'

It is as if stars are exploding around me. I am so happy I squeeze Louis's hand and laugh.

'Happy, happy news! These are roles of a lifetime!'

Louis and me are the best at drama in our centre, and we have always wanted to play Romeo and Juliet. But Louis doesn't look happy. I notice that he is sniffing in a sad way. I turn his face so that our eyes can meet and I see they are wet.

'Why are you sad? We've been waiting for this for so long. Remember when we wrote a letter last term asking Mrs Green to let us do this play?' I was talking so quickly it made me breathless.

'But the play is on at the end of the term. That is three months and two days away.'

'So?' I have a strange feeling swirling around my belly and my brain. I don't like it.

'Do you remember what Stepmonster said?' Louis asks.

The feeling is getting hot and it makes me frown. 'Why are you talking about that?' My voice is loud.

'Well, I asked my mom and my dad about it and they said that maybe you will be too sick to do the play, and then they explained to me about that word.'

I do not need to ask him what word. I know what he is talking about. It makes me go tight all over my body and I want to shout at him but I can't because I love him.

'Dad says a nicer way to say that word is to say that someone passes away.' He starts to cry and snot is coming out of his nose.

His sound is very loud and it is making me hotter and hotter and hotter until I have to put my hands over my ears and shout, 'I am not passing away! No way. Not me!'

Louis puts his hands over his ears and shouts back. 'But my mom and dad said you are. Also, I couldn't save you with the cow's heart.'

The beeping all around me is getting louder and the air around me is shrinking and hard to swallow.

'I am not passing away and I WILL BE JULIET in the play.'

My fire is burning in my eyes and I can't understand why because I have never felt this way at Louis before.

'I will not die! I will not die! I will not die!'

Anger, anger, like hot and spicy Sì chuān chicken exploding in my mouth, like summer sun blazing on my head, like stamping feet and jumping music, like a sore throat, like the sound of thunder stuck in the sea, like everything lost.

Like Mum in her box in the ground.

The beeping around me becomes so fast it is ringing in my ears beep beep beep.

The door opens and two nurses rush in. One takes Louis outside. Another speaks softly to me but I cannot hear what she is saying because my heart is like the sound of drums in my ears, and everything is fast around me. She takes my hand and puts an injection into the tube there. After a few seconds, the beeping slows down and becomes like a soft tiptoe. My room is lazy and blurry and I feel like I am swimming in the air.

Marlowe

Two days later, Uncle Johnny and I met in the lobby of the Wing Fat Building, a small and dingy office block in Wan Chai.

'Thank you for coming.'

Uncle Johnny was fidgeting with a loose thread on the sleeve of his leather jacket.

'No need to thank me,' he replied, glancing over his shoulder.

The elevator was old school, with a spring wire gate for a door. I pressed the button for the ninth floor and held on to a railing as the rickety lift rose upwards. Uncle Johnny fingered the button on his jacket nervously. I had never seen him like this before. He'd seemed so calm when we rang Mr Zhāng a few days earlier.

The doors opened. Worn navy carpet lined the corridor. We walked to room 101 and knocked on the door. A man with slicked-back hair and a toothpick in his mouth opened it. Uncle Johnny said something to him in Cantonese. The man nodded and we entered. The room was empty but for three collapsible chairs in the centre and a suitcase.

The man gestured to the chairs and we sat. I clutched Harper's medical records in my sweaty hands as Uncle Johnny and the broker conversed in Cantonese, Uncle Johnny with an American accent and the broker with a thick Shanghainese accent, words emerging from the back of his throat and spilling over one another like choppy waves.

Uncle Johnny turned to me. 'Mr Zhāng says that it's better if the transplant can be done in November or December.'

I felt the air leave my lungs. 'That's ages away! We don't have that long.'

'I know.' Uncle Johnny spoke to Mr Zhāng again. After several long minutes he spoke in English, 'He said you should take Harper to China and wait for the organs there.'

'How long will it take?'

'He says if she can get to Shanghai soon, it will only be a matter of days.'

I wanted to jump from my chair and hug Mr Zhāng.

'Marlowe,' Uncle Johnny said, 'I have to say this all sounds a little –'

But I didn't let him finish. 'Tell him we'll do it,' I said.

Mr Zhāng asked for Harper's medical records, then told Uncle Johnny she would need to have a pre-transplant blood test and an immunological evaluation in China. A cash deposit of US$35,000 had to be paid within twenty-four hours. The remaining $30,000 would be payable once the surgery was scheduled. There might also be smaller fees once we arrived in China, Mr Zhāng warned.

Uncle Johnny looked at me, brow creased, eyes filled with concern. 'That's a lot of money, Marlowe. Are you sure about this?'

'Yes.' I glared at him and he took a step back, his eyes searching mine. 'Yes,' I repeated in a softer tone. My stomach tightened. I imagined Olly beside me, taking my hand and telling me everything would be okay, that I was not alone.

But I was alone. Uncle Johnny and Bì Yù were only helping reluctantly, and Dad and Wài Pó were against the idea. If Olly were here, would he really say that everything would be okay? *Stop*, I told myself. I had to stop thinking like this. It wouldn't help me in any way.

Uncle Johnny and I left the room and made our way out of the building. It took me a minute to adjust to the light.

'Marlowe?' Uncle Johnny turned to face me. His expression had changed. His eyes were quieter now. 'Promise me, no matter what, you'll stay in touch?'

I nodded and found myself exhaling deeply.

'Thank you for helping me.'

As I watched him walk away, I was aware once more of my aloneness, but this time, it felt different.

I looked at my watch. I didn't have long to set things in motion. At the bank, I took out Mr Zhāng's deposit and organised a transfer to Bì Yù's account. I was told it would take one to two days to go through. My heart raced. That was cutting it fine. I then made it to the travel agent, with only fifteen minutes left before she closed. I felt a tightening in my belly as I paid for our flights. Those pesky thoughts returned: *Was I doing the right thing? There would be no turning back now.* Yet something was driving me, something deep, primal. Like a serpent in one of Harper's stories, it had curled itself in my belly and no amount of logic could override it.

Harper

Louis has not come to visit me today. Maybe he is still a bit upset in his heart with me after what happened yesterday with my anger. We have our engagement party soon and I think it is not good to start an engagement with bad feeling, so I take out my pen and paper and write him a small note:

> To my sweet Louis,
> I am sory.
> I am sory that I was angry and that I hurt your feelings.
> Plees forgiv me.
> That is all.
> From
> Harper明华Míng Huà Eve

I put a very important URGENT word on the envelope and will ask my dad to give this to Louis as fast as he can.

There is a knock at my door. It is the lady who brings us food. Her name is 'Angel Chow'. I think it is strange that she is an angel because her food tastes like cardboard and looks like poo. But I do not tell her this personal private information.

She leaves the room and I push her food to one side. I use my mind to think about all my favourite foods:

Oodles of udon noodles
Baskets of egg tarts
Spring rolls, handmade by Wài Pó with love
Steamed chicken with ginger and spring onion sauce
Hawaiian pizza
Chocolate cake
Red bean soup.

Now, I see myself with Louis in the kitchen. The table is set for two with a candle in the middle. Our first course is the spring rolls. We have one plate each. I dip the fried roll into sweet chilli sauce and take a crunchy bite.

YUMMMMM.

Louis and me smile and cheers with cans of Coke. We are not shy as we feed each other spoonsful of steamed chicken and rice, slices of Hawaiian pizza and we even share one long noodle, sucking on it until our lips touch. The walls are whispering to one another as we kiss. We finish the hot and spicy udon noodle soup – hot and spicy hot and spicy hot and spicy – and then have one egg tart.

Dessert. Louis looks into my eyes and gives me a slice of warm chocolate cake topped with custard and a little vanilla ice cream. His eyes are sparkling.

We cross arms and give each other red bean soup. It is warm and sweet.

The taste of ginger and cane sugar are still on my tongue a long time after I finish eating.

Even though I am not allowed to have these foods right now because the doctor says they are not good for my heart, I can still eat them in my eyes-wide-open dream, shared with Louis, with love.

Marlowe

The sound of a gunshot echoed through my mind. As the elevator rose through the hospital, I kept thinking of the kneeling prisoner.

One Mississippi, two Mississippi… I wouldn't let myself go there, not today. Even though Harper had to have her engagement party in hospital, I wanted it to be special. I had to focus on enjoying myself, for Harper's sake.

As the doors opened onto her ward, it took me a moment to adjust to the vibrant sound of Bob Marley's 'Three Little Birds'. Silver balloons were tied to the handle of Harper's door. Bouquets of red roses filled the corners of her room with colour. At the foot of her bed was a table covered with packets of crisps and chocolates, a CD player and a large photo of Harper and Louis holding hands.

'We'll have the bridal suite for two people, please. Two people in love.'

Louis, who was wearing a light blue suit, stood with his back to me, clutching the telephone by Harper's bed.

'Yes, I will pay with a credit card, but I need to know that you will put roses and chocolates in the room for us because that is a very special thing to do.'

'Louis, what're you doing?'

He immediately hung up the phone and turned to face me. I watched as he casually slid a credit card into his pocket.

'Oh hello, Marlowe. And how are you this fine afternoon?'

I asked him again what he was doing and his cheeks turned red as he told me it was something private. I was reminded of the time a few years ago when Wài Pó had banned Harper from drinking Coke to cut down on her sugar intake. Louis had snuck into the house with a backpack full of cans of Coke and gummy bears.

Harper emerged from the bathroom. Although she was still in her hospital gown, she was wearing make-up, a beaded necklace and a yellow flower in her hair. For a second, it was as if she was no longer sick. It took me a few long seconds to compose myself.

'My goodness, you're a stunning lady.' Louis kissed her on the cheek.

'Marlowe, I'm so glad you are here,' said Harper, 'but you are early.'

I helped her back into bed. Her nose twitched as she pushed her glasses back into place.

'I came to help you set up,' I said, 'but it looks like you have it covered.'

'After we get engaged this evening, we are going to go to the Mandarin Oriental hotel,' she told me.

I could have told her that the doctor probably wouldn't discharge her tonight, and that the likelihood of her going to a hotel would be slim, but I decided not to be a spoilsport.

Louis looked at a watch on his wrist and told me their friends would be arriving soon.

'Whose credit card were you using to pay for the hotel?' I couldn't help but ask.

He glanced at Harper. 'I didn't do a bad thing, you know. I just had to borrow it from my dad. I don't think he will mind.'

I ducked my head to hide my smile.

'Hello!'

I turned. Adam, Harper's friend from the vocational centre, was standing in the doorway. He was dressed in a *Star Wars* shirt, red tie and jeans, and moved with the help of a walking frame.

'Adam!' Harper held out her arms and gave him a hug.

'You look as beautiful as ever,' Adam said.

'Where is everyone else?' Harper asked.

'They went to buy you a cake and some Coke.'

My sister always had so many friends. Friends who loved her.

'Wah!' Wài Pó entered, carrying a flask and a plate of egg tarts. 'You've transformed this room. How beautiful.'

When I'd left the house, Wài Pó was still asleep in her room. There was no way she could have whipped up a dozen egg tarts in the time I had been gone. As Louis grabbed the plate from her and helped himself to one, I looked at the foil casing and saw the sticker of a famous Hong Kong baker on the side. Wài Pó had always refused to buy egg tarts from a store. They were *her* specialty, so much so that she had told me once that she'd rather be hit by a bus than eat tarts from a commercial baker.

'God only knows what junk they put into them to make them look more yellow and creamy, to make them tastier. No, mine are the real deal.'

'It's only egg tarts,' I told myself. There was no need to get upset.

But I was.

Wài Pó walked over and patted my arm. 'Look at your sister.' She gestured to Harper. 'She's happy.'

My sister was happy, very happy, and she deserved to stay that way.

The sounds of chatter trickled in from the hall, and a group of people in colourful clothes entered the room. Harper's friends had arrived.

'I'm so happy you all made it here to be with me on my special day,' she announced, before breaking into a coughing fit.

Out of the corner of my eye, I saw Dad enter with Louis's parents, Deborah and Michael. They seemed very cheerful, which only accentuated Dad's moroseness.

'The parents are here.' Harper waved. 'Everyone, please meet Louis's very friendly, happy-like-the-sun mum and dad, Deborah and Michael, and my very handsome, charming dad.' The group rushed to them as if they were movie stars.

Dad cleared his throat. 'Irene's sorry she can't make it today.' His eyes darted about the room. 'Got held up.'

'Yesssss!' In an uncanny fit of energy, Harper thrust her arm into the air.

I wanted to do the same, but then I saw Dad's face harden, his head bow.

'I would like you all to please make a circle around Harper's bed.' Louis signalled to Adam to hit the music. *The Lion King* began to play.

'Crap, Adam, that's the wrong song!' Louis shouted.

Adam flicked through the tracks until he found Whitney Houston's 'I Believe in You and Me'.

'Thank you all for coming.' Louis adjusted the red rose in his left lapel. 'I want to share with you all a very special moment in time.' He took a ring case out of his jacket and dropped to one knee.

My cheeks were aching. I hadn't smiled this much in so long.

'I can't see you,' Harper called from her bed.

Louis got up, opened the case, and took out a yellow sapphire ring.

Wài Pó moved closer to me and whispered, 'Where did he get that from? That is certainly not cheap.'

'Harper Míng Huà Eve, I love you from the bottom of my heart. Before I met you, I had a feeling like I did not belong, but now, with you, I feel like I do. You make me sparkle.' Louis's chin quivered. 'You are the most beautiful girl in the whole world, and now I want to ask you to be my Juliet.'

My eyes began to sting. I looked away. Why was I getting so emotional? Normally I hated sentimental talk. Not that I wanted to get married, but if Olly were to propose to me, or I to him, it certainly wouldn't be done like this. And yet, my body was expressing something different. My body was, in this moment, with Harper and Louis, living this with them.

'Yes, of course I will be your Juliet!' Harper's glasses slipped down the bridge of her nose. With one hand, she pushed them back up, while she held the other hand out for Louis. He gently uncurled her IV drip and placed the ring on her finger. They shared a passionate kiss. Everyone clapped and cheered.

For the first time, I wondered what it would feel like to have a ring on my finger. I suddenly had an overwhelming urge to call Olly and tell him everything. It was ridiculous that I was keeping my plans secret from him. I had to call him as soon as I got home. I let myself imagine him here with me, his arms wrapped around me.

'Congratulations. I'm so happy for you both.' Dad embraced Harper. He was smiling proudly.

Would I ever be able to make him this proud?

Harper raised her hand. 'Look, my ring shines in the light.' She held it to the lamp at her bedside. Yellow fragments bounced against the shadowy parts of the walls. 'Maybe there are fairies in the room.'

I moved over to stroke her forehead. Her skin was moist with sweat and her breathing seemed laboured. Maybe I should summon a nurse to check that everything was okay? I wondered if Anita was working today.

Anita.

If I could talk to Anita myself, she would reassure me that I was doing the right thing for Harper.

Swallowing the lump in my throat, I kissed Harper and said I needed to get more Cokes but I would be back soon.

Slipping from the room, I walked down the corridor to the nurses' station and asked the woman there if she knew where Anita was.

'She's around here somewhere,' the woman said vaguely. 'I saw her a few minutes ago.'

'Thanks. I'll try to catch her later.'

Reluctant to interrupt Anita on her rounds, I kept walking down the corridor until I reached the hospital chapel. I pushed the door open and stepped inside.

The scent of burning wicks hung lightly in the air. I took a seat in a pew. Although I wasn't religious, my eyes were drawn to a statue of Mary holding baby Jesus at the front of the room. Mary gazed lovingly at the baby in her arms. He rested his chubby little hand on her chest. And suddenly, it was as if I could feel her heartbeat.

'Marlowe.' A hand touched me lightly on the shoulder. It was Anita. She slid into the pew. 'You were looking for me?'

We sat for a while in silence as I tried to find my words. Although I had decided this was the course of action I needed to take to save Harper's life, as much as I tried to avoid it, I kept thinking of the prisoner kneeling.

'How can I do this and still sleep at night? How can I give my sister a heart in this way?'

'Try not to feel so bad,' she said. 'These people have a chance to undo their wrongs by saving another life.' She put her hand on

209

my shoulder and I felt a deep warmth stir in my chest. I slowed my breath and silently counted from one to ten again.

'Harper can either live or die. You have a chance to save her now. Just remember that.'

I looked back at the statue. My thoughts were scrambled for a minute or two until I slowly realised it wasn't Anita I had been looking for.

I watched as a candle that had burned down to its wick slowly extinguished. Yellow flame turned to grey and smoke wafted through the air. I let the curling shapes take me back.

⊷

The North Point Funeral Parlour had been filled with elaborate wreaths of white flowers. It was as if Mum had just won a prize.

An altar had been arranged at the far end of the room. A large photo of Mum was displayed on a stand – she looked youthful and was smiling. Below this were small vases of flowers and burning incense. Guests lined up, bowing three times at her altar and then at my father who stood with Aunt Lǐ Nà and Uncle Bǐng Wén, all bowing back. Wài Pó could not attend. She was at home, locked in her room. Before we left the house, I asked Dad why and he said she was sick. But when we got to the funeral parlour and I asked one of her friends, she explained that: 'It is very sad to have white hair seeing black hair off. Your Wài Pó cannot be expected to attend such an unnatural and painful event.'

'I'm sure Mum wants her here,' I said, and left Wài Pó's friend at the entrance to collect white money packets from incoming guests.

I knew where Mum was. She was in a wooden coffin in a small room at the back of the hall. Aunt Lǐ Nà had talked to Harper, Bì Yù and I before the event, explaining every custom and detail that was to come. Only close relatives and family could visit her there. The thought made me nervous, so I followed a helpful Bì Yù around the funeral parlour, holding her hand whenever I could. Occasionally, I would glance over my shoulder at the room behind the altar, toying with the idea of seeing Mum.

A loud crash made me turn. Harper had tried to remove a white iris from a standing wreath. As adults rushed to clean up the mess, I pulled Harper aside and helped her fix the flower in her hair.

'Heaaavennn,' she whispered.

'She's not dead,' I said.

Harper shook her head and pointed at the ceiling. 'Heaaavennn.' She was repeating what Dad had told her: *Mummy's in heaven now.*

'No, she's not in heaven. Mum wouldn't leave us.' My pulse was racing.

She looked at me blankly.

'Don't you understand, Harper?' I was breathing fast, really fast. 'Mum wouldn't leave us.' The room began to spin. What was happening to me? It felt as if I couldn't get enough air. 'Get Bì Yù,' I shouted. 'I think I'm dying! I can't breathe.' But Harper just cocked her head to one side, looking at me with serious eyes. I pointed. 'GO!'

Harper ran, while I gasped for air.

Soon I realised I was running too, running fast towards the coffin.

'Mā ma!' I shrieked. I clutched the edge of her coffin, stood on my tiptoes and peered in. Mum was dressed in her best clothing – a sparkling navy garment she often liked to wear when on stage. Her face was still, serene, her eyes closed.

'Mā ma! Wake up.' I reached out to touch her cheek. It was stiff and cold. I pulled my hand away.

No.

I froze.

'Marlowe!'

Someone was calling my name, but I couldn't take my eyes off my mother. How strange and waxy she looked, sleeping in her open casket. All signs of her illness were covered. The angry red marks on her face were barely visible under a thick layer of make-up.

I had always been told I was a petite nine-year-old, but my body felt heavy then, as heavy as a mountain of books that I could not read.

'Come now,' a voice whispered. A hand took mine and led me to a chair. 'You're having a panic attack. I want you to take deep breaths.' I felt the hands of a woman brush the hair from my damp forehead. 'Follow me.' She breathed in and out again, slowly. 'Gooooood,' she said.

My shoulders dropped.

'Count to ten with me now. One, two...'

Three, four, five...

My breathing deepened.

'That's good, can you feel yourself calming down now?'

I could. *Six, seven, eight.*

'You're doing really well.'

Nine, ten, eleven...

'Good, very good.'

I focused on a flake of paint peeling from the ceiling. As I breathed slowly, I could feel the emotion leave my body and it was as if my insides had turned cold.

'I'm all right now,' I said.

And I walked towards my father and took my place by his side. Together we greeted the arriving mourners.

—◆—

'Marlowe, are you okay?' Anita asked.

I nodded.

'I'm glad I found you. There's something else I meant to give you.' She took a slip of paper from her pocket on which was written a phone number. 'If you fly Cathay Pacific, here is a number you call to book an in-flight medic. Harper will need one in order to travel given her condition.' Anita looked at her watch. 'I'd better get back.' She stood and I rose too. 'Harper's due to be discharged in the morning.' She gave me a brief hug. 'Good luck.'

As she left the room, I sat again. The chapel was quiet. I decided to stay for a little while longer, staring at the statue of mother and child.

Harper

An EKG machine is something the doctors put on my chest in the hospital. The EKG has wire hands that record the energy in my heart with swooping and jumping lines on paper.

The doctor told me my heart is like an engine, but sometimes even the best engines have problems. In my brain, I see my heart. This time I decorate it with feathers, hanging shells and flowers that grow out of its top. Tubes bigger than the ones connected to my IV drip move blood in and out of its pumping system. Its skin is made of red velvet and in its belly are beating drums: da dum da dum da dum da.

Plum-red blood rushes into my engine like the waves of the ocean – swish swoosh, swish swoosh – and out again – swoosh swish, swoosh swish.

I put my hand on my chest. I think that the doctor does not know everything about my heart.

I am going to be married soon and an EKG machine cannot hear and feel what I can. My hum is like the low moon at night, when it kisses the ocean. This is when my sound turns into a song.

Marlowe

As soon as I arrived back home from hospital, I shut the door to my bedroom and dialled Olly's number. The phone only rang once before he answered.

'Marls?'

As soon as I heard his voice, longing hit me like a blow to the spine.

'Hi.'

'Oh, thank God. I've been trying –'

'I know. I'm really sorry.'

He had so many questions, but I asked him if I could tell him something first.

'Of course you can.' His voice was soothing.

'I'm taking Harper to China – she can get her transplants there.' I told him about Anita, Mr Zhāng and how I would be funding the whole thing using the inheritance from my mother.

The silence on the other end of the phone was dense and full.

'Olly?' I felt light-headed.

'Sorry, I need a moment.' His voice sounded cold. I thought I could hear traces of disappointment. A moment quickly came and went.

'Olly, what's going on?'

'I'm just a little shocked. I mean, my girlfriend has just told me she's about to take her dying sister to China where she will purchase a heart and lungs for her on the black market.'

His words stung.

'I was hoping you might be more understanding.'

'Understanding? What you're talking about is unethical... Is it even safe for Harper?'

'I can take care of things myself.'

'Don't be like that.' Another long breath. 'Look, let's talk about this rationally.'

He didn't understand. No one did. 'I –' My voice broke. 'She's my sister.'

'I know, Marls.' His voice softened. 'But what you're doing is illegal, and who knows if you can really trust this Zhāng guy?'

'Bì Yù will be there, and she –'

'Does Bì Yù even know exactly what's going on? How much have you told her?'

He knew me too well.

'I've got to go,' I said.

Stop, a little voice whispered. *Take a breath.* But I couldn't.

'What? You're going to hang up, just like that?'

'I'll talk to you later.' As I ended the call, I felt an ache in my chest. I curled into a ball and buried my face in the maroon jumper.

Harper

Home.

My heart is like a tall church with wide-open arches and walls that whisper happiness.

Marlowe

A suitcase lay open on my bed, half packed with my clothes and waiting to be filled with Harper's. Two tickets to Shanghai sat on the desk in front of me. I was staring at the phone in my hand. After our phone call the day before, Olly had rung me several times, but I hadn't answered. In the end he had sent me an email, which I'd read on Dad's computer.

> Marls,
>
> I'd really like to speak to you. I've given our conversation some thought. I'm sorry I got upset. I've realised I can't look at your actions in a logical way. This isn't a logical situation. I didn't consider your feelings and the reasons why you've chosen to follow this path. Your relationship with your sister is a part of you I didn't get to know well enough while you were in London. To be honest, I'm still worried about this trip you're taking to China. I've done some research. It's such an unregulated industry. I worry things could go badly for Harper.
>
> Please let me come with you.
>
> Please, please call me.

I walked the length of my room, back and forth, trying to decide what to do. I didn't want him to talk me out of the decision I'd made – but I needed to hear his voice, to know that he still loved me and even if I had trouble completely feeling it, I still wanted to hear that I wasn't alone. Finally, I dialled Olly's number. He answered straight away, as if he'd been waiting for my call again.

'Are you okay?' he asked. 'I'm so worried about you. Please let me help.'

The kindness in his voice bled out from the phone and filled the air around me. I allowed myself to entertain the idea of him coming, just for a moment. How could I tell him that, while I was grateful for his offer, I needed to do this on my own?

'I'm sorry… I don't think that would be a good idea.'

Pathetic. Harper was so much better with words than me.

I heard him exhale, soft and slow, but to my relief he didn't argue. I promised him I would call once I had arrived in China and hung up.

Next I turned my attention to the suitcase. It was 2 pm, and the flight was scheduled to depart that night at 7.15, but I couldn't finish packing until Dad and Wài Pó left the house. Dad had told me they had an appointment that afternoon and I was impatient for them to go.

The minutes seemed like hours until at last Wài Pó called out from downstairs, 'James, I'm calling the taxi – do hurry.'

I heard a creak in the corridor outside my room and then there was a knock at my door.

'Marlowe?' It was Dad.

The suitcase.

'Darling, are you in there?'

I quickly slid the tickets into my desk drawer and shoved the case under the bed then opened the door.

'Hi, Dad.'

'Are you all right?'

'Fine.' I walked over to sit on the bed, nudging the suitcase further back with my heel.

He came to sit beside me. 'You know,' he said softly, 'just because your sister's sick...' He clasped his hands together. 'Well, it doesn't mean...' He unclasped them again. 'What I'm trying to say is that it doesn't mean you can't have a life of your own.'

'Thanks, Dad.'

'She seems as stable as she can be for the moment. Why don't you call some of your old school friends and arrange to catch up?'

Was he serious? Did he really expect me to go out and have fun when my sister was dying in the room opposite mine?

'Sure,' I said, barely able to find my voice. I stood up and moved towards the door, hoping that he would take the cue to leave, but he didn't.

Wài Pó called from the foyer. 'Five minutes, James!'

'You don't want to be late, Dad,' I said.

'Darling.' He tugged at his shirt collar, as if it were too tight. 'There's something I need to talk to you about.'

I tried to hide my frustration. He never wanted to talk. Why now?

'Wài Pó hasn't told you about our appointment today, has she?'

I shook my head and glanced meaningfully at my watch.

'We're going to meet a real estate agent.' He looked down at his feet. 'There's no easy way to say this, but we are thinking of selling the house.'

I felt as if the wind had been shocked from my lungs.

'We should have told you earlier, but I was worried that –'

'But – but you can't!' I said. Mum was all over this house, it was all I felt I had left of her. 'How does Wài Pó feel about this? I can't believe she would have agreed to it.'

'It was your grandmother's idea actually. We don't need such a big house anymore and, to be frank, we need the money. Harper's illness has been a great financial drain.'

Wài Pó's idea? Really? I clenched my jaw. 'When?'

'As soon as we receive an acceptable offer.'

'What about Harper? Is there even going to be a room for her in the new place?' My head was spinning. *What about Mum?* I wanted to know.

Dad seemed to shrink under my gaze. 'Of course there'll be a room for her.' He lowered his head. 'How can you even ask –'

'James!' Wài Pó called from downstairs. 'The taxi is here!'

He stood. From his breast pocket, he removed an envelope.

'I never was very good at talking.' He handed me the letter. 'I hope this helps to explain things.' He nodded once, then left the room.

Another damn letter. Harper and Dad were always writing letters. I took it and put it straight into my handbag. I had no intention of reading it. There was nothing he could say that would make this right.

I touched the locket at my throat. *Mā ma*. It felt as if I were losing her all over again.

I took a deep breath, exhaling my emotion before pasting a smile on my face and striding across the hall into Harper's room.

Tina Turner was playing. Louis was singing along, using a hairbrush as a microphone.

'Looouiiiisssss!' Harper teased him for being out of tune, yet he continued to sing, dancing around the room as if he were on stage. As she laughed, it occurred to me that although I had often seen my sister happy, I had never seen her *this* happy before.

How could I take her away from him?

Catching sight of me, Louis stopped singing to call, 'Hi, Marlowe! Do you like my singing?'

'It's beautiful,' I said. 'But I need to talk to you guys about something.'

As I drew close to Harper, I noticed her lips had turned blue and she was struggling for air. I quickly turned on her portable oxygen machine. She had lost so much weight, the clear mask looked like it might swallow her chin and nose.

'Why are you putting that on her face again?' Louis asked. He took Harper's hand in his. 'She's not in hospital anymore.'

'Louis, please,' I snapped. 'When she gets breathless and her lips turn blue like this, you have to tell me, okay?'

'I'm sorry,' he whispered. 'I didn't see that.'

I sat with Harper until her breathing returned to normal and her lips regained some colour. She grew drowsy, and as she drifted off to sleep I removed her spectacles and put them on her bedside table.

'I can take care of her.' Louis stood beside me, eyes red-rimmed. 'I can take care of her when she is sick.'

I couldn't reply. Instead, I watched my sister's chest rise and fall.

Harper

In my sleep, I find Mum. She is in our garden, singing my Chinese name.

'Míng Huà, Míng Huà, Míng Huà.'

She is holding out her hands for me to take, but I don't want to touch her.

I tell her I need to be alone. For the first time, I do not want to be with my mum.

I tell her I am happiest in my room, in my home, with all my things, with Marlowe and Dad, Wài Pó and my love, Louis.

But then Mum tells me to look around. In this strange place we are in, Marlowe, Dad, Wài Pó and Louis are nowhere to be seen.

Marlowe

Our suitcase was ready and waiting at the door, but there was one more thing I needed to do. When Dad and Wài Pó came home and we weren't there, I was sure it wouldn't take them long to figure out where we'd gone. On a scrap of paper I scrawled the details of a train journey to Beijing and stuffed it into my desk drawer. Then I called a cab and went to wake Harper.

She was on her side, her eyes twitching under their lids and her palms pressed together as if in prayer. Part of me wished I could simply leave her in peace, but then she rolled over, coughed and her wheezing intensified.

'Harper, time to wake up.'

Her eyes opened, but she looked past me. A thin line of blood seeped out from the split skin in the crease of her lip. She closed her eyes again.

'It hurts, Mum.'

'It's me, Harper – Marlowe.'

'My chest hurts.'

I patted her cheek. She opened her eyes again, and this time looked directly at me. It took her a while to focus. As she sat up in bed, she coughed again.

'I had a very terrible dream. Where's Louis?'

I dabbed her lips with a tissue.

'He had to go home, but he gave you a kiss goodbye while you were asleep.' I took her hand. 'Harper, you know how you're very sick?'

She looked at me blankly – the look she gives when she doesn't want to acknowledge something or doesn't like where a line of questioning might lead.

'I know a doctor in Shanghai who can make you better, but we will need to go there.'

'Shanghai?' She shook her head weakly. 'I don't want to go there right now. Anyway, the doctors here can make me better like they did when I was in hospital.'

'But they didn't really fix you. Your heart's still sick.'

'I'm happy here. I don't want to go anywhere.' She folded her arms across her chest.

I should have thought this through more carefully, I should have prepared what I would say…

'But, Harper…'

'No.'

She was always so damn stubborn.

'I already told you, Marlowe: the doctors will help me here and you and Dad and Wài Pó and Louis too.'

I sighed and looked at my watch. Time was running out. I looked around my sister's room, trying to think of a way to convince her. There was a collection of porcelain dolls on a shelf, arranged in pairs 'so they can whisper to each other at night'; shrivelling plants and odd things that she kept ceremonially by the window – I never understood what she was trying to do with them; a bookcase full of books. On the walls were colourful paintings she'd made at the vocational centre and photos of everyone she loved: our parents, Wài Pó, Louis, me, her friends, our cousin Bì Yù… And then I knew what to do.

'Oh no,' I said. 'I've messed up. I've already booked us the tickets to Shanghai and told cousin Bì Yù we were coming…'

'Bì Yù?' Harper lifted her head. 'I haven't seen her in so long.'

'And now she's expecting us. I don't want to disappoint her. How about we just go and see her and I'll bring you back in a few days? I don't want to waste the money I spent on the ticket either.'

I felt terrible about manipulating her, but it was for a good cause, I reminded myself.

'And you know that story you wrote about the plum tree in China? Well, maybe we could go and visit your special plum tree in Zhōngshān Park together, as inspiration for your writing.'

Harper flung back the covers. 'Every writer needs inspiration. And I would love to see Bì Yù.' She sat up. 'We would only go for a few days, right?'

'That's right.'

'And no hospitals, okay?'

I nodded.

'Okay, let's go to Shanghai. But we have to bring my writing book. I am sure I will have a lot of stories to write down on this trip.' She reached into her bedside table and retrieved her creative writing book. 'Oh, but I'll have to tell Louis that I'm going.'

'I already told Louis,' I said hastily. 'He's excited for you.' The lying made me nauseated. 'But if we don't leave now, we're going to be late.'

I helped her out of bed and got her dressed.

When I went to turn off her lamp as were leaving the room, she grabbed hold of my hand.

'Leave it on, Marlowe.' She pointed to her porcelain dolls. 'So they don't miss me when I'm gone.'

Part Two

Harper

Marlowe and I are sitting in a very nice aeroplane called Cathay Pacific. I have a window seat and I can see that this plane is flying high in the sky. Its wings are not made of feathers but the same kind of shiny hard stuff as a car or a fridge or a microwave.

In between us is a kind lady named Susan Tong. She told me she is called a 'flight nurse'. This means she is here to help my sore chest on the flight. I noticed she is very good at helping me with my oxygen mask. She has round glasses and her eyes look like little planets from outer space. She is quick and clever at reading the signs of my body and puts an extra blanket on my lap to keep me warm.

There are four other people travelling with us who are a bit sick like me, and a man with small eyes and a toothpick in his mouth, who Marlowe knows. He gives me a strange feeling, like ice running down the back of my neck. I don't talk to him, but I would like to ask the other people what their names are.

Suddenly, we all wobble in our seats and the plane shakes. I feel a shiver in my belly and chest.

'Are you all right, Harper?' Susan asks.

'Harper?' Marlowe looks at me. The blacks of her eyes are small and serious. This means that she is feeling panic. 'It's only turbulence, there's no need to worry,' she says, holding the sides of her seat tightly.

'I am fine,' I say. 'You should relax.' But I know that she can't relax, because I see her moving a lot in her seat. I think it would be nice if Susan took care of her too. So I ask her to please give Marlowe my blanket – not for warmth, but for comfort and love. Susan smiles and unwraps a new blanket for my sister, who takes it and puts it around her shoulders.

The plane calms down again and becomes still. I look at the night clouds under the moon outside my window. They are in the shape of a woman with round hips and long hair. I feel an itch in my fingertips. I get out my autobiographical storybook and let the ink from my pen fall onto the page.

> There was a beutiful lady who onse upon a time had a sore chest and was sick. She didn't know it yet but she had ~~majic powers~~.

I stop and put my pen down for a minute. The word 'magic' is not quite right. I think in my brain about other words I can use. I see a tiger in the snow, like in the *National Geographic* programs that Marlowe watches. It jumps into the air and catches a bird from the sky. The tiger runs fast. In my mind, I can see its strong muscles move under its fur.

> There was a beutiful lady who onse upon a time had a sore chest and was sick. She didn't know it yet but she had ~~majic powers~~ corage.

Yes! That's it! Now I can feel the energy of my blood all over my body, warm and smooth, filling all my corners with the heat and colour. I have an electric idea. I look back through all the pages of my autobiographical storybook and I write the beginning of the beautiful woman's journey.

> Even though the yung woman was sick in her chest, she found her corage and desided to go on a jorney. Her body filled up with power like a leeping white tiger.

My hand hurts. My head hurts. I put down my pen, close my book and stop my Shakespeare writing for now.

Marlowe

Lions, six of them, were sitting around me on hot concrete. In the distance, buildings touched the sky – unfamiliar buildings, not Hong Kong buildings. I placed my hand on the back of the closest male; his hair was coarse beneath my skin. My body was tight, still. Both afraid and mesmerised, I did not move. Goosebumps rose like a rash up the sides of my arms. Suddenly, I felt cold.

The lion stood, positioned himself, then urinated on the side of my body. The warmth was soothing. I reached for him, unafraid now. His animal breath was close and hot as I leaned in to touch his mane. The lion placed his paw on my chest, slowly pushing the air from my lungs. He lowered his head to my navel. A low and steady growl rumbled at the base of his throat and then his teeth sank into my hip. Pain pierced my belly and shot through to the base of my thighs.

—•—

I opened my eyes. Another cramp gripped me and I clutched my abdomen.

'Are you okay?' Susan placed her hand on my shoulder.

'Fine.' I stood. My seat was marked with blood. Immediately my cheeks felt hot.

'Oh dear.' Harper pointed. 'You've got your period.'

'Shh,' I hissed before frantically rubbing the spot on my seat until my hands burned, but the thing about blood is it always stains.

Harper removed the oxygen tube from under her nose and told me it might make me feel better if I tried it. Immediately, I reached over to fix it back on, but Susan got there first, swiftly placing the tube back in place.

I wrapped the arms of my jumper around my waist. 'I won't be long. Will you be all right, Harper?'

'Yes, I will be fine. Susan is a kind lady who knows how to help me.'

As she spoke, her chest rose and fell heavily, carrying air through her lungs as if it were filled with stones.

Another cramp rippled through my belly. *You have too much yīn in your belly*, Wài Pó whispered, *not enough yáng. This is no good for childbirth*. Just as well, I thought, as I shoved two Panadol in my mouth.

As I walked down the aisle, I passed Mr Zhāng. He was drinking a whisky and reading the in-flight magazine. His eyes were like black orbs. When I looked at them, I felt like I was walking through empty tunnels that led nowhere. He seemed so casual, so carefree, sitting there. I wondered what he had done with our deposit, along with the money he'd collected from the three other sick 'clients' who were seated in the rows behind him. There were two men who looked to be in their late fifties and one woman. Their presence made me feel both comforted and on edge.

In a small bathroom cubicle that reeked of lemon air freshener, I cleaned myself. The lighting was dim, and the walls vibrated with the drone of the engine. I placed the toilet lid down, disinfected it with a soapy tissue and sat. Arms wrapped tightly around my waist,

I found myself rocking back and forth. Only in this strange kind of silence did I realise how thin I had become, how loose my shirt was, how my jeans slid down my hips. I left the bathroom and headed straight for the galley.

I asked for a snack, and the flight attendant gave me a packet of Pop-Pan crackers which I ate quickly, leaving nothing but a tiny morsel of seaweed and a few crumbs in the foil wrapper.

'Nǐ hěn è!'

I turned. An old lady was telling me I was very hungry in Chinese. She then asked if I was from Shanghai.

I shook my head and smiled sheepishly at the lady, then hurried back down the aisle to my seat.

For years I had avoided speaking in my mother's mother tongue; the memories it evoked were too raw. But I knew that Bì Yù couldn't be with us every minute of the day, and although Harper could speak, I didn't want her getting too involved, so for Harper's sake I would have to try. The shiny red corner of a Chinese–English dictionary stuck out of my handbag, a reluctant purchase from the bookstore in the departures lounge. I drew it out and opened the cover. I had the sensation that I had opened a door as Mum's voice came spilling out in Chinese. I could hear her singing folk songs, reading me the stories that were read to her as a child. I could hear her whispering that she loved me.

The pilot announced our descent to Shanghai Pudong airport.

'Zhōng Guó,' I mouthed. *China.* I turned to check Harper, but Susan was already tending to her.

A young woman who sat in the row next to mine, peeled an orange with her thumb, its zest flavoured the stale air. Next to her was a small boy who could have easily been her son.

I flipped through the pages. '*Chéng zi.*' Orange.

I recalled how Mum used to peel oranges for me as a child.

With a heavy thud, the plane touched down. The tyres screeched along the tarmac.

'*Wǒ mén huí jiā le,*' the young woman said to the boy. 'We've come home.'

'*Jiā,*' I repeated.

'*Wǒ mén huí jiā le.*' The little boy grabbed another segment of orange from his mother.

'*Jiā,*' I said again, a little louder this time.

Harper turned towards me. Breathlessly she said: 'It's nice to hear you speak.' She took my hand in hers.

Suddenly, the woman looked at me and smiled. 'Where are you from?' she asked.

I froze. 'England.'

The woman tilted her head to one side. 'Eh?'

I remembered what my mother had taught me. 'Yīng Guó.' It was only half a lie.

❯❮

We followed Mr Zhāng through the arrivals hall. There were security guards in every corner, watching. Harper's wheelchair squeaked incessantly, drawing unwanted attention. I tried to ignore the narrowed eyes staring at her. Was it fear I could read on their faces? Or was it pity? Even though they were gawking at her and not at me, I felt exposed. If this was what I was feeling, I couldn't imagine what must be going through her mind. Did she notice? I put my hand on her shoulder and gave it a quick squeeze, something Dad would do.

The three other clients of Mr Zhāng were able to walk and they followed behind us, talking jovially as if part of a holiday tour group.

Chinese words rolled around their tongues like hot food, always moving never lingering. I wished desperately they would just be quiet.

'I don't want to be in this thing.' Harper folded her arms squarely across her chest. 'Wheelchairs are for old, old, old people.'

A skinny man walked up close to her, too close, staring without blinking. The crowd pushed him on, but his head remained turned in her direction.

'He likes my outfit,' Harper announced.

I gripped the handles, pushing faster. I no longer felt exposed and vulnerable; now I was downright irritated. 'Nearly there,' I said.

Outside the arrivals hall, the air was thick with cigarette smoke. Cold wind grazed the side of my face. I adjusted the scarf around Harper's neck, then tightened my own.

'It's very important to stay warm, Harper. It's colder here than in Hong Kong.'

At the pick-up zone, a cacophony of car horns was blasting. Harper placed her hands over her ears. I too felt assaulted by the noise.

'*Biǎo mei!*' Sister cousins!

Bì Yù was standing next to her little red Honda, waving.

I had told her that we would make our own way to her apartment. I'd wanted to avoid introducing her to Mr Zhāng until it was absolutely necessary.

Harper called to her and waved excitedly. I looked at Mr Zhāng and then back at Bì Yù. Frowning, he said something that I didn't understand in rough Chinese.

Bì Yù ran towards us, smiling. Her apple cheeks were framed by shoulder-length black hair, with a streak of electric blue. As her gaze moved from me to Harper, her face tightened and dropped. She kneeled in front of Harper, so that they were at eye level, and put a palm on my sister's cheek.

'I've missed you,' Harper said. She patted the blue streak in Bì Yù's hair and laughed.

Bì Yù's smile was strained now. She seemed at a loss for words.

'I like your necklace.' Harper, who was never at a loss, filled the silence, touching Bì Yù's turquoise beads.

A white van pulled up beside Mr Zhāng. The other clients got in. Mr Zhāng turned to us and spoke rapidly. He was making shooing movements towards Bì Yù. 'That's not very nice,' Harper muttered.

Bì Yù looked at him and then at me. 'Marlowe, who is this man? He says I can't come with you. Where are you going?'

'We're going back to your house Bì Yù and I don't think that we should invite him.' Harper pointed at Mr Zhāng.

I pulled Bì Yù to one side and whispered: 'His name is Mr Zhāng. He's arranging Harper's transplant.'

Her eyes widened. *'Him?'*

'Yes. Why?'

'I was expecting a doctor.' I could see her mind ticking as she glanced at Mr Zhāng.

'He's taking us to see one.'

'Now? It is so late.' She spoke to him in rapid Chinese.

He shook his head violently and said something back.

Bì Yù's forehead creased.

I took out my wallet, and discreetly pulled out a hundred-dollar bill.

'Please tell him you'll be very discreet if he lets you accompany us.'

She did as I asked.

Mr Zhāng spat his toothpick out and took the money.

'He says I am to follow him in my car.' She looked at me, her face troubled. 'We're going to the Shanghai Middle Hospital and are to meet him in the lobby.'

We were quiet on the drive to the hospital. My cousin gripped the steering wheel tightly and glanced frequently at the rear-view mirror. I followed her gaze to Harper, who sat in the back seat listening to music on the radio.

Outside my window, cars zipped past at high speed.

'Bì Yù, let me explain,' I said.

'Later,' she replied, looking once more at Harper. 'Let's talk later.'

I turned to look out the window. Shanghai grew more and more unfamiliar to me with each visit. There were more buildings than I remembered, and they were taller and closer together. Billboards along the side of the road advertised luxury cars, cigarettes and real estate.

I turned back to face Bì Yù. 'You know I would never do anything to hurt Harper,' I whispered. 'I'm doing this to save her life.'

When the car stopped at a red light, she looked over at me and shook her head. The expression on her face said, *We are not children anymore*.

Bì Yù double-parked in the street outside the hospital. It had begun to hail, pebbles of ice pounding the roof and smacking against the windows. Harper had her hands over her ears.

'You guys get out here,' my cousin said. 'I'll go find a park and meet you inside.'

Harper peered out the window. 'This looks like a strange place to live,' she said.

'I don't live here,' Bì Yù said. 'This is the hospital.'

I turned to look at my sister.

She looked back at me, wounded. 'You promised, Marlowe. You promised no more hospitals.'

I couldn't bear to see the pain and confusion on her face. 'Let's go,' I said, reaching for the door.

'I don't want to go in there.' Harper's arms were crossed. 'You said that we were here to visit Bì Yù. You promised no hospitals. You lied. Lying is hurtful and mean and horrid. Sisters don't lie to each other.'

Shame made my cheeks burn. I got out of the car and walked around to the other side to open Harper's door. The hail had stopped as quickly as it had started, but the air felt damp and cold. I couldn't let it sink into Harper's weak lungs.

'Well,' I said, trying not to let my frustration show, 'let's just get out of the car now and then we can discuss what to do next. We can't stay here any longer. We're causing a traffic jam.'

A car behind us sounded its horn but Harper just sat there, refusing to move.

Come on, Harper. Don't do this now.

'Go on, Harper,' Bì Yù said. 'I'll meet you in there soon.' How did she always manage to sound so calm?

A second car began to honk, but Harper still wouldn't budge.

'*Kǎo hóng shǔ!*'

I turned. At the entrance of the hospital was a man selling *xiāo yè* – late-night snacks. I saw Harper's childhood favourites: steaming hot yams. Wài Pó would have called this a gift from heaven.

I ran over to the stall. The smoky air was thick and sweet above the man's stove. I quickly purchased the yams and raced back to the car. Luckily, a place by the kerb had freed up further along the road, and Bì Yù had quickly claimed it.

Harper stuck her nose into the warm bag and inhaled.

'Lying is bad,' she said softly. 'I am hurt in my heart that you did that.'

'I'm really sorry, Harper.'

Bì Yù said quietly, 'This is a drop-off area. We can't stay here for too long.'

I nodded. 'Come on, Harper,' I said. 'Let's go.'

'I think I will try one yam first.' Harper reached into the bag. 'Ouch, hot. We have to wait for it to cool.'

Damn it, Harper. I snatched a steaming yam from the bag and blew on it furiously, trying to ignore the heat that seared through my fingertips. As I handed it to her, a man in a uniform tapped on Bì Yù's window. He pointed to his watch and gestured to say that she had to move on.

Harper inspected the yam. 'What's this bit?' She pointed to a small fleck of black in the orange flesh.

I closed my eyes and swallowed hard, resisting the urge to shout.

'That's just the way it is; it's part of the yam.' I reached over and removed the fleck.

Harper chewed slowly. 'Yum. This is very nice.' She nodded. 'I'm still a bit mad at you about the hospital, Marlowe, but I have decided to let it go.' She sat up and held out her hand for me to take. 'Let's go now.'

❧

The Shanghai Middle Hospital reminded me of a large shopping mall. Although the shops had closed for the night, the lobby was dotted with makeshift stalls selling items such as wheelchairs and walking sticks.

Mr Zhāng was nowhere to be seen.

After Bì Yù parked the car, she joined us inside. We walked fast. I pushed Harper in her chair. We passed what looked like a closed pharmacy. Its windows were covered with bars.

I looked at Bì Yù for help. She bit her lip.

'It's a big hospital; there are four wings. Perhaps we're in the wrong one?'

I thought about the deposit I had paid Mr Zhāng. What if he had run off with it? Was it possible this whole thing was a sham? Adrenaline surged through my body, making the tips of my fingers and toes prickle.

With Bì Yù leading the way, we headed down a wide corridor, hoping to find another lobby.

'Where are we going?' Harper asked.

'Me and Bì Yù just want to see a doctor to ask him if he can make you feel better.'

Harper didn't respond. Her silence made me uneasy. I didn't like the person I was becoming.

Eventually, she turned to look at me. I stopped pushing her wheelchair and kneeled down.

'What is it?' I asked.

She pushed her glasses up the bridge of her nose then took my hand.

'I tell you what.' She patted my hand gently, like she knew exactly what was going on. 'I think I will be all right with seeing the doctor here for a little while, because I think I can look at this with my writer's eyes and get some inspiration for my story.'

I exhaled. Harper was looking at me sympathetically, as if *she* felt sorry for *me*.

'But, Marlowe, I don't want to talk about the things we talked about in Hong Kong? No transplants. I want to keep my heart that is in love with Louis, okay?'

'Okay.' I looked away.

We began moving again, Bì Yù striding ahead.

'You sure we're going the right way?' I called.

She turned and shook her head, then approached a man in a white lab coat. He pointed to a corridor that led off to the right. We raced through it and soon enough, we were in another lobby, with cherry wood floors and marble walls.

'There.' Bì Yù pointed to Mr Zhāng, who was standing with a nurse and the three other patients.

I felt limp with relief.

'Him?' Harper shook her head. 'Why do we need to see him again?'

'He's helping us get you in to see the doctor, Harper.'

When Mr Zhāng saw us, he immediately addressed Bì Yù in a torrent of Chinese. Harper looked at Mr Zhāng and shook her head. 'So rude,' she said under her breath.

'What's he saying?'

Bì Yù frowned. 'He says we can't accompany Harper to see the doctor.'

'What? No way!' I tightened my grip on the handles of the wheelchair. 'Tell him we can't leave her because she has Down syndrome.'

'Up syndrome,' Harper corrected me. 'And I can go places myself. I don't need you to follow. I'm not a baby anymore, you know.'

Words flew back and forth in Chinese.

Finally Bì Yù told me that he'd agreed to let me accompany Harper, but that she would have to wait behind.

'Fān yù yuán,' I said firmly, pointing at Bì Yù.

They both looked at me blankly.

'Do you mean interpreter?' Bì Yù asked. '*Fān yì yuán?* I've already told him that.'

'I've changed my mind.' Harper got up from her wheelchair. 'I would like to go back to Bì Yù's house now.'

I shook my head wearily. 'Harper, you said you'd stay.'

'No, I've had enough.' She dropped her empty paper bag, tottered forward a few steps, then collapsed.

Harper was helped onto a gurney by white-clad nurses. They wheeled her through double doors into a long room lined with beds. Harper was borne away to a recovery area while Bì Yù and I were instructed to sit in a waiting room nearby.

The room was completely bare, other than a white table with matching chairs.

'When we get home,' Bì Yù said, 'we need to have a serious talk.'

I nodded, anxiety swimming in my belly.

She looked around. There were no windows, not even a sign on the wall. 'I get a weird vibe about this place.'

Me too, I wanted to reply, but I was too scared to admit it. *What have I done?*

The door opened abruptly and Mr Zhāng entered with a stony-faced nurse. He addressed Bì Yù, his tone firm, like he was issuing instructions.

'He says if anyone asks, we have to tell them Harper is being treated for an infection, nothing more.' Bì Yù shook her head as Mr Zhāng continued speaking. Translating rapidly, she told me that all consultations were to take place in private with the doctor. We would meet him tomorrow at 3 pm at the Red Lantern Hotel. They would run more tests on Harper tonight. All further testing would need to be paid for in cash.

'Ask him when the surgery will take place,' I urged.

She relayed my question.

Mr Zhāng was silent for a few seconds. He ran his tongue over his yellow teeth then muttered something in Chinese.

'He says we'll find out tomorrow and to bring the rest of the money then.'

Mr Zhāng turned to leave.

'Where the hell is he going?' I asked.

Bì Yù shrugged.

'Wait!' I shouted.

Mr Zhāng turned to glare at me. The corner of his left eye twitched. 'Quietly!' he growled in English.

'Tell him I won't leave until I know when my sister will be getting her heart and lung transplants.'

As Bì Yù spoke, her voice was shaking.

I watched helplessly as he left the room without acknowledging what Bì Yù had said. I had no idea if he was coming back.

◆

After twenty long minutes, Mr Zhāng returned. He smiled and began to speak, more slowly this time.

Bì Yù started to say something in reply, but Mr Zhāng cut her off.

'Bì Yù, tell me what's going on.'

She turned to look at me. 'Harper can have a heart and lung transplant on Thursday.'

'Really?' My voice rose in excitement. 'She can have the surgery that soon?'

'Yes.'

'Well, tell him thank you.' I smiled at him. 'Thank you!' Who cared if he was slimy? He was saving my sister's life

But Bì Yù grabbed me by the shoulder.

'Hold on, Marlowe – he says he wants you to pay the remaining money. How much did you pay him already?'

'Don't worry about it. I… we're going to save Harper's life.'

She became very still. I struggled to read the expression on her face.

'He says not to be late for the appointment at the hotel tomorrow.'

Before she could say anything more, a nurse entered and said a few words. My cousin stood so I did too. The nurse led us to a room where Harper was sitting up in bed drinking an apple juice. She told us Harper was ready to return home.

'I'm feeling a bit better now,' Harper announced. 'Let's go. It's late and I'm very tired.'

She was seated back in her wheelchair and we were led out of the hospital via a different route. We passed several wards lined with beds, all occupied.

'There's a lot of people here,' Bì Yù muttered under her breath. 'Are they all transplant patients?' She asked the nurse in Chinese, and the woman replied with a simple, 'Yes.'

'A lot of people here have broken hearts,' Harper said.

As we left the building and walked towards the car, Bì Yù put her hand on my arm. 'Marlowe,' she said softly, 'this isn't right. You have to tell your dad what you're doing.'

'No,' I said. 'That's not an option.'

'Then talk to *my* dad,' she pleaded.

'We've already discussed this,' I snapped. 'No one can know.'

Bì Yù glanced at Harper to make sure she wasn't listening then whispered in my ear, 'It's common belief among Chinese that one must be buried with their organs intact, for the afterlife. You know that, don't you?'

I nodded, unable to look her in the eye.

'So where are all these organs coming from? There were so many transplant patients in there.'

I shrugged. I couldn't tell her the truth.

Harper spoke up. 'All this whispering,' she said. 'I just don't like it.'

—

Bì Yù's apartment was on the seventeenth floor of a new building opposite Zhōngshān Park, one of Uncle Bǐng Wén's new developments. The walls smelled vaguely of fresh paint, the floorboards of varnish.

She showed me to my room and then went to settle Harper in the other spare bedroom.

I started to unpack, shifting piles of neatly folded clothes from our suitcase to the dresser drawers.

After a few minutes, I noticed Bì Yù standing in the doorway, a large duffel bag at her feet.

'Never again.'

I undid the zipper and the musty smell of money wafted out. The notes were soft against my fingertips.

'They asked what I was doing with all that money.'

'What did you say?'

'I was helping my cousin pay for her university tuition fees.'

'Thank you.' I didn't know what else to say.

'Harper's asleep. I've made us some tea.'

'Do you have somewhere safe to store the money?'

'Shanghai is a safe place. Plus this building is secure. I'd just put it in your room somewhere.'

Why was she so relaxed? I wanted her to be more concerned.

'Come for tea, we need to talk.' She left without shutting the door behind her.

The room was small; there weren't many places to hide things safely. There was the small wardrobe, a single bed and a bedside table. That was it. I opened the duffel bag, lifted up the mattress, then poured the bills from the bag over the base of the bed. It was a clichéd place to hide the cash, but I had no other option.

I left the room, gripping the locket at my chest.

In the room opposite mine, Harper was asleep. I walked over quietly to check on her, adjusting the oxygen tube under her nose.

'Not long now,' I murmured.

I watched her breathing. Her lips were curved in a smile as she slept. I envied her serenity.

In the living room, I sat on the floor in front of the sofa and Bì Yù sat behind me. She ran her hands through my hair and started braiding just like Mum taught us to do when we were small.

'You're not telling me everything.'

Damn Bì Yù. It was so hard to lie to her. And I didn't like doing it. I needed her to understand what I was doing, to accept it.

I turned to face her, wanting to tell her everything, but I didn't know where to start.

'How do they get the organs so quickly, Marlowe?' she prompted me. 'And why do they cost so much?'

I answered her questions as simply as I could, recounting what Anita had told me and then the research I had done on Dad's computer.

She was very quiet, then, nudging me to turn around, she took my hair in her hands once more and continued braiding. When she was done, she put her arms around me and drew me close.

'Thank you for telling me the truth,' she said.

To my surprise, she didn't sound angry, and she didn't try to talk me out of it. The relief was overwhelming.

'Does Olly know about this?'

'Most of it…'

She bit her lip. 'I don't like the hospital and I certainly don't like Mr Zhāng, but I'll do everything I can to help.' She tightened her grip around my shoulders. 'Whatever it takes to save Harper.'

For a moment, it was as if I could smell Mum's perfume close by, like a warm breeze carrying the sweet scent of jasmine.

Overcome, I pulled away from her embrace and stood up.

'I'm thirsty,' I said as I headed towards the kitchen. 'Where do you keep your glasses?'

'In the cupboard to the left of the stove… Marlowe?'

I stopped and turned. 'Yes?'

'There were just so many people in the transplant ward.'

Not this again.

'That's a lot of prisoners to execute…'

'I suppose.' I shrugged.

'I didn't know the government executed that many people. And the wait time is so short. How can the demand be met so quickly?'

I would not think about this anymore. I entered the kitchen. With its black-and-white decor and clean lines, it looked trendy and arty, just like Bì Yù. As I reached for the cupboard, something on a nearby shelf caught my eye. Behind handmade mugs, a vase of dried flowers and several cookbooks, I saw a pink Minnie Mouse flask.

Minnie's red skirt with white polka dots had faded with age. I took the flask from the shelf. It seemed so small.

—

Outside, the occasional explosion of fireworks sounded in the sky as people across Shanghai continued their Chinese New Year celebrations. It was early morning and I longed to be watching the fireworks, but I was stuck in a smelly hospital, staring at Harper from the doorway of her room. She had just returned from surgery; her tiny chest was covered in bandages and there were tubes running everywhere. Her face was the same colour as the snow that lined the streets below. *Poor little Harper.* Was she in a lot of pain? I wanted to ask, but the words froze in my throat.

Mum, Dad, Wài Pó, Uncle Bǐng Wén and Aunt Lǐ Nà crowded around her bed, but Bì Yù and I stood in the doorway holding hands. My little sister looked so still, so lifeless, that it scared me. Bì Yù must have felt the same way, because she was gripping my hand as tightly as I held hers.

Mum turned to face us. 'There's nothing to be frightened of, girls. Even though she's just had major surgery, Harper will be okay. We just have to be gentle with her.' As she moved slowly around the bed, I thought that Mum looked very thin and tired. A small hole in the back of her tights ran down the middle of her calf.

She stroked Harper's forehead.

Dad turned towards us. 'Come on, girls.' He beckoned us closer, but I couldn't move.

'Bì Yù, *gùo lái*,' Uncle Bǐng Wén ordered.

My cousin took a deep breath and let go of my hand.

She marched bravely to Harper's side.

As I watched, she bent over to place an ear to Harper's chest. Straightening, she turned to face me and smiled. 'I can hear her heartbeat.'

Quickly, I went to her side. Harper lay sleeping, breathing heavily. I was itching to wake her up, to tickle her – anything to get a response.

Mum stepped closer and put her hand on my shoulder. 'We have to let her rest now, darling.'

The next morning, my parents and Wài Pó returned to the hospital, leaving me at home with my aunt, uncle and cousin.

'Why can't Harper come home?' I asked.

'She needs to stay in hospital until she gets better, darling,' Uncle explained.

'I have an idea,' Bì Yù said as we played in her room. 'The hospital is only giving Harper western medicine. Let's make her some Chinese medicine too, so she can get better twice as fast.'

We went down to the kitchen and gathered everything we could find that looked medicinal: goji berries, chrysanthemum flowers, ginger, ginkgo, cinnamon.

'Now we have to boil it up into a tea,' said Bì Yù.

When we were done, we poured the concoction into a pink Minnie Mouse flask, ready to be delivered to Harper.

My dad returned home for lunch, leaving Mum and Wài Pó at the hospital, and that afternoon he took me back to visit my sister. I carried a backpack with some of Harper's toys and put the flask in too.

When a doctor came to talk to the adults, I saw my opportunity. While they were distracted, I took the Minnie Mouse flask from my backpack and began pouring the medicine into Harper's half-open mouth.

To my horror, she immediately started to gasp and wheeze.

'Mā ma, come quick!'

The adults turned. When Mum saw the brown liquid streaming from Harper's mouth, she screamed. 'What is it? What have you done?'

'I gave her some medicine,' I said, 'to help her get better more quickly.'

The doctor, meanwhile, had rolled Harper onto her side. 'Quick,' he was saying to Dad, 'press the emergency call button.'

As Wài Pó ushered me from the room, I was still clutching Bì Yù's flask.

Glancing over my shoulder, I saw my little sister heaving and choking.

I wasn't allowed to visit Harper in the Shanghai hospital again.

Harper

The morning sun is low and the shape of a half-eaten cookie. Curly smoke comes out of buildings below, moving through the air like long, hot fettuccine pasta straight from a pot.

In my bed, I feel cold. I say Louis's name over and over again and I close my eyes. I imagine his body is giving warmth to mine. We lie together, like tangled vines whispering floating words to each other. Holding hands, we listen to the sound of two breaths moving at the same time.

Marlowe

It was 9 am and Bì Yù was heading off to work, promising that she would be back in time to come with me to the Red Lantern Hotel.

'See you back here at two thirty,' she said.

As soon as the front door closed behind her, I dialled Uncle Johnny's number. When he answered I told him we had safely arrived in Shanghai.

'How are you and how's Harper doing?'

'We're all as good as we can be considering.'

I heard the front door open and close again. A few seconds later a thin, middle-aged woman entered, carrying a bucket filled with cleaning products and a mop. She smiled at me and said something in Chinese, then held up a cloth and headed for the bathroom. Bì Yù hadn't told me she had a cleaner. My pulse raced. I didn't know who this woman was. I started thinking about the money I had hidden.

'So, has everything gone okay so far with Mr Zhāng and the hospital?' Uncle Johnny asked. 'Tell me what's going on.'

I told him Harper's surgery was scheduled for Thursday.

'Marlowe, I've done a little digging into transplants in China.' He paused. 'I'd like to send you some articles. They have some sensitive content. Perhaps sending them by post would be better than via email.'

Articles? I'd read articles. I didn't need to read any more articles. Harper's surgery had been scheduled. I didn't want anything to get in the way of that.

'I've read a lot already –'

'Please. I feel it's important.'

I recited Bì Yù's address, just to make him happy.

'Thanks. Keep me posted. You have my number, if there is anything I can do… Please be careful, Marlowe.'

The cleaner emerged from the bathroom and opened the door to my bedroom. Oh no – I couldn't let her see the money.

'Thanks, Uncle Johnny – I've got to go.'

'Wait!'

For God's sake, what now?

The cleaner was vacuuming around my bed now. She was way too close for comfort.

'Have you spoken to your dad?' Uncle Johnny was asking.

'What?'

'I was thinking of stopping by the house to see him. You know, it's been so long.'

The cleaner had shut the door. Why would she do that?

'Sure. Sorry, Uncle Johnny, I really have to go.' I ended the call and ran to the bedroom. Flinging open the door, I saw that she was making my bed.

'Stop!' I shouted.

She looked up at me, frowning.

'Stop! You don't need to clean in here.'

She started talking rapidly in Chinese but I shook my head and pointed to her and then to the door.

'What's all this shouting about?' Harper appeared in the doorway, breathless.

'Nothing,' I said, as the cleaner, giving me a baleful look, collected her things and left the room.

'You're acting so strange, Marlowe,' Harper said. 'And I heard you speaking to Uncle Johnny. Why didn't you let me speak to him? I would have liked to say hello and let him know how I am doing and feeling in my heart.'

It hadn't occurred to me that she might be listening.

'I'm sorry, Harper.'

'You said I had surgery scheduled for Thursday.'

I froze. *Think of something to say quick.*

'I told you I didn't want a surgery and you promised no more hospitals.'

I couldn't think of something to say. I couldn't come up with the words.

'Why didn't you talk to me about this?'

'I'm – I'm sorry, Harper. I just want to get you the medical treatment you deserve.'

She looked so sad.

'You never think about me anymore or what I want.'

She was right. Yet she couldn't possibly advocate for herself and seek the best medical care as well as I could.

'Harper,' I said, 'wait.'

But she walked off to her room without looking back.

Harper

As I am sitting here on Bì Yù's cosy couch, listening to her sounds while she makes breakfast, I remember a dream I had last night of my sweet Louis. He was dressed in a blue suit, and he looked so handsome. He was reading to me in Dad's garden. His words were like yellow flowers, blooming soft petals against my cheek. I felt the earth underneath us turning. We were moving, always moving, but when I put my head on his shoulder, together we were still.

Marlowe

Harper had been in a short, deep sleep on the couch beside me, and as her chest rattled away, it was incredible to me that she seemed oblivious to the struggle that was taking place in her body. And then I caught myself, as I thought about this more, I wondered if in fact she wasn't so oblivious. There was a strength to her that I often overlooked. Despite everything she had been through, she held onto joy and optimism. I thought about a long chambered heart of a butterfly, spanning from its head through to its thorax, diffusing gooey hemolymph around its body efficiently. Such a fragile creature that in many ways is so robust. If only humans were made in this way. If only Harper could have been made in this way.

The phone rang, snapping me into the present. I held my breath. It had to be Dad. Or was I being paranoid? I had turned off my mobile phone so he couldn't contact me. Yet, I still lived in fear that he would find us before I had got Harper her transplant. I let it ring out, but after a pause of only a few seconds it started to ring again.

Harper woke up. 'Who's calling?' she asked groggily.

'It's a wrong number.' I got up and took the phone off the hook. 'I'll make us some tea.'

We sat at the dining table sipping tea from Bì Yù's hand-crafted ceramic mugs and nibbling on sesame crackers. The cleaner still hadn't finished her work; she was now mopping the floors. Her presence was irritating me.

'Let's go to Zhōngshān Park,' said Harper. 'I want to see the plum tree.'

I looked at my watch. We would have to leave for the Red Lantern Hotel in a few hours. I was reluctant to let Harper get any more exhausted than she already was.

I shook my head. 'It's way too cold today. We shouldn't take any chances with your health.'

'But, Marlowe, you promised.' She stood up, her breathing laboured from that small effort. 'I'll go on my own then.'

'Wait.' I grabbed several wedding magazines Bì Yù had bought for Harper. 'Don't you want to have a look at these together? I think you would look stunning in this one.' I opened to a page of a woman wearing a puffy white gown and held it out. Harper was immediately transfixed. She sank back onto the couch and started leafing through the magazines.

I had Bì Yù's laptop in front of me, but just as I was about to open my emails the cleaner entered the room and began dusting. Hadn't she already done that? Why was she still here?

'Her name is Ān Chén,' Harper announced as she cut out magazine clippings of women in both Chinese and Western wedding dresses and stuck them into her notebook. Every so often, the rasping of her breath would overcome the sound of scissors slicing paper.

'How do you know?'

'I asked her. It's nice to know people's names.'

She smiled at the cleaner, who smiled back.

'Do you like this one?' Harper pointed to a photo of a woman with pink flowers in her hair. She was standing in a field of daisies, the afternoon sun glowing behind her. One hand was lifting the skirt of her dress, and the delicate silver embroidery was illuminated by the golden light. She looked like she might be stuck in a dream.

I quickly turned the page. 'I like this one.' I pointed to a woman wearing a clean, simple dress that clung to her curves, it had a qí páo-style top and I thought it was very elegant.

'No, that dress is boring,' Harper declared. She turned back to the previous page. 'Don't you see?' She ran her fingertip over the dreamy lady. 'This dress is all about the magic of love.'

Ān Chén moved into the kitchen and I heard the clatter of dishes in the sink.

I logged into my email.

'Marlowe?' Harper asked, as I was waiting for it to load, 'Do you think you will have a wedding one day?'

I shook my head.

'I wish I could come to your wedding one day.'

Her words hit me in the gut. As if she could sense this, she stretched out her hand for me to hold.

'If I ever got married, my wedding wouldn't be much fun,' I told her. 'I'd keep it small and simple.' *If I ever got married? Since when was I going to get married?*

I opened a message from Olly. We'd spoken briefly last night when Bì Yù and Harper had gone to bed. Our conversation was tense. Despite promising he would try to understand and support my actions, it seemed he was finding it hard to.

> Marls, please call me. Please. I really need to talk to you about something.

I told him everything that had happened, even Harper telling me she didn't want a transplant and that I never listened to her. Of course he was concerned. I shouldn't have told him so much yesterday. I was sleep deprived. I wasn't thinking clearly. I closed his email and opened a new message from Professor Lipin.

Dear Marlowe,

I hope your sister is recovering. I've been getting updates from Olly, who said that you may have found the appropriate treatment for her. I am keeping my fingers crossed for you all.

I've tried to call the Hong Kong mobile number you left me several times without being able to reach you. I was disappointed to learn from your last email that you would be leaving the PhD program. If the reasons are primarily financial, I'd like to assure you that there are funding options available to you – especially now. We've had a call from the Devon pesticide and insect control authority. Thanks to your hard work, they've agreed to stop using insecticides.

We are starting the *arion* conservation program again this summer, and I would like to offer you a paid position as my assistant. Since it's still a few months away now, and from what Olly has said there's a chance that your sister will have recovered by then, I thought there would be no harm in asking.

Finally, I have saved the best news for last. It gives me great pleasure to inform you that you have won the Royal Zoological Award. Marlowe, this is such an honour and it couldn't have gone to a more deserving candidate. The results have not been announced publicly yet, but you should be receiving formal notification from the Zoological Society of London shortly.

The award ceremony will be held next month. I do hope you'll be able to attend.

I look forward to hearing from you as soon as possible.

Best regards,

John Lipin

I stared at the computer screen until the words became blurry and reality sank in. All my hard work over the last few years had finally paid off: the conservation program was going ahead; there was hope for the *arion*.

An image of Grandpa came to mind, his hand on my shoulder, his face pink with pride. Although I'd been dismayed to learn that I had been entered for the award, now that I had won it, it felt damn good. And being invited to work with Professor Lipin on the conservation program was a huge honour. A new feeling swelled from my torso, making me stand tall. I didn't feel the need to hide anymore.

I would have to ring Olly.

'What's so funny?' Harper asked.

I became aware of my face – my cheeks were tight from smiling.

'Come on, what is it?'

I took her hand. It was cold; too cold. I felt myself deflate. Suddenly I was finding it difficult to breathe. It was as if I was feeling what she was feeling, as if I was suffering from the very same heart defect.

'Oh, nothing.'

She shrugged and returned to her wedding magazine. 'You always say that.'

The realisation hit me then. I wouldn't call Olly because I wouldn't be returning to London to collect my award, finish my PhD or take part in the conservation program and bear witness to the revival of the brilliant blue butterfly in its natural habitat.

⸺

'You thief! *Nǐ zhè gè zéi!*' I was holding a wad of bills in my hand, waving them at Ān Chén as I shouted in a mix of English and broken Chinese. I had counted the money and we were one hundred renminbi short.

'Give it to me!' I demanded, holding out my hand. 'I know you took it.'

She threw her arms into the air, screaming.

'*Nǐ fēng le ma?!*' Her fringe clung to her sweaty forehead.

'Marlowe... Marlowe.' I heard Harper's voice close by. The sound of her sobbing. 'Leave her alone. Stop it.'

But I couldn't stop. My body was thick with heat. My hands were shaking. I wanted to empty her pockets myself. I was breathing in short, fast gasps. Furious words spilled out of me. The room was becoming a blur.

The front door opened and shut, footsteps ran through the apartment.

I felt hands on my shoulders. It was Bì Yù, urging me to sit on the bed.

'Marlowe, you have to breathe.' Her voice was calm.

I closed my eyes. Opened them again. I could see Harper standing in the doorway, tears rolling down her cheeks. Ān Chén was standing beside her, one arm around her shoulders, the other at her chest. Money scattered at my feet.

Bì Yù was rubbing my back while talking very softly, very calmly to Ān Chén.

'*Duì bù qǐ, duì bù qǐ,*' she was saying.

'Why are you apologising?' I demanded. 'She took my money! Money for Harper!'

'Marlowe, look.' Bì Yù took an envelope out of her bag and passed it to me. 'Ān Chén has nothing to do with this. I realised this morning that we were short because of the transfer fees and took out the remaining amount from my account today.'

I looked inside the envelope. Sure enough, the money was there. My world became still.

What was happening to me?

'Oh...' I was light-headed.

I stood unsteadily and made my way across the room to Ān Chén, but she backed away as I drew near.

'I'm so sorry.' But as I spoke, I realised my apology would be of no use.

❥

The Red Lantern Hotel was situated directly opposite the hospital. An overpowering scent of floral detergent filled the lobby, which had mauve-tiled floors and large urns of fake roses.

We took the elevator to the eleventh floor, as instructed by Mr Zhāng, and walked down the corridor to room 1109. I gripped the duffel bag tightly. Harper had refused to sit in her wheelchair and was leaning heavily on Bì Yù's shoulder, oxygen tank in hand. I could hear her sucking in breath. It made my insides turn.

'No hospitals today, right?' She had been asking me this every five minutes during our journey over here.

'Right,' I promised.

'Good.' She sighed. 'I really don't like the hospitals here, you know.'

Mr Zhāng answered the door at our knock and we entered. The curtains were drawn and the room was sparsely furnished, apart from more fake roses next to a large TV. I scanned the room for the surgeon we were supposed to meet, but there was no one else in the room.

'Where's the surgeon?' I asked, and Bì Yù translated the question for Mr Zhāng.

He looked away as he spoke. 'That's good news,' Harper said.

'The surgeon is unable to make it,' Bì Yù told me.

'What? Why?' Suddenly, I felt as jittery as if I had just downed four shots of espresso.

Harper plonked herself on the bed and turned on the TV.

Mr Zhāng gestured for Bì Yù and I to sit on the hard wooden chairs arranged on each side of a small table.

The broker put a new toothpick in his mouth before responding to my question.

'He said the operating surgeon is a very busy man,' Bì Yù translated. 'I asked him the surgeon's name but he said he could not reveal it.'

Surgeons were busy, I understood that, yet I couldn't ignore the sense of foreboding building in me.

Mr Zhāng gestured to the duffel bag.

'He says if you want to lock in the surgery tomorrow, you have to pay now.' She paused. 'Marlowe, before you hand over all that money, let's stop and think about this for a minute. The whole thing feels like it's getting out of control.'

I felt myself becoming irritated.

'I don't have a minute! Have you seen how sick Harper is?'

A small crease formed on her brow. 'Of course I have, I –'

Mr Zhāng interrupted, tapping a long fingernail on the shiny face of his Rolex.

I thrust the duffel bag at him, trying to quell my apprehension.

He counted the money in front of us. When he was done, he nodded.

Bì Yù, who sat at the edge of her chair, spine erect, spoke to him in Chinese.

The broker replied.

I looked over at Harper, who had fallen asleep on the bed. The oxygen tube under her nose had come loose and was nestled in the crease of her lip. I quickly got up and fixed it in place as gently as I could.

'Ask him what time the surgery will be scheduled for tomorrow?'

Bì Yù listened to his response, then reported, 'He says he will call us in the morning to let us know. But Harper needs to return to the hospital today for more tests so they can prepare.'

'Does she need to fast tonight?'

Bì Yù asked him, and I saw Mr Zhāng shake his head.

'Tell him she's always needed to fast before any significant procedure.' Air felt hard to grasp.

Mr Zhāng's voice got louder, faster.

Bì Yù said, 'He insists she doesn't need to fast. Not tonight. He repeated that we have to keep this whole thing a secret.' She added, 'I don't like this, Marlowe. I don't like this one little bit.' She leaned in and whispered, 'Are you really sure we should have given him all that money? Now he's asking for more for these new tests.'

I wasn't sure, but I wasn't about to admit it. 'Yes, damn it,' I snapped. I took Harper's hand in mine. I had to put my doubts aside.

The only way Harper was going to get her transplants was if we followed Mr Zhāng's instructions.

—⋈—

Back at the Shanghai Middle Hospital, I sat alone in a small waiting room off the transplant ward, rocking back and forth. The sounds of Harper's screams echoed through the hall.

'Don't touch me, leave me alone! *Fàng kāi wǒ! Fàng kāi wǒ!* Leave me alone! I don't like this place. I want my Louis – someone please get me my Louis.' And then, 'Marlowe, where are you? You promised no more hospitals!'

My insides felt hot. I swallowed bile as it churned up into my mouth. I was trying not to imagine how betrayed she must be feeling – conned into coming to this awful hospital against her wishes. It was cruel. I knew it was cruel.

I stood and shut the door. Her muffled screams tore through my chest. It was as if there was no boundary between us. Her pain was my pain. Her desperation, her frustration, her dependency – the feeling of being trapped, of having her free will harnessed by me. I placed my headphones into the small tunnels of my ears, as far as they would go. Although they were attached to my MP3 player, I did not listen to music. Silence enveloped me like a soft, cotton blanket. I sat on the floor and leaned my back against the wall. I brushed the tears from my cheeks, but they just kept coming.

I opened my handbag and rummaged for some tissues. It was a mess in there: hair ties, lip balm, Panadol, old receipts, my scarf, a notebook… and Dad's letter. I wiped my nose on my sleeve and opened it.

Dear Marlowe,

I've had much on my mind that I've wanted to share, but when I'm with you, I struggle to find the words to express myself. I'll try to say what I need to in this letter, but please forgive any clumsiness.

Most people thought it was me who had trouble accepting Harper's birth. I fit the stereotype of the stiff-upper-lipped Brit who couldn't handle emotion. But when I held her for the first time, looked into her eyes, the fact that she wasn't 'perfect' didn't disturb me at all. It made me want to wrap her up and tie her to my chest so that I could keep her close and safe.

As your mother lay in her hospital bed, listening to the doctors tell us we had a 'retarded child', I saw her eyes turn glassy. I knew then that she was stuck in a nightmare, waiting for her 'real' daughter to be born instead of this 'flawed' one. *She will never learn to read, never learn to write...* The doctors rattled off a list of things she would never be able to do.

When they left, I sat next to your mother and took her hand. I suggested we name our baby Harper, after Harper Lee – as you know, she is one of my favourite authors.

Your mother didn't smile. She looked away and reminded me that the doctors had said Harper would never be able to write.

I wish she could see Harper now, sitting at the table, writing furiously, words spilling from her in a language that knows only love.

You see, my darling girl, my love for Harper is as strong as yours.

I do hope one day you will be able to understand my position in all of this.

Yours always,

Dad

My body felt weighed down by Dad's words. I put the letter to my nose, searching for the scent of home, but all I could smell was ink. Suddenly I felt like a small child, desperate for her father to come and make it all better. *Silly.* I took a breath and folded the letter, slipped it back into the envelope and slid it into the side pocket of my bag.

'Marlowe?' Bì Yù was standing in the doorway, panting. 'Why aren't you with Harper?'

I shook my head and looked at the floor between my knees.

'Did you get the money for the tests?' I asked.

She nodded.

'But I can't keep doing this – I'll run out.' She sighed, then held out her hand. 'Come on.'

—✦—

Harper was asleep when we entered her cubicle. The nurse attending to her told us she had been given a sedative to calm her down but we could take her home now.

She then handed me the bill. Bì Yù peered over my shoulder. Every item that had been used in Harper's care, including cotton buds and the thermometer, was listed.

'What the hell?' Bì Yù grabbed the bill from my hands. 'This is daylight robbery.'

I felt a flutter in my abdomen as I handed over the cash my cousin had given me. The woman took it and hurried off.

It will be fine, I told myself. *This is all part of the process.* Mr Zhāng had warned me from the beginning that there would be extra costs. The important thing was that tomorrow my sister would be given the new heart and lungs that would save her life.

I turned to wake her.

Harper

In the car on the way back to Bì Yù's home from the hospital, Marlowe does not say anything when I tell her I will *not* be going to hospital again. I feel big anger flames burning in my heart.

She talks in whispers to Bì Yù in the front seat. She thinks I cannot hear because I am sitting in the back, but I can. I hear the word transplant.

Transplant transplant transplant.

I want to shout at them and say: 'I won't let you do that to me and my heart.' But I can't shout. The injection I was given in the hospital makes my body feel like it is made of bricks. Everything around me is slow and heavy. I understand in my mind that I can't shout anymore, I can't say what I need to, because if I do, the doctors will come and inject me with more of that wicked potion.

When we get home I am tucked into bed. Marlowe sits with her legs crossed by my feet and she is biting her nails – something Stepmonster says is unladylike. I think to myself that Stepmonster is right. Marlowe is un-lady-like. She looks thin and grey in the face and her eyes are empty. She ties her hair up in an ugly bun. No, she does not look like a lady. In fact, she does not look much like my sister anymore. I see and feel now that the air and space between us is broken.

Marlowe

While Harper was resting in her room, Bì Yù was in the kitchen making pork and chive dumplings by hand. I was sitting at the dining table drinking whisky. Normally I hated the stuff, but today I relished the burn of the hot liquid in my throat and the way it quieted the swirling in my mind. Just when I felt myself growing calm, the phone rang. After I had taken it off the hook, someone must have placed it back. *Harper?*

'Bì Yù, no!'

But it was too late. She had already answered.

'Hello?... Oh, hi, Uncle James.'

I froze.

'You're in Beijing?... Oh, I see... Yes, I'll let you know if I hear anything.'

'I hate this,' Bì Yù said.

All I could say was 'So do I.' I sounded so pathetic.

The phone rang again.

Bì Yù answered once more.

'Mā ma!' She spoke in Chinese to Aunt Lǐ Nà. All I understood was Bì Yù saying, 'I don't know.' She was covering for me. When she hung up the phone, she didn't bother coming out of the kitchen.

'I'm ready to go home now.'

It was Harper, standing behind me. I didn't want to turn and face her. I couldn't.

'I said I want to go home now... Marlowe? Why are you ignoring me? I want to go home I want to go home I want to go –'

'Enough!'

I turned and saw the word strike her like a blow to the stomach. Her beautiful brown eyes filled with pain.

Who was I becoming?

'I'm going home, Marlowe,' she said, her voice subdued.

Taking her in properly now, I saw she had her coat on and was standing with her oxygen tank in one hand, backpack slung over her shoulder. For a moment, I fantasised about letting her walk out of the apartment. A refreshing sense of solitude washed over me, reminding me of the silence I relished in the lab when staring down a microscope lens at the compound eyes of the *arion*. I drew in a breath, a full and deep one, and then I saw my sister walking through the door.

'Harper.' I leaped up.

She walked down the corridor towards the elevator.

'Harper!'

She ignored me and kept walking. The elevator doors opened and she stepped in. I followed.

'Harper, please.'

She looked away, pretending I wasn't there.

I grabbed her arm.

'Let go of me!' she shouted.

The doors were closing.

'Harper, this is silly,' I said sternly.

'I want to go home. Why can't you respect me?'

Respect. She hadn't used that word with me much before.

'How exactly do you plan to go home without me?' Bitter. I could taste it.

She took her wallet from her backpack and showed me a wad of US hundred-dollar bills.

'Where the hell did you get that?'

'Louis. He took it from his dad. It's money for our marriage.' I could feel gravity in the pit of my stomach as the elevator descended. 'I'm going back to my Louis. He looks after me when I'm sick. He loves me with his brave heart.'

'How dare you,' I said through gritted teeth. 'All I do is look after you!'

Harper folded her arms.

'You used to look after me. Now you're just... you're just' she took a breath from her oxygen mask – 'an empty heart.'

I took one step too close. I laughed bitterly at the irony. It was thanks to me that tomorrow she would have a working heart.

'You'd be dead without me,' I said.

The elevator doors opened, but she didn't move; she just stared at me without blinking or breathing. My words seemed to have winded her.

'I'm only doing what's best for you,' I added.

She sank to her knees on the floor of the elevator.

I felt numb. The doors closed and we travelled back up. Time moved painfully slow, and all I could think about was how I was supposed to stop myself from becoming someone I didn't know.

Harper

Last night something strange happened. Marlowe came into my room. I pretended I was asleep, but I wasn't really because I was thinking of my Louis and sending him love through my closed eyes and open heart.

I felt her fingertips on my forehead, brushing away my hair, making my appearance tidy. She was whispering something. I turned to move closer to her sound.

'I'm sorry,' she was saying. 'I'm so sorry.'

I did not open my eyes because I could feel pain coming from her voice, so hot it felt cold.

'Please, please, don't leave me. Don't die on me. I need you not to die, please.'

Her words travelled into my chest and every time my heart made one beat it hurt so bad that I had to squeeze my mouth shut so I did not scream.

She crawled under my covers with me, like I used to do with her when we were small. She wrapped her arm around my waist and held me tight and it felt so cosy I went to sleep.

When I woke up in the morning, she was gone.

—✦—

A strong flame has been burning in my belly. It makes me want to leave Marlowe. Last night, I tried to go back home to my Louis, but I couldn't. Not because I do not know how. Of course I know all about calling up a travelling agent and with my words telling her I will be getting on a plane, economy class, to Hong Kong International Airport. I have seen my dad do this. But he uses a card from his wallet and reads out the numbers on it to pay for a ticket. I do not have these numbers.

But that is not the reason I didn't go. Deep in my heart, when I tried to leave Marlowe, I felt something inside me pulling and pulling.

It is like we are magnets, and right now the powerful forces and energies between us keep bringing me back to her.

—◆—

This morning the phone rang early. Bì Yù answered it and had a conversation that sounded angry. And then she and Marlowe started shouting. I didn't like the sound of the loud voices so I went to my room, but even though I shut the door, I could still hear them.

'I don't trust him, Marlowe. He can keep delaying all he wants. He can just run off with all the money now.'

'It's only one day. Don't overreact.'

I wondered what was happening in one day, but I knew I could not ask this right now or Marlowe's flames of anger would hit me and maybe mine would hit her.

'Ugh, you're so frustrating!' Bì Yù said. 'You're not thinking clearly anymore. He could keep saying one day forever.'

'I don't need to listen to this. I'm going out.'

Then I heard the door slam. It made me jump. After a while, when I felt the air in the house drop to the floor like sinking dust,

I crept out of my room and into the living room. I was getting a bit bored in the bedroom to be honest.

Now, lying on the couch with my warm, pink socks on, I feel my fire burning. Its flames are on low for now because Marlowe is still out. The house feels peaceful without her, but this is personal private information I will keep locked in my head. I am tired of the anger anger anger that is swimming around her whole body, inside and out. She can't see it, but I can.

An envelope arrives via a Speedy Gonzales postman for Marlowe and Bì Yù opens it. Inside are some cut-outs from a newspaper and a letter. I know this is not a good thing to do. Mail is personal and private. If your name is not on the envelope, that means you should not read it, but Bì Yù does. She reads the newspaper cut-outs first and I can tell she is holding her breath because her chest is still. Then she puts the cut-outs down and reads the letter. Suddenly she runs to the kitchen. I can tell she is making a phone call because I hear her say, 'It's Bì Yù. Marlowe's gone out and I opened the letter you sent. I need your help.'

I think to myself that I have not heard Bì Yù ask for help before.

'Harper was due to have her procedure today,' she says, 'but it's been moved to tomorrow. Marlowe's already paid the money, but… I'm just not sure about it anymore.'

I wonder what she means by the word *procedure* and think I must look it up in my dictionary soon.

'I know Marlowe is desperate to get this done, but my gut tells me it's wrong.' Bì Yù's words are fast and shaky. 'I couldn't work out how the hospital can have so many organs available for transplant at such short notice, while in the rest of the world people have to wait years. I didn't think we executed that many criminals.

'But one of those articles, you sent said that it's not just criminals who are being executed – that it's political prisoners and people from labour camps too. Do you think it's possible that the organs...'

I don't want to listen anymore. There are too many words that don't make sense and it is making me tired. I go back to my room and crawl into bed.

——————

After a while, Bì Yù comes to my room and asks me to sit with her at the kitchen table. She shows me a book called *The Anatomy of the Human Heart*. There is a photo of a heart and lots of words. Some of the words are a bit strange and long, but Bì Yù explains the meaning of it all: that my heart is a muscle inside my chest and I need it to be full of life. When it stops beating, this is called dead. I tell Bì Yù that I already know about the human heart and I tell her that I am not going to be dead because the doctors are going to fix me. I also explain to her about dead. I tell her that just because your body becomes dead, your hum is not gone. Like my mum. Sometimes she is with me. When I am in the garden by the jasmine bush, I can smell her perfume.

When I finish speaking, I notice something different in me. I am calmer now; the dead word doesn't scare me so much today. I said this word three times out loud and it didn't upset me.

'Don't you think the heart looks like a plum, with vines and roots that reach all over your body?' I ask.

Bì Yù looks at me. 'Your heart is sick, Harper. You know that, don't you?'

I nod my head. *Not this conversation again. Does everyone think I am stupid in my brain or what?*

'And Marlowe wants to get you a new one from another person. This is why she has brought you to Shanghai.' She leans her body in so she is close to me. 'I don't want to scare you, but she wants to get you a heart in a very bad way.'

Bì Yù's eyes look a bit small and sideways, like she is doing something secret.

'I already told Marlowe I don't want the transplant thing. I don't want someone else's heart and I don't want it in a bad way.'

I ask Bì Yù to get me a glass of apple juice and she does. I drink it in one go.

She looks at me, and her eyes are soft.

'Harper, if you don't want this heart transplant, you have to be firm with Marlowe.'

I think to myself that Bì Yù does not understand a few things. First of all, even though I keep telling Marlowe that I don't want someone else's heart, she will not listen. This is something that happens a lot in my life, maybe because I am not as quick at speaking out my words as someone who doesn't have the Up syndrome. Marlowe used to be someone who listened, but now she has forgotten how, just like everyone else. The second thing is that now I think I understand in my heart and in my mind why Marlowe won't listen. It has something to do with the pain that she whispered to me last night when she thought I was sleeping.

I decide it is best not to use words to say any more to Bì Yù, so I lift up my glass and ask her for one more apple juice.

—

I go to my room, take out my autobiographical storybook and open to the page where my pen was last touching. I read it again:

There was a beutiful lady who onse upon a time had a sore chest and was sick. She didn't know it yet but she had corage. Even though the yung woman was sick in her chest, she found her corage and desided to go on a jorney. Her body filled up with power like a leeping white tiger.

It is time for me to add in a few more words. I can feel them running from my brain and into my hand. I needed to find my plum heart before it was too late.

There was a dark forse that was trying to stop the brave woman from finding her plum hart.

I close my eyes and see a faceless man wearing a large black cape. In his hand is a glass globe, spinning.

The dark forse was a man called deth. He had no eyes to see and no fase to be toched. He held a glass world in his hand, it was moving rond and rond and rond. He told the lady her time was runing out. And then she culd feel a drumming thumping drumming all the way from her roots, up her trunk and to the sky. In this moment she relised how brave she was for she was not scard of deth. But she new she needed to protect her hart, before he took it for himself.

279

Marlowe

I yearned for the night. It was like a cave I longed to crawl into. Sleep had become elusive – hard for me to catch, hard for me to hold. I sat at the edge of my bed, facing the window, watching the warm lights in the apartment blocks outside flicker on and off. The quiet, the absolute quiet, sank deep into the pit of my belly and rooted me to the earth. I became aware of my body, slow and pregnant with guilt, and I was too tired to run from it, too tired to halt my unravelling.

Am I going mad?

In the early hours of the morning, I took a notepad and pen and tried to doodle my way out of insomnia.

I found myself writing the word 'Help' over and over.

Harper

I am homesick and I miss my Louis, Dad and Wài Pó. I know I cannot ask Marlowe anymore about going to Zhōngshān Park because she is very upset about it. But I am not angry with her now. I think I am just sorry. When I look at her, she looks sad, so sad. I feel her hurt inside of me, so deep, right down past my feet to the bottom of the earth and to the middle of all things in this universe. This makes me feel like maybe I should just do what she wants. Maybe I should just have the transplant thing and take the new heart. Maybe then her pain will go away.

I sit on Bì Yù's couch with her Hello Kitty cushions and her warm pink blanket, watching Marlowe. She has been by the phone, or moving back and forth, back and forth, across the living room. She says she is waiting for an important call but I don't know who this call is supposed to be from.

Bì Yù comes home from work early, smelling like coffee. She said she went to work this morning, but I notice she is not wearing the smart clothes she normally wears with her red coat. She is still in her tracksuit. I have a feeling there is something going on with her too because she seems a bit quiet and her eyes are still, like she is trying to figure something out in her brain.

Bì Yù and Marlowe talk quietly for a while in the corner of the room. Their words are hissing at each other.

'He's not answering my calls… I'm going to the Red Lantern.'

'Wait. We need to talk. I've been doing a lot of thinking, and I'm just not sure I'm okay with this anymore, Marlowe…'

'Enough already!' Marlowe storms out of the living room and goes to get her coat.

Bì Yù starts burning joss. The smell is hot in my throat like chilli paste. I think of Wài Pó; she sometimes burns joss too. I close my eyes like she taught me to do for meditation, and I listen to my very own humming. It sounds like a loud whoosh and a thud.

A whoosh and a thud.

And then the whoosh comes without the thud and the inside of my body feels like I am falling. It is quiet, I think. Then my thud returns and I feel a small prickle in the tops of my fingers and toes.

How long before my sound runs out?

My face is hot and my stomach heavy. My eyes feel like they are going to leak tears. Right now, more than ever, Marlowe really doesn't like tears. So I swallow, pick up a magazine and stare at the face of a serious-looking man on the cover. He looks back at me with eyes that are hard like stones. I wonder if Marlowe wants to get me a heart from him.

She storms back into the living room with a tight face full of frowning.

'Harper.'

I notice some of her hairs are thick together in what looks like a bird's nest and she is wearing the same clothes from yesterday. This means she is losing care for her physical appearance. Wài Pó says this happens when your mind is too full and your spirit is thin and flat.

'Why is the suitcase packed again?' She stares at me. The air comes out of her mouth in a huff.

The sounds of my body move quickly and I lose my breath.

'I told you I want to go home.' Even though I am saying this, I do not think I would leave Marlowe anymore. Her spirit feels shaky. She needs me now. But I want her to know that I can go home without her if I really want to.

'Home?' She looks at me as if she has never heard this word before. 'We've already been through this, Harper. I thought we'd moved on.' Her voice is sharp and her tongue is quick. She is so full of anger these days. She grinds her teeth; I hear it like the sound of Wài Pó grating white radish for turnip cake. 'Do you really not care about getting better?'

'I know you care and I also care about you, but I... I... just...' I look away.

From the corner of my eye I see her walking towards me; her body is softer now.

'All this is for your own good. You'll have your transplant soon and then you'll be better again.'

'So you want me to go back to that hospital to have a transplant?'

'Yes. I'm going to go and try to sort it all out so that you can.'

I am pleased that she has finally told me the truth, but that hospital scares me. I think to myself about how I didn't book a flight because I was hoping Marlowe would do it for me. I was hoping one day she would see my feelings and the way she is hurting my spirit. But now I know her spirit is hurting too and I am the one who can fix it with a transplant thing.

Bì Yù walks into the living room. Her eyes are large and still, like marbles. 'Marlowe please, we need to talk. I just can't let this go. It's really been bothering me how so many organs can be available on demand. Did you read the articles Uncle Johnny sent about the other executions?'

Marlowe spun around. 'You read my mail?'

Bì Yù's eyes go sideways again. 'That's not the point. The thing is it might not just be criminals who are being executed. If it's people from labour camps, they could be political prisoners, Uighurs, unregistered Protestants and Catholics, Tibetan Buddhists, Falun Gong practitioners…'

'Am I the only one who cares enough to save Harper's life?' Marlowe's voice is low and sizzling. 'If she doesn't get this transplant, what do you think is going to happen?'

This again. Everyone is always talking to each other about saving my life without talking to me.

'If you go through with this, you'll regret it,' Bì Yù says. 'Please, Marlowe, you have to believe me – I've only got your best interests at heart.'

'ENOUGH!'

Marlowe slams her fist on the table. It makes my plum heart thump and my skin prickle. She has never made this sound of anger before. Her noise gets into me through my ears and races over my body. I throw my pen and writing book to the floor and quickly put my hands over my ears. I shut my eyes and mouth but it is too late. The sound in my body is taking over. The thumping is now in my vines and roots and it is like a gong going louder and faster. My skin hurts and I am sure the sound is going to burst out of me with all of my plum blood spilling everywhere.

'QUIET!' I scream and lie on the floor.

My insides understand the quiet.

My outsides understand the quiet.

The world is still.

I open one eye only. Bì Yù is next to me, her eyes and her mouth wide open. I turn my head. Marlowe is on the other side. Her eyes are wide open too but her mouth is moving.

'Harper, are you all right? Talk to me. Do you have pain in your chest?' Her sound is soft because my hands are still covering my ears.

'Marlowe has never made a fist noise before,' I say. Then I close my eyes. The world is breathing with me and the ground is flat under me.

Time is slow now. I open my eyes. Bì Yù is still there but Marlowe is gone. She is by the door, buttoning her coat. I stand up. She sees me then turns her head in a quick way.

'I'm going for a walk.'

I look out of the window.

'You must not go. There are grey Shanghai clouds outside the window which means that soon they will burst open and make you wet.'

But Marlowe doesn't care. Her coat swallows her up and she shuts the door to Bì Yù's apartment behind her. It is loud, like all of Marlowe's thoughts have been left inside for us to hear.

Bì Yù looks at me. 'Harper, would you like me to make you a longan and red date tea?'

The red date is good for the red blood, so I say yes and I wait – not for the tea, but for the loud to go.

The kettle is singing, then screaming and whooshing at high speed. I put my hands over my ears for this part. Again, the noise gets inside my ears and inside my head. It itches and burns and I squeeze my teeth tight and cross my legs and my toes so that no noise can get in.

'Harper.'

One hand is on my shoulder, the other has my tea. I see steam rising from the cup under her face. I let my hands drop from my ears and take a sip of tea. It is sweet and deep.

'Thank you.'

She smiles but I see that her eyes are not smiling; they are small and watery.

'You're welcome.' She kisses me on the cheek and I catch a whiff of her perfume. It is like pretend roses, the same smell as the pink lotion on her bedside table. I think to myself that she should come and smell some real roses in Dad's garden.

The air is calm now, so I take out my writing book and I make an entry.

Februrary I don't know what day anymore in the yeer 2000
The hart is a musle inside your chest. There is only one for each of us. Only one each.

And now I must put my pen down, because all of a sudden, I feel sadness in my throat. I cough to get it out but it just grows bigger and starts to feel hot. My face is getting tighter and it is rising rising rising to my eyes until water escapes in a big way, running all over my cheeks. Luckily, Marlowe is not here to see.

Marlowe

I had spent a day with my stomach in my mouth, waiting for Mr Zhāng to call. When he never did, I took a cab to the Red Lantern Hotel in search of him. Bì Yù should have been with me, translating, but she refused to come. Why did my family abandon me whenever I needed them most? I was tired of people letting me down. I wasn't going to let the broker be one of them.

In the hotel lobby I asked the receptionist to call Mr Zhāng in room 1109.

She told me he had already checked out.

It took a moment for her words to register, but when they did, I ran to the toilets and vomited. I thought of everything I had done to get to this point. I'd paid him all the money Mum left me, I'd dragged my gravely ill sister all the way to Shanghai and I'd lied to my family. The possibility that it was all for nothing, that Harper might not get her transplant after all, made my insides turn cold.

Overwhelmed by sadness, I left the hotel and got into a cab at the rank outside. But instead of giving the driver the address of Bì Yù's apartment, I asked to be dropped at Zhōngshān Park.

I followed a path through the park, raising my head to admire a wide pink arch made by the branches of plum blossom trees.

This is Harper's special place and I refused to bring her here.

I sat on a bench and studied the closest tree. She would spend hours in this park when she was small. It was always her favourite place in Shanghai. I recalled the many childhood holidays spent in Shanghai and the family picnics we had in this park, Harper sitting under these trees, singing to herself.

And I have refused to bring her here.

How consumed by the past I had become. My memories were like beads on Harper's necklace. Sometimes, they caught the light and shone. Sometimes they fell, broke, and I would have to pick up the pieces.

In front of me, a young couple walked hand in hand. He moved his arm to wrap it around her waist and nuzzled her cheek. She smiled, her face glowing. His lips hovered over hers, teasing for a kiss. She laughed and leaned in. I couldn't take my eyes off them. The sight of them made me ache.

Beads of memory twinkled. One fell, and I was back in London, with Olly.

—

Fairy lights pulsed red and green. We were at a Christmas party in a Holborn share house. It was late, music throbbed, the spiced scent of mulled wine lingered. We were standing in the middle of the room, a throng of sweating bodies writhing around us to the beat of the music.

Olly took my hand. His body swayed to the music and mine followed, guided by his. Dancing became easy this way.

After a while the music changed to something slower, softer. I could feel myself turning red. *I can't do this. I don't know how.*

He drew me close.

'Don't think so much,' he whispered.

I closed my eyes and let the weight of my body sink into his. For a while we moved together and I realised I was no longer thinking about how to dance.

We felt so natural together, easy and tender. Was this love? Was this what my parents had felt? Was this what Harper felt with Louis?

I had never felt this way before. Never wanted to.

'Marlowe.' Olly was smiling in a lopsided kind of way; it made me dizzy. Our eyes locked. I wanted to look away but I couldn't.

'I love you.'

Before his words registered, I felt his lips flutter over mine.

Wait. Be careful.

It was as though the floor was shifting beneath my feet.

'I'm so lucky,' he murmured. He ran his fingertips over my cheek, brushing the hair away from my face. 'I really love you.'

I froze as the words hit me. A current ran through me, sharp and icy. I bolted from the living room, down the hall and through the front door, out into the cold. Frigid air assaulted my lungs with each gasping breath. I sat on the steps with my head between my legs.

It didn't make sense. I recounted the seconds, minutes and hours I had spent with Olly, wanting to tell him I loved him but was unable to. Perhaps it was cowardice, perhaps it was fear – although I had no idea what I was afraid of. And now that he had told me he loved me, it was the perfect time for me to say it back. Yet I hadn't... couldn't.

The front door opened and then Olly was sitting beside me on the step.

'I'm sorry. I didn't mean to make you feel uncomfortable.'

'It's my fault.' Although I knew this much, I couldn't explain myself further.

'You don't need to say it back; I still –'

'Thank you.'

Thank you?

He smiled again, always lopsided, then ducked his head so I couldn't see his face.

◆

Wind grazed the side of my cheek like a fine blade to the skin. As I crossed the busy road to Bì Yù's apartment block, dodging bicycles, motorcyclists and cars, my eyes met those of an old lady crossing in the other direction. She smiled at me, and dimples appeared on her cheeks.

Dimples.

I smiled back, clutching the locket at my throat.

Bì Yù was cooking dinner when I entered. How she could do something so mundane when we were in the middle of a crisis baffled me.

'Spaghetti is for dinner,' Harper said from the sofa. She looked pale; her hair was plastered to the sides of her head with sweat. Did she have a fever? I went to her and put my hand to her forehead, but she pulled away.

I tried to remember where I had left the thermometer. On the kitchen bench, I thought.

Smells of sautéing onion, garlic and basil wafted up from the stove. Bì Yù was emptying a pot of pasta into a dish. She saw me and set the pan back onto the counter. Her eyes were soft. I felt the harder edges of my frustration melt.

'Did you find Mr Zhāng?' she asked.

I shook my head.

'So what now? Will you take her home?'

'I can't let her go,' I said, avoiding her eyes. I picked up the thermometer and cleaned the tip with my shirt.

Her face tightened. 'But do you really want to save her like this?'

We stood there facing one another, without making eye contact, without speaking. I listened to the humming of the refrigerator, the sound of the exhaust fan sucking up steam from the cooling pasta, the sound of her breath, of my own.

The sound of the clock on the wall. *Tick tick tick.*

I tried to quell the voice in my head telling me that Mr Zhāng had run off with my money. I put my hand on the phone and looked at Bì Yù.

'Please.' My voice cracked. 'I know you don't agree with what I'm doing, but I need you. Please.'

She stared at my hand on the phone for what felt like hours, then she brushed my hand aside, picked up the phone. I handed her the slip of paper Anita gave me and Bì Yù dialled the number.

It rang out.

Shit.

My stomach lurched.

'Try again. Please try again.'

She pressed redial.

Again, it rang out.

I took the phone from her and dialled the number myself. The number I had rehearsed in my head over and over again, each night when I couldn't sleep.

'*Wéi?*'

Thank whatever God might or might not exist.

I thrust the phone at Bì Yù.

She spoke in rapid Chinese. Paused. Spoke again, her voice rising.

'Bì Yù!'

She slammed down the phone.

'What did he say?' I demanded.

She was panting.

'Tell me' – I tried to keep my voice steady – 'exactly what he said.'

Her cheeks were red, eyes flashing. 'He said there was a problem with the donor. We have to wait another three days. It's time to stop, Marlowe.'

Stop. But I couldn't.

I knew she was going to argue with me again and I didn't want to hear it, so I walked out of the kitchen with the thermometer and took Harper's temperature. It was elevated, but not dangerously so.

Leaving her on the couch, I went to my room. There I sat on the bed and counted my breaths until I was calm again.

Harper

Am I sleeping? Resting on the couch, my eyes are closed and my breath is like water. I see the man with no face, more real than he looked in my storybook. He moves like a shadow. When he is gone, I feel my body change.

My heart is tired, more tired than ever before. It feels like a long and slow sigh of air.

My time is running out. But now I can say I am really not scared.

Why? I am not sure, but I feel that my heart is full: full of all the people I love. I think to myself that love is many things and one thing it does is take care of those you love. I will take care of my Marlowe. Even though I haven't told her yet, I made my decision to be okay about having the transplant she wants. I will be better, not sick but alive in this body.

'Better is a good thing,' I say out loud, but then something moves like electricity in my blood. With someone else's heart, will I be able to love like I do now?

I don't only love people, I love my words too.

Will I be able to write like I do now?

I need to finish my story. I really do, but every time I try, I can't get the ending right.

Something is missing. Now, instead of trying to write in my

storybook again, I take out a dictionary, my flowery paper, an envelope and my coloured pens and write Louis another letter.

To My Dear Louis,
My hart does miss you. When I see your fase in my mind the beeting inside my chest is fast. I know this is a sine of romanse.

Marlowe says I have to have someone elses hart very soon. I do not want this new hart but now I feel calm all over me like melting buter because I will do this trans-plant thing for Marlowe. She needs it more than me.

Some times love meens a word called sac-ri-fice. After I looked this up in the dictonry I understod in my brane that sac-ri-fice is when you give up your own hopes and dreems so that another person will be happy. And this is what I wil do for my Marlowe.

I have the dictonry in my hand now and I wanted to tell you abot a brave thing I am doing. I looked up how to spell the word dead. D.E.A.D. It meens no longer a live. See, I am riting it now to tell you I am not scared of this word anymore. Not scared to rite it, not scared to say it. Even tho I understand in my hart and in my mind that I need a trans-plant to stay in my body and a live with two feet on the grond I still am not afrade anymore if I am not in this body and all that is left of me is my hum. My hum that will be in everything
the wind
the see
the sand
the air
in you.

I don't no wen this hapened or how but I want you to no
that I do not have long before the beetng of my very own hart
will run out. Even tho it is sick, it is full of love for you.

My sweet Romeo,

I love you.

Harper明华Míng Huà Eve

When I put my pen down, I suddenly know what I need to do to find the ending of my story. I need to see my plum tree before it is too late.

'Knock, knock.' Bì Yù comes into the room. 'How're you feeling?' She stands behind my chair and puts her hand on my back. Everyone keeps asking me this question.

'I'm fine.' I don't tell her about the stuff that came out of my coughing this morning, sticky and the colour of roses.

'What are you doing?'

I hide my letter under the table. Marlowe says I am not allowed to send people letters while we are here because this trip is a secret, so I am saving them for when I get home and will deliver them in person. It is a bit confusing if I think about it, because Marlowe said Louis knew about my trip to Shanghai but then she said I am not allowed to tell him where I am.

Bì Yù looks under the table.

'Can I see? I won't get angry, I promise.' She smiles. I can feel her words; they come into my ears and through my veins like warm water and it feels nice. In this moment, I know that it is safe to give her the letter.

'This is a love letter to Louis. But don't tell Marlowe.'

Bì Yù's smile is bigger now. She looks at me and does not blink. I am sure she is thinking hard in her brain. I see her eyes move slowly back and forth, back and forth over my words and her breathing seems very still.

'What's wrong?'

'Nothing.' She is shaking her head, but I can see from her face she is not being honest.

'What is it, Bì Yù? Are you mad at me for writing the letter? I'm sorry.'

'No, I am the one who should be sorry.' She folds up my paper and hands it back to me. 'I just realised, I am doing the same thing to you that Marlowe is, but in a different way.'

I don't really understand what she is saying but I nod and smile.

'I have been so caught up in finding the truth behind what is happening with all these transplants in China that I never really listened to you and what you want.'

I want to tell her it is okay because I am already used to this thing of people not listening to me, but before I have a chance to get my words out, she is already saying she is sorry and asking me to forgive her.

'Neither you nor I want this heart transplant, but our reasons are different. My mistake was that I should have tried to understand and respect yours.'

'It's okay. I have changed my mind. I will do this transplant for Marlowe.'

She looks at me and she shakes her head. 'My dear Harper, you don't have to do that.'

'I know. This is my decision and you can listen to this one now. Thanks.'

I see her eyes moving, searching my face, and now she is trying to find her words. Slowly she bows her head. I see she has given up.

'Would you like me to send this letter for you?'

My heart jumps and it sings. Then I remember all the other letters I wrote that I had to hide in a secret place under the bed. I get them out and give them to Bì Yù. Her hands become full.

She sits on the bed. Her fingers move slowly through them. Her face is long and her chin is nearly at her chest.

'Could you send those letters too?'

'Of course.' I like the way she touches them, like they are little baby animals and she is their mother. 'Harper…' She looks up at me. 'When you have finished writing your letter, why don't you put my address on the back of the envelope?'

'Okay.' She is full of good ideas.

'You could even tell Louis in your letter that you are in Shanghai staying with me…' She blinks a lot. I know this means she is thinking something nervous and it is making me feel nervous, like all the blood in my body is whooshing at high speed. 'Just so that Louis will know you're safe.'

I think about this in my brain for a bit. 'This means I am going to upset Marlowe. She said our trip is a secret.'

'She won't need to know. This will be *our* secret.'

There are so many secrets in China. I am feeling like all the secrets are knotted in my body, all the way up to my neck, and soon they might unknot themselves and spill out of my mouth.

Bì Yù writes her address on the back of one of the envelopes and tells me to copy it.

'Do it as quick as you can, before Marlowe comes out.'

I nod a yes at her.

'Will you send this by Express, DHL, Speedy Gonzales post?'

'Of course.' She smiles and leaves my bedroom.

I add a bit quickly to the last letter.

PS Louis I cannot wait to marry you at sunset.

Louis I am in Shang-hi.

There are so many secrets.

    Love, Harper

I copy the address onto the back of *all* the letters. I do it so many times that after a while I don't need to copy because I can remember in my mind the order of the words that tell Louis how to get to Bì Yù's home. When I am finished, I leave my room to give Bì Yù my letters, but then I stop in the hallway, because I hear her on the phone. She is in the kitchen, talking in a hushed way.

'Hi, Uncle James? It's Bì Yù. I'm so sorry – I've made a big mistake. I was confused... I thought I was helping Harper, but I'm not. She and Marlowe are with me, waiting for a transplant.'

Dad? I want to run to the phone and call his name but air is too hard to catch.

'It is supposed to be scheduled for three days' time, but who knows? The broker's really shady. Marlowe's determined to go through with it and I can't make her see sense, but maybe you can... That would be great. Let me know your flight details.'

Her voice is long and soft and slithery, like a big S for secret. I am beginning to think this is the language of my whole family.

Marlowe

Warm light oozed down the middle of my face. I heard fingers plucking the strings of a guitar; the sound was gentle, familiar.

I opened my eyes to the sky. It was not the blue I was expecting, but bright yellow.

I stood, and found I was wearing an ivory lace gown that reached my feet. Why was I wearing lace?

I heard someone call my name. Following the sound of the voice, I saw Olly sitting on the edge of Cleeve Hill, singing. His lyrics told me I was old, as old as the Jurassic rock on which he sat.

Dry grass fell from my body as I walked. I brushed hair from my face and a daisy fell too. Momentarily, I wondered if I was Harper, but Olly was singing my name.

By the time I reached his side, the sound of his voice had faded and all I could see were his hands: outstretched and cupped together. Coaxing them open, I found a monarch pupa. I could see the outline of a black-and-orange wing inside the waxy casing.

The pupa should have been hanging from a twig or a branch; Olly must have disturbed it. Yet I wasn't outraged – I was mesmerised as I watched the delicate creature struggling to break free from its self-made womb.

I tried to keep my breathing shallow, so as not to disturb the birthing. Time seemed distorted, sped up. The pupa was like a lung, cracked at its base. With an expand and contract, it pushed itself out, head first. Its wings were small, wet and creased, its abdomen rounded with fluid. I waited until it beat its wings, pumping the stored liquid through its veins. And then up, up it flew. The sky had changed colour and was now the same orange as the monarch's wings. Camouflaged, the butterfly was now invisible.

When I lowered my gaze, I saw Mum standing before me. Her long hair loose around her shoulders. She was wearing an orange cheongsam. I wanted to tell her that was the wrong colour, but I couldn't speak. My throat was gripped by a raw longing for her. She took my hand and fastened a gold bracelet around my wrist; I knew it had been given to her on her wedding day. She kissed me on the forehead and told me everything was as it should be.

As she turned to leave, I tried to call to her, but no sound emerged. I kept trying, but the more I tried, the further she got, until she was gone.

Harper

'Mum! Mum!' Marlowe's voice is screaming from across the corridor.

I open my eyes and sit up in bed.

'Muuuuuum!' Her sound is high then falls sharply.

I make my feet wriggle out of the warm sheets and, with all my strength, I lift my body out of bed. I see little white stars in the corners of my eyes and my world feels thin and dizzy as I walk as fast as I can to her room.

She is asleep in her bed with her arms crossed over her heart. Her forehead is tight and her bottom lip sticks out. I have not seen her like this before and it makes something inside of my heart rip and it feels like I have been cut open already, bleeding bleeding.

As I stare at her, I think in my mind that there is a rotting seed inside my Marlowe, and this time, I can make it better.

Marlowe

'No! I'm not calling him for you!' Bì Yù and I were standing by the phone. 'This isn't what Harper wants – we have to respect that.'

The feelings bubbling inside of me as I stared at her were so intense, so convoluted, tangled, torturous, that I struggled to make sense of them. I feared if I opened my mouth I would say something I'd regret, so I didn't speak as she left the kitchen. I heard the sound of chair legs against the floor as she sat at the dining table. I exhaled. She hadn't totally abandoned me.

I dialled the number for Mr Zhāng with the phone on speaker.

'Wéi?'

I struggled in broken Chinese to ask when we were to admit Harper to hospital for her surgery. As usual, his response was delivered so fast I couldn't keep up. He ignored my attempts to interject, to ask for clarification, talking over the top of me.

Before I knew it, Bì Yù was back in the kitchen, shouting into the speaker. I had never seen her so angry before. Mr Zhāng seemed stunned into silence. Then the line went dead.

'What's going on?' All I could muster was a whisper.

'He said there was another problem with the donor; there'll be another delay and he has to increase the fees. He also said that Harper's tests showed she needs a kidney transplant as well. I told him he was a scumbag and asked for a refund. That's when he hung up.' Her face was pale.

A cacophony of emotions began to swell inside me and words came pouring out, unfiltered.

'Go on – say I told you so, tell me how badly I've failed! Tell me how I've been ripped off, how I've squandered my inheritance and wasted everyone's time. Tell me how unethical I've been, tell me how morally –'

'This isn't about you!'

Her words stopped me short. I stared at her, breathing hard. No, it wasn't about me. What was I thinking? This was about Harper. I felt the gears shift in my mind.

'Please, call him back and tell him Harper can't wait any longer.'

'I know you're hurting, Marlowe, we all are.'

I hated that look she was giving me, the pity on her face.

'You're so *simple*,' I snarled.

I watched Bì Yù's face change as my insult sank in. I opened my mouth to apologise, but it was too late.

'I'm tired of all this. Why don't you just relearn the language your mother taught you and speak to him yourself? I'm sick of doing your dirty work for you.'

She strode from the room.

'How dare you!' I shouted at her back. I followed her into the living room. 'How dare you bring Mum into this!'

'Marlowe.' Suddenly Harper was standing between us. 'You don't see with your mind and heart that you are the one who is upset about Mum.' She was breathing quickly as she spoke, and I felt like my lungs were catching up. 'You think you are fighting for me, but really you are fighting for Mum.'

Bì Yù must have put her up to this. She wouldn't... she couldn't...

'Everything in your body is becoming dark and rotten with this.'

There wasn't enough air. The room felt tight and small.

'Stop it.'

'Her body is *gone* and you are broken. Your heart is broken.'

Shut up. Just shut up.

'I don't need to listen to this.'

'You never listen!' Harper strode out of the room.

I tried to count, to empty my mind, but it wasn't working.

Mā ma. You felt close. Too close.

'Why do you think you are going to the ends of the earth to save Harper when she doesn't even want to be saved?' Bì Yù asked softly.

Mā ma. The longing made me want to heave.

'No.' I shook my head. 'No.' I tried to think of something to say but my mind was blank.

I went to Harper's room – I had to tell her she was wrong; this was not about Mum, it was about *her*.

But Harper's room was empty.

Empty.

I went back to the living room.

'Where did Harper go?' I felt a curl in my stomach.

Bì Yù's eyes widened.

'Where did Harper go?' I repeated.

'Harper!' I ran through the apartment, calling her name, searching. I could hear Bì Yù doing the same.

We met again in the living room. 'She's too weak to go anywhere by herself,' I said frantic. I felt my knees buckle and before I knew it I was on the floor.

'Marlowe!' Bì Yù ran to me. 'I'll go after her – she can't have got far. You stay here in case she comes back.' Bì Yù headed for the front door.

How could I have let this happen?

I went back to Harper's room, hoping to find some clue to her disappearance.

On the desk, her autobiographical storybook lay open.

In my drems I smell roses. Their sweetnes is all arond me when I wake up in the morning and it stays with me when I go to sleep at nite time.

Did mum smell roses when her body was sick?

My body is doing strang things like rite now my moth and tong are watering for apples diped in salt. Wài Pó says this is wat mum was eeting when I was inside her belly. This is how I no that she is coming for me soon.

I wrote about the man with no fase called deth. But now I wonder in my mind and in my hart if he is a she and she is mum?

I have been thinking a lot in my mind about what hapens when the body is no more. I think to my self about the spases in betweene things. A plase in between plases. This is were storys come from. This is were mum lives. This is were I think I will go wen my time in this body is over. I was scared of this plase and somtimes I still am, but most of all I am scared for my Marlowe.

Even tho I have desided to do the trans-plant, I still ask myself if I shuld get this new hart? This hart that belongs to someone else? The hart that has its own loves and does not no about the things that I love. But I worry about leeving Marlowe alone becos she does not no how to here the mesages from the in between. How to reed the signs. If I go, she will not no how to here my hum. She will not here me wispering in the trees, she will not see me in someone elses feet when they have the gliter nail polish on and she will not feel me under the lite of our one and only moon. My Marlowe does not under stand these things.

My hart is broken, but so is Marlowes. I think in my mind that hers broke when she was 9 years old when mum left her body. Marlowe has never been abel to fix her broken hart, but I can. I can fix it for her. But I will never tell her this. She does not no how to here it.

There is still so much I want to tell her. I want to say I have seen her long hope and it has been like two big arms holding me. I want to tell her I am sorry about my hart and that even though I have the Up syndrome, I could not stop it from being sick.

Marlowe and I are con-nec-ted by an invisibel, sparkelling thred and when my hart is gone, im scared hers will go too.

This is why I will take the hart that is not mine. This is why I will do it.

I will fix my Marlowe. I will make things better again.

An unfamiliar calm washed over my body. I felt my feet on the floor, as if I was aware of the ground beneath me for the first time.

'What have I done?'

I touched my cheeks; they were wet and warm. I let my fingertips linger on my skin, accustoming myself to the texture of my sadness.

I closed Harper's book, noticing as I did the title she had written on the cover: *The Plum Hart.*

I grabbed my coat and ran for the door.

Harper

Cross the road to reach the park on the other side. Look up, then you will see an arrow pointing to the gates. Turn the corner and at the entrance to Zhōngshān Park is a big gate.

I repeat in my mind the instructions Ān Chén gave me when I asked her how to get to the park.

I leave the lobby of Bì Yù's apartment. The sky is angry, shouting balls of ice from the sky. They hit me hard on my head and shoulders. I walk slowly as I am alone, no one is pushing me in my special chair today. My breath is difficult to take in and let out. It was a good thing I brought the air tank for my lungs.

Cross the road.

I look to the left and I look to the right. The streets are more quiet than normal. I can see puffs of warm air leaving my lips. As I am walking on the wide road, an old man on a bicycle goes past me. On the back, in a basket, he has two little white dogs. I have to stop and watch because they are so cute.

I hear a beeeeeeeeeeeeep of a car horn, too close. I drop my air tank when I put my hands over my ears. A man gets out of a blue taxi. Even though my hearing is shut, I can still make out his sounds. He spits rude words into my face in Chinese: rude words that would make Wài Pó very upset.

My poor little heart is moving fast and heavy in my wet chest. I am feeling a bit dizzy now. I cough, pick up my air tank and put the mask over my mouth. The shouting stops.

Beeeeeeeeeeeeeeeeeep comes again. I want to lie flat on the ground, but then I hear Louis's calm voice in my head. He says, *My dear, sweet Harper, all you have to do is put one foot in front of the other one.*

I remember him saying this the last time I wanted to cross the road in Hong Kong, and I was a bit scared by all the noises. He told me to count my steps: 'One, two, three, four...'

So, this is what I do.

The cold feels like big fish with sharp teeth, biting at my bare skin. I pull the hood of my jumper over my head and walk on. Five, six, seven... My hood keeps falling off and I only have two hands, so I stop again to fix it.

Beeeeeeeeeeeep. I drop my special air tank again and my mask falls down with it. My chest is tight like there are big hands around my heart, strangling it. With all my strength, I move as fast as I can to the pavement. Eight, nine, ten... I'm nearly there. I can feel my heart shiver and shake. I might be sick. Eleven, twelve, thirteen... there is a fire in my throat... fourteen... whoosh. My heart skips one beat and I arrive onto the pavement. It is very hard to get air into my lungs, so I sit on a bench. I want to tell Louis about how brave I have been and the thought makes me feel happy. But I cannot feel happy for long, because in front of me I can see my poor, old air tank getting knocked about by wheels of the cars on the road. Poor old air tank.

I try to remember what Ān Chén said to do next: *Look up, then you will see an arrow pointing to the gates.* I stand, but I am a bit wobbly. It is like the blood from my head is travelling at high speed into my feet. I grab hold of the side of the bench but do not sit down. I have to keep walking, before it is too late.

As I walk, I listen to the sound of my breath. It is like a grumpy old man growling. I look up and see a green arrow the same colour as the trees, I follow it around the corner. *Turn the corner and at the entrance to Zhōngshān Park is a big gate.*

I see it in front of me! It looks strong, tall and has a dark brown roof and cream walls. The colours together remind me of vanilla ice cream with melting chocolate on top.

The sounds from the street outside become quiet. Above me and around me are trees, their long arms, vines and roots reach together and touch above my head in a half-moon shape, covered in pink blossoms. The petals fall to the ground like whispering snow. It feels like a wedding day, so bright and full with colour. I forget about all my body pains for a moment and continue down the path as if I am floating. I remember how Mum used to bring me, Marlowe and Bì Yù here to play when we were small. After Mum died, Wài Pó brought us. I still feel Mum's spirit with me when the leaves on the trees pat and shiver like the sound of falling rain.

Her blossoms are a darker shade of pink than the rest. No plums yet, but I know when the season changes, they will come. There is a deep mark that Marlowe and Bì Yù made on her trunk when they were small. It is in the shape of a star. They did it with a pen knife and the sharpness of it made me cry. I told them that was a very mean thing to do.

'I am so sorry,' I say, touching the star with my fingertip.

My hands wrap around her trunk and I lean in. She is rough, but she feels warmer than the air.

Even though I am wearing a thick coat, I am sweating. My body is hot and cold hot and cold hot and cold.

I move my hands all the way down to where the base of her ripples under the soil. This is where she takes life. She is a strong tree.

My chest hurts again, like a tight tight tight squeeze. I crouch down onto my knees. My sound thumps loudly in my head: Da dum da dum da da dum. I feel a danger in my heart. No, it can't be.

I look up again.

Oh, my special tree, look at how you have grown. Your branches are so long now, and full of colour. I sit by her on the earth and lean my head against her trunk. Da da dum dum, da dum da dum…

I am so tired now. So very, very tired.

Marlowe

I was hit by a blast of cold air as I ran from Bì Yù's apartment building. I was standing by the kerb, waiting for a break in the traffic, when I saw Harper's oxygen tank on the far side of the road. It had been run over and the mask had cracked and split. 'No!'

I crossed the road and my mind went wild with images of Harper: on the ground, bleeding, having been hit by a car… or lying frozen and blue-lipped in a remote corner of the park, unable to breathe.

I ran through the large gate into Zhōngshān Park and remembered walking through it holding Mum's hand while Harper and Bì Yù raced ahead. I heard Mum's voice say, 'Míng Yuè, look up.' Above us was a canopy of blossoms in magenta and soft pinks.

The path forked and without thinking I chose the right-hand path.

Then I saw the flash of a red coat in the distance: it was Harper, slumped against a plum tree. Bì Yù was already by her side.

I sprinted, my legs on fire.

The sight of Harper shocked the breath from my lungs. Eyes closed, she looked eerily serene, her bruised lips parted in a half-smile.

My fingers fumbled at the cool skin of her neck for a pulse. I held my breath… then exhaled. It was faint, but it was there.

'You wait here – I'll get an ambulance.' Bì Yù turned and ran.

I took off my coat and wrapped it around Harper's limp body, then I sat beneath the tree.

I lifted her onto my lap, drawing her close to share my warmth.

'Oh, Harper,' I whispered, 'forgive me.'

—

The siren wailed overhead as we squeezed in beside Harper's gurney in the ambulance. Two paramedics dressed in black and white stabbed the skin on her arm with a large needle as they tried to find a vein. Her eyes opened and closed as she drifted in and out of consciousness. Blood oozed from her puncture wounds and I felt the veins in my own body shudder. *Don't hurt her!* I wanted to scream, and at the same time, *Hurry, please fix her, try harder for a vein!* Wires threaded out from her chest under the blankets.

'They can't find a vein because she's too dehydrated.' I grabbed hold of Bì Yù's hand and gripped it tightly. Bì Yù stroked my hand, like Harper would. Her touch was comforting.

Harper's rasping breath grew louder. 'My sound.'

I looked up.

Harper's eyes fluttered open. 'My sound.'

'Tell me…' I steadied my voice. 'What are you trying to say?'

She pointed to her chest. 'Listen.'

I put my ear to her heart. The beating in her chest was faint, its rhythm erratic.

Abruptly an alarm started to blare. She was flatlining.

I opened my mouth to scream, but no sound came out.

The paramedics moved swiftly, pumping Harper's chest and filling her lungs with oxygen.

I found my voice. 'Fix her! You have to fix her!'

Bì Yù pulled me close and held me tight. I didn't know if it was my body shaking or hers.

I should have been more persistent; I should have got her a transplant earlier.

But then I thought of the last entry in Harper's storybook. I closed my eyes. I heard a voice in my head: *I am water. I am water.* I saw Mum's face. She was smiling at me.

'I'm so sorry, Harper.' Words spilled out of my mouth. 'I should've listened to you. I'm so sorry.' I recalled now how she had begged me to take her home, how she had told me over and over that she didn't want someone else's heart. 'I'm so, so sorry.' But my words were futile. They couldn't change anything. They couldn't take me back in time.

Suddenly, the alarm stopped and beeping from the heart monitor resumed. The male paramedic told us that they had found a sinus rhythm. The female paramedic ceased performing CPR.

I exhaled. *She's back.* A swelling in my throat found its way to my eyes. We swayed to the left as the ambulance swiftly turned a corner and came to a stop. The doors swung open and chill air rushed in. As the medics slid the gurney from the back of the ambulance and wheeled it into the hospital, I ran alongside it, gripping Harper's hand. Doctors met us at the door, speaking quickly.

I looked at Bì Yù. 'She can't die here,' I said. 'I need to take her home. She needs to say good—' *Goodbye.* I found myself choking on the word. 'I need to call Dad. I need to tell him…'

'Don't worry,' Bì Yù said. 'I've already spoken with him. He's on his way. They're all on their way.'

My shoulders slumped in relief.

Harper's hand twitched in mine. I looked down, her chestnut hair was splayed over the pillow. Her face was smooth, unmarked by tension. She seemed so peaceful.

'I'm so sorry,' I whispered.

We had reached the entrance to the ICU. The doctors told us we couldn't come any further. Bì Yù took me by the shoulders. Harper's hand slipped from mine. I watched as she disappeared from sight. Large doors swung back and forth until they finally settled.

Part Three

Harper

Outside, the sun looks like an old man; clouds float over his golden chin making a long beard. I think to myself that I am glad to see the day falling into night. I have missed the sky, the air, the world outside the hospital in Shanghai. Most of all, I have missed all of my loves: my family and my Louis. I am so glad in my heart to be home.

Here, in the living room, I am lying in my special hospital kind of bed that they made for me, facing the garden and the sea. I think to myself that if my life were a book, I would be in my final chapter. I had so many plans:

Learn how to play the guitar.

Open a cafe with Wài Pó.

Get married to Louis and move into our own house.

Watch Marlowe get married.

Publish *The Plum Heart*.

I close my eyes and see my mum's face. With a brave heart, I tell her: 'I am too young to die.' I ask her: 'Who will I be when I'm gone?'

But she does not reply.

Thoughts in my brain turn off and on like Christmas lights. But one that keeps coming to me is that my illness is like a puzzle that I am not meant to solve. It is okay if the pieces do not fit together and now I feel like maybe I can leave them that way. After this, I have easier thoughts. The other day I found one grey hair on my head. Is dying making my colour fade?

I think to myself that I should catch a few of these thoughts and record them on paper, like building a wonderful bridge with my pen from this world to the next and back.

I take out my autobiographical storybook and make a last entry for the day.

Marlowe

I took a seat at my desk, now overlooking the garden. I could hear music playing in Dad's bedroom – a recording of one of Mum's pieces, something she had composed herself. The timbre of her piano was bright and rich, the notes cascading with a lightness and ease that could only have come from a pianist who was happy. Time stood still and I let myself flow with the music, letting myself go in a way I never had before. I wasn't trying to understand how it worked; I was just listening, really listening, perhaps in the same way Harper would. *Don't think so much.*

I was reminded of that Holborn Christmas party and how I was able to let go with Olly.

I looked at my watch. Olly would be here in an hour. I felt a flutter ripple through my belly. I opened the door and made my way along the hall to the landing. The house was full with the sounds of my family. Wài Pó, Bì Yù, Aunt Lǐ Nà and Louis's mother, Deborah, chatted to each other in the kitchen. Uncle Bǐng Wén and Louis's dad, Michael, sat in a corner of the living room drinking whisky. Occasionally, Uncle Bǐng Wén made his way to the kitchen to tell the ladies to keep their voices down so as not to disturb Harper. I found myself becoming acutely aware of Irene's absence. Dad had said she felt that she kept making mistakes with Harper, kept hurting her, and that we were all better off without her.

Hurting her.

Was Irene really able to acknowledge this? A part of me couldn't quite believe it; it sounded too good to be true. Then I thought of the mistakes I had made over the last few weeks. I too was fallible. I too had made some bad choices. Yes, I should reach out to Irene; after all, I was the one who drove her away. The only thing stopping me was Harper. If I had learned one thing in Shanghai, it was to respect her wishes. She should be the one to decide if she wanted Irene to come home.

I leaned against the banister and watched my sister in the living room below. She lay in the new hospital bed we had bought for her, facing the garden. She had asked for it to be placed in the living room so that she could be in the middle of things, so that she wouldn't have to be alone during this time. Her palliative care nurse, Samantha, was injecting something into Harper's cannula. She spoke softly to Harper, gently stroking the skin as fluid entered her veins. I said a silent 'thank you' for Samantha. She was making Harper's remaining time on earth a little easier; she was giving us all a chance to enjoy Harper's company and spend time with her in the comfort of our home.

'Coming through!' Louis bustled into the living room carrying a tray piled high with chocolate chip cookies. He held a crumbling biscuit to Harper's lips.

She took a small bite, then shook her head. 'No more.' Her voice was gravelly and old. Although I had accepted Harper's decision not to pursue a transplant, the pain of watching her deteriorate and knowing there was nothing I could do to stop it hurt me more than I felt my body could hold.

'Never mind, my sweet lady, I'll eat what you can't.' He finished the cookies at an alarming rate. She carefully leaned over to wipe the crumbs from his chin. Watching them together struck me hard in the ribs. The two of them planned to wed in a few days. They wouldn't have long together as a married couple and I had taken precious moments away from them. Since we had arrived home, I thought of our time in Shanghai with regret. Seeing Harper and Louis like this, I wished that I had never separated them.

'Grief can make us do strange things.' Dad was standing next to me. I didn't know how long he'd been there. His presence was quiet – even more so since we had returned from China. 'I want you to know that I am... that I feel...'

Oh God, he was trying to have a deep and meaningful.

'I'm so...'

Come on, Dad.

'I'm so proud of you.' He put his arm around my shoulder and drew me close.

His words stunned me.

'How can you say this after everything I've done?'

He was quiet for a moment. 'It's not easy... it's not easy saying goodbye.'

My chest tightened. This was too much; I wanted Dad to stop voicing what I needed to leave unsaid. But instead of pulling away, I found myself wanting to lean in. I buried my head in his chest and breathed in: cologne, bitter coffee, laundry detergent and, finally, the garden: sweet florals and fresh salt air. Our home. My father: the one who stayed, the one who never left. His arms wrapped tighter around me.

When I pulled away, he looked at me and smiled. 'How do I look?' He adjusted his blue bow tie and smoothed his salmon-pink shirt.

'A bit overdressed,' I said.

'I want to make a good impression.'

And just like that I was smiling.

Harper

I hear the soft, quick, pit-pat of Marlowe's feet coming down the stairs. I always know when it is her sound, even though hers is the quietest of all of us. Sometimes I think to myself that she belongs to the air and not the earth.

I ask Louis if he will give me some time alone with my sister. The love of her heart, Oliver, is coming soon and I am very excited about this but I want to be with her by myself before I have to share her.

Louis says, 'Okay,' and he kisses me on the forehead and tells me he will go to the kitchen and help everyone cook dinner. I know this means that he will be tasting all the food and get full in his stomach before the meal is put onto the table.

Marlowe comes around to the side of my bed and takes my hand. She is wearing a blue jumper, the kind of blue that lives inside a jewel and swims deep deep deep. The kind of blue that matches her eyes. She has always been the most beautiful woman I have ever known with her pearl rice skin, marble eyes and long, coffee-coloured hair, and the way she moves quietly, easily... the word is *graceful*. And when she smiles, her hum spreads out from her gentle heart and fills the room. Even though I love my body and its brokenness, and I think I am also a beautiful woman because I love my eyes and my hair and my skin, I have never glowed as brightly as she does. The sad thing in my heart is that I know my Marlowe will never see herself the way I do.

The grandfather sun has sunk into the ocean, and the night has taken over our day. It is just me and my Marlowe left in the living room. Samantha, Uncle Bĭng Wén and Michael have left us alone.

'Want to watch the *National Geographic* channel together?' she suggests. 'We could learn something useful. There's a good program on the melting of ice caps in Alaska and its effect on the natural habitat.' She likes those two words very much: *natural habitat*. If I did not feel so tired, I would look them up in a dictionary, but for now I find them a bit boring so I have to shake my head.

'No, thank you.' A bit of my hair is loose over my face and she brushes it away. Her palms brush the top of my head in a way that makes my body feel safe and calm. Then I have a bright thought. Beside me on the bedside table is a wedding magazine. I turn the pages and show Marlowe a lovely photo of a woman in a fluffy dress. Her hair is done in a low French braid bun. A very special low French braid bun.

'Can you do my hair like this?'

She nods and smiles. She has always been good at braiding because this is something that she learned from our mum who used to do her hair every morning before school. I remember when I was old enough to have my hair braided, Mum would ask Marlowe to do it. She stood next to her and watched. If she did something wrong, Mum would tell her, and if she did something right, she would also tell her. Mum did that with a lot of things before she left, showing Marlowe what she needed to know.

She begins to move her fingers through my hair: over and under, over and under.

'What a nice feeling.'

323

Warmth comes into my body from her fingertips. I close my eyes and can see the face of Mum smiling with dots on each cheek. These are called dimples. *Over and under, over and under…* I can hear her voice. *That's it, be gentle, don't pull too tight.*

There is a rhythm Marlowe uses, like the da dum da dum of my heart when it was not broken.

Over and under, over and under.

And the warmth again, all over my body.

Mum, I say in my heart, *see how she is taking care of me? See how she is doing all right?*

In my mind, it is as if I go through moving photos of Marlowe over the years. The young Marlowe had more energy and spirit. She would buzz around the place like one of her insects. As she got older, the feeling of her changed: like the bark of a tree, her outer skin is now a little rough. I think to myself that she is not like Louis; you cannot tell what she is feeling unless you know her, unless you are like me and can understand what she wants to say but won't let herself. To a stranger I think she might seem a bit hard to figure out. But she isn't. She's quite simple really.

Marlowe

After braiding Harper's thinning hair, I climbed onto her bed and slipped beneath the covers. Navigating carefully around the IV drip and the coloured threads of the heart monitor, I snuggled in beside her.

'I am excited in my heart to meet your Oliver.'

'You can call him Olly.'

'I'd like to call him by his full name because that is the name his mother gave him. Also, Olly is your word for him and that should be in the love between him and you.'

'Okay. Understood.'

'I want you to have this.' She handed me her storybook, open at the last page.

There is a tree in a snowy park in Shang-hi. It is a brilient tree with long branchs and pink flowrs. It is tall and wide and holds many memorys and wishes and speshel secrets from those peple who visit.

The beutiful lady that we met at the begining of this book visits the tree. She stands underneth it near the trunk. A long branch bows down to her. On the end of it she sees a plum. It is in the shape of a hart. She opens her hands and lets it fall into her palms.

Imm-or-tal the tree wispers.

> The lady takes one bite of the plum.
>
> Wen she is finished eating, she reches her hand thrugh the snow into the soil were it is warm. She makes a cosy little hole and plants the hart plum seed.
>
> One day she nos her seed will grow grow grow into a tree and this is how she will live on, imm-or-tal forever.

Beside me, Harper's eyes have closed. Her breath is shallow, eyes racing under their lids.

'May your branches be thick and full with blossoms and colour.' I ran my index finger over the cool skin on her forehead. 'May your fruit be ripe and whole.' I took her hand in mine. The ache in my chest radiated through my body, rising to my throat. 'May the heart of your trunk beat with the pulse of the earth, the sun, the moon, the stars… and everything.'

I lay with her as she napped, looking at my watch every so often. *Now, Olly has landed… He must be going through immigration… Baggage claim… Getting on a bus…* Then, just as the moon dropped into view, the doorbell rang. I leaped out of Harper's bed and ran for the door. I flung it open.

Olly.

My heart stopped.

He let his bags fall to the ground and reached out to pull me into him. I filled my lungs with his scent – traces of thyme from our lab, our London home, his peppermint shampoo, the honeyed sweetness that always lingered on his skin.

He lifted my chin and I couldn't tell where my breath ended and his began.

'I need to tell you something.' Time was something that I was developing a new appreciation of, and I couldn't waste any more of it, with anyone. I inhaled and counted to three, trying to steady the pounding in my chest. 'You know I love you, right?' Words that came so easily to Harper, but words I had to learn how to say.

'I know you do.'

My body sighed.

He looked over my shoulder. I turned and saw everyone had gathered at the door, and they were beaming at us. I wasn't anxious as Olly greeted them, like I'd thought I would be. When he reached Wài Pó, she took his hands into hers and told him that she could tell he was a very smart and kind man. I felt overwhelmed by something… was this happiness? Was it regret that I hadn't let them meet sooner? Or was it just the kind of sadness that had become an ever-present friend?

Olly had reached Dad. At first, they just looked at each other without speaking. Then Dad put his hand on Olly's shoulder and smiled. 'Welcome home.'

Olly nodded. 'Thank you. I'm so glad to be here.' He looked around in his quiet thoughtful way, then he asked: 'Can I meet Harper now?'

Harper

Oliver Michael Sutton. That is his fullest name and part of it is the same as Louis's dad. Oliver is sitting next to me, really sitting next to me, in the flesh. Everyone is in the living room with us, eyes on Oliver meeting me. I cannot see them all because some of them are behind my bed. Even though I am happy I am in the living room, sometimes I find all the feelings very strong, like all the bodies around me are too loud even in the silence and it makes me very tired.

As I am looking at Oliver, I am surprised by the feelings in my heart. Seeing him here, it is like I am now a still ocean that has no need for its waves.

I can hear my own heart and mind tell me that because of this man, my Marlowe will be okay when I am gone.

'Can I hold your hand?' I ask him.

His skin is a little rough and I see that he has dirt under his nails. That is a bit disgusting, but I don't mind because I like the way he holds hands. It is not too tight, not too loose, not too hot or cold. It is dry and warm.

I study his face. He has some freckles like Louis does on his long nose. He has eyes that are just like my Marlowe's – big and round. They are the colour of freshly steamed choi sum. He has a wide mouth and smiles like a happy fish. If I were to use two words to describe him, I would say he is calm and gentle.

'You are a handsome man,' I tell him, 'with the angels of happiness all around. A perfect match for my Marlowe.'

'Eight thirty pm!' Louis comes into the room at full speed. 'Dinner today is much later than normal… but better late than never!' He puts his arm around Oliver's shoulders and takes him into the kitchen. I feel like I want to tell Louis off for doing that as I was enjoying Oliver sitting with me, but I know food is important, and even though I am not eating as much as I used to, Louis still enjoys this activity and it is important that he has things which will keep him happy.

'We'll come back soon.'

The living room lets out a long sigh. Its air is lighter now that there is no one but me in it.

'This is nice,' I tell myself, but just as I am enjoying my time alone, my dad comes into the room carrying a plate of food. It is steamed chicken and rice and vegetables, one of Wài Pó's excellent dishes. I can smell it; I can smell the ginger, the rice wine, the spring onion, the soy. But it does not make my stomach growl and ask for food. My tummy is quiet. How I miss the feelings of hunger and happiness when eating.

'Can I offer you some dinner?' Dad asks.

'Maybe later.'

'Just one bite?'

I give him a look with my eyes. This look my dad knows well. It means not to ask me this same question twice or I will get a little bit upset.

Dad puts the plate on the coffee table.

'Just because I am not eating, it does not mean you have to stop eating.'

'I know. I'm just not very hungry either, darling.' He looks out the window, something he does when his mind and his heart are talking to him. Then I start to have a bad feeling in my chest, because I think I know why my dad is not hungry.

'Dad? Where's Irene?' This is something I should have asked him much earlier.

'She's staying with her friend Tammy.'

I like Tammy, she is very sweet and always brings me a homemade cake or biscuits when she comes to visit.

'Why?'

He looks away again.

'Well…'

I wait, but no words come. He touches the bow tie on his neck. I know this means he is a bit nervous.

'Is it because of me?'

'Oh no, darling, don't you worry.' He looks down at his hands.

But I do worry. The last time I saw her, she was not a stepmonster. She was very kind to me. I know this is the way my dad sees her too. I can see it in the sadness of his downward head.

'I know she feels bad in her heart.'

'She does.'

'Ask her to come. Ask her to come tomorrow.'

My dad lifts his head. 'Thank you, darling. She would really like that.'

Marlowe

I stood in the kitchen doorway, watching Olly make eggs for breakfast. Wài Pó stood beside him, occasionally interrupting his rendition of 'Into the Mystic' with questions about his life in London, his family, his work. As he dolloped spoonsful of butter into the pan, she gasped, then threw her hands into the air and laughed.

'You only live once! Put more!'

I realised that for once she wasn't chewing nervously on a hawthorn candy or a White Rabbit. It occurred to me that she seemed happy.

A tap on my shoulder. Louis.

'Um, Marlowe. Stepmonster is here.'

'What?'

'She's at the doorway, but I did not let her come in.'

'Why?'

'Because she is a stepmonster.'

'Louis!'

I rushed to the door.

Without make-up on, Irene looked like a ghost. Her lips were the same colour as her pale cheeks. Her dark eyes seemed to sink back into their sockets, rimmed with grey. She was dressed in sweat pants and trainers. After I got over my initial shock, I found myself missing the Irene I knew: red-lipped, stiletto-heeled, brimming with confidence.

'I know you don't want me here, but your father said Harper wanted to see me… and I would really like to see her too.'

When she spoke, she seemed small, vulnerable. Without thinking, I gave her a hug. 'I'm glad you came,' I said.

'I'm glad you came too.' Dad was standing in the doorway behind us.

I didn't know exactly how long the two of them had been apart, but I knew I needed to give them space. As I walked back into the house, I turned to look over my shoulder. Dad had taken Irene's hands in his and was gently caressing her palms with his thumbs. I lost my breath for a moment, recalling how he used to do this with Mum. I let myself realise for the first time that Mum wasn't the only woman Dad had ever loved.

❧

I told Harper that Irene had arrived, and she smiled and nodded.

'Thank you,' she said.

We sat together for a while before she cleared her throat. 'I want to ask you something.'

'Shoot.'

'What do you love about me?'

'You're my sister.'

'No.' She shook her head before asking again: 'What do you love about me?'

I thought for a while. How was I supposed to put it into words? I closed my eyes and saw my sister when she was small, dancing in the snow. Her lips were blue and she was about to collapse yet she was not in distress; in fact, she seemed to be somewhere else completely, somewhere I wished I could go. In that moment, I understood the difference between us. It was as if life's loneliness would never touch her. She was the embodiment of happiness. She made it seem simple. As snow fell onto her hair, her forehead, the tip of her nose and her scarred chest, she laughed. I'd thought I felt envy back then, but as I sat with my sister as adults, trying to put these feelings into words, I realised it was something different. She had one foot in this world and one in another – and this 'other world' was one I would never fully understand, no matter how hard I tried in my laboratory. But how was I to put this into words?

'You are magic,' I say. 'Very few people will ever be able to see the world like you do.'

She smiled. 'I like that.' A laboured breath. 'Marlowe?'

'Yes.'

'When I'm gone, you won't forget that… that word for me, will you? I mean… that magic word.'

Would I?

'I won't forget.' I thought of the day my parents brought her home and how, since then, she had enmeshed herself in every fibre of my being. 'I won't forget.'

'Good,' she sighed before resting her head back on the pillow.

'Harper?' Irene walked into the room barefoot. Neither of us had heard her coming.

Harper smiled at her. 'I'm glad you came to see me, Irene.'

I'd never heard her address Irene by her given name before.

'I'll leave you guys to it.' I stood and turned to leave.

'No, stay,' Irene said. 'What I have to say is for you too.' She sat beside Harper's bed and I pulled up a chair beside her.

'I owe you both an apology.' She lowered her head.

'I have had a lot of time to reflect on things. When Marlowe started talking to us about getting you a new heart in China, Harper, I couldn't believe that she would go through with it. And then, when she took you to Shanghai, I began to remember you both as you were years ago, when I first met you. I realised there was so much I didn't understand about what you had been through before I came into your lives.'

I thought about how much I used to loathe her, how often I had wished that Dad had never met her, but now I wondered if this was less about Irene and more to do with the simple fact that she was not my mother.

'Thank you for speaking about your feelings,' said Harper. 'And now, I think I need to tell you something back.' She is silent for an uncomfortable amount of time before she speaks again. 'One: I am not mad at you anymore. Even though I did have some anger at you in my heart about some of the things you said to me, this has gone now because I understand in my heart and in my mind that some things in life are hard and not everyone feels the same way I do and that is okay.' She takes a congested breath. 'Two: this is the most important one. I think that the reason my dad has not married you is not because he does not love you in his heart, but because he is scared about you losing your physical body in the same way our mum lost hers.'

Irene nods, and in a very soft, very hoarse voice she says, 'Thank you.'

'Irene?' Harper says.

'Yes?'

'I have to tell you one more thing. But this is a personal private thing that I am thinking in my brain.'

'Okay...'

'I think that you need to wash your hair and your face and your body and put on one of your red dresses and some pointy shoes. You look bad right now and you don't smell so great. This is the worst look I have ever seen you in, ever.'

Irene laughs. A full, belly laugh, and then, when she snorts, I find myself laughing too.

Harper

I am standing in my dad's special study room with all his books. Marlowe, Wài Pó, Bì Yù, Irene, Aunt Lǐ Nà and Deborah are with me too. In front of me is a long mirror Irene has brought here from her dress shop. I am looking at my beautiful self, wearing my wedding dress. It is like all my birthdays, all the Christmases, all the Chinese New Years and all the days that glow brightly have come together in this one special moment. My hair is in a French braid. My lips are the colour of strawberries from the lipstick that Marlowe painted on for me. There is still an oxygen tube under my nose and the tank is by my side. It is an ugly tank, so Bì Yù said she will carry this for me when I walk down the aisle. Even though I feel a bit wobbly on my feet, it is the first time I have been standing on them in a while, so I am happy.

'You look stunning,' Marlowe says.

'Yes I do.' My hands brush my dress again. It feels thick and smooth under my fingertips. Around my waist, the dress is a bit tight, but then at my hips it puffs out and is long long long behind me. I am in swirly lace from my head to my toes and I feel like a princess from the royal family.

The window is open. I can smell the sea and the earth and jasmine. *Mum, are you here? Are you with me now on my special day?*

336

Wài Pó gives me a bunch of flowers in the colours of pink and red. She tells me the roses are from my dad's garden. Marlowe adds a few thin stems of a very cute and tiny blue flower to this bunch.

'These are forget-me-nots,' she says. 'This is your something blue.'

Forget-me-nots. And then I feel a swimming, happy kind of sadness in my heart. My mum is here. My mum is with me on my wedding day.

'Thank you,' I say to my Marlowe. As I look at her, I think again in my brain about how beautiful she is. Her long hair is tied up on the top of her head the way ballerinas do. Inside this bun she has put a few small yellow flowers. She is wearing a light blue dress that comes to her knees.

Wài Pó takes my hand in hers. Even though she is gentle, I have to say a small 'ouch' when the needle inside my hand moves.

'Sorry,' she says as she puts a very soft, long white glove over my hand. It looks like a very nice white glove and has perfectly round buttons on the side of it. She takes my other hand and puts another glove on that too.

'I wore these on special occasions when I was your age.' She kisses me on the cheek.

'This is your something old,' Marlowe says.

Aunt Lǐ Nà takes out a small red chest and opens it. Inside there is a gold bracelet. I know this is a Chinese thing to do because this is what happens in a Chinese wedding.

'For you.' She puts the bracelet onto my wrist. It is heavy and feels uncomfortable but I don't tell her this personal private information.

'Can I?' Irene stands behind me holding a very shiny pearl necklace. When I nod, she puts it around my neck and clips it at the back. 'This was my grandmother's, my mother's, then mine. It was supposed to be your something borrowed, but I would like you to have it.'

Pearls from the ocean. I run my hands over each wonderful treasure. I feel like a lucky lady with all my jewels and gifts.

'And now it is my turn,' Bì Yù says. In her hand, she holds a hairpin. It is silver with a butterfly on the side of it. Under the light, it glitters. 'This is your something new.' She stands on her tippy-toes and puts the pin in my hair.

Something old, something new, something borrowed and something blue. And now I think to myself that I cannot wait for my Louis to see me with all my jewels and beautiful things on our special day.

'One more thing.' Deborah hands me a book. It is called: *One Hundred Love Sonnets* by Pablo Neruda. 'I thought you would appreciate these words; it is something to feed the lover and the writer in you.'

I feel something in my chest. It is like a waterfall.

'Knock knock.' I turn to see my handsome dad standing in the doorway. He is dressed in a very smart blue suit the same colour as Marlowe's dress. It is the same colour as their eyes.

'My precious girl,' he says with his voice that sounds a bit broken. 'Are you ready?' He pushes a wheelchair for me to sit.

'No.' I shake my head. 'I want to walk.'

'Are you sure?'

I take a breath and nod. Then he holds out his arm for me to take.

'Now I am ready,' I say, because in my heart, I have been ready for a very, very long time.

Outside, the wind is blowing in from the sea. I can taste salt in the air.

'Thank you, sea,' I say. 'You give us pearls and shells. You are the home for all the creatures in your waters, like dolphins and whales and crabs and seahorses. You move in a fast way and a slow way and I love it when I am standing on the beach and your water licks my feet.'

I look up. The sunset has arrived in pink and orange and gold.

'Thank you, sky,' I say. 'You give us sun and rain and clouds that tell us of stories and shapes and patterns. Today, you have made a wonderful sunset for me to marry the love of my heart, Louis.'

My dad walks me through the garden. All around the greenery are candles and fairy lights. Behind me, Marlowe is holding my dress and Bì Yù is holding my oxygen tank in a very careful way. We have only done a few steps together, but my breathing feels tight and my chest feels heavy, so I have to stop for a while. We wait together by the fishpond, where the koi are swimming around in the water waiting for bread. I used to give them bread when I was small but I don't do this anymore.

A drop of sweat runs down the side of my face. I feel a swirling in my belly.

Come on, Harper, I tell myself. *Come on.* But suddenly I don't feel like I can go on. I take another step, but my legs feel shaky and weak.

'Wait,' my dad says. Then he lifts me up, all in one go. 'Let me carry you.'

I laugh, because I think this is a funny way to go down the aisle to meet my love, Louis. I wrap my arms around my dad's neck and lean my head into his chest. His sound is strong and brave, like a soldier's heart.

My dad walks slowly, stepping on the stone path one foot at a time. We pass the old banyan tree, which is covered in coloured lanterns. It is so beautiful that I feel certain there is some magic swimming in the air around it. Thank you, old banyan tree. Thank you for being my friend.

Dad walks on. We pass the bush with red flowers and come to the place where Mum's temple used to be. A sound comes from my mouth, a high sound. In front of me, a new temple has been built. It is made from wood and is the colour of whipped cream. There are red roses all around its arches. Inside, the love of my heart, Louis, is standing tall. His chest is proud. There are chairs all in front of the temple, lots of them, filled with people I love.

'I can walk now.'

Dad gently lowers me to the ground. My dress makes a swishing sound as Marlowe and Bì Yù make all the folds straight.

Music starts to come from a violin and a white piano just like the one Mum used to have. Even though their faces are puffy now and they have some grey hairs, I recognise these people from when Mum was with us on this earth. They are her friends Maxine Tam and Ronnie Chen. As they play, I remember this song in my heart. It was one Mum used to play for me.

I look at the crowd of people in front of me, all here to celebrate this special moment in time. I see all my friends from the vocational centre and from my work at the library, and some of the kind nurses from the heart hospital that I have been going to since I was small. Then there is Oliver, Uncle Bǐng Wén, Aunt Lǐ Nà, Deborah and Michael, and Wài Pó with all her mahjong ladies. I see Uncle Johnny; he winks at me and it makes me smile.

I think to myself that all our guests are so smartly dressed.

'Thank you all for coming,' I say.

'Shall we?' Dad holds out his arm for me to take and we start walking down a carpet made from pink rose petals. The music changes, and Wài Pó stands at the entrance to the temple. She opens her mouth and the most beautiful sound comes out, made from her voice. My chest tingles and it is like shooting stars have filled my heart. Dad squeezes my hand and I squeeze his hand back.

As I get closer and closer to Louis I can see his face clearly. He is crying. *No, Louis,* I want to say, *today is a happy day, this is not a day to cry.* But then my own feeling rises up up up in me and I find myself telling my heart to hold on.

'I am happy here on this earth,' I say.

With silent words, I tell my heart that I don't want to leave. I beg my heart to let me stay.

Marlowe

As bridesmaids, Bì Yù and I stood to the left of Harper in the pagoda we had built for this day. It still smelled of fresh timber and sour, drying paint. Harper and Louis were facing each other, holding hands, the celebrant behind them. Louis's alarm watch then beeped, loudly.

'Oh, shoot.' He switched it off. 'Sorry, everyone,' he said. 'That was just my digital alarm watch reminding me that it is time to get married. Good news! We are ahead of the schedule.'

The celebrant, a woman with funky blue-rimmed glasses, began to speak. I struggled to focus on what she was saying. I was watching Harper. She looked so beautiful. Her features were soft and her almond-shaped eyes made her look like she was forever smiling. Blush and lipstick added colour to her otherwise pale face. With her hair in an elegant French braid and dressed in an ivory lace gown, she looked a bit like Grace Kelly. It was as if she had never been sick.

I felt Bì Yù's hand take mine.

'Repeat after me.' The celebrant spoke to Louis first. 'I, Louis Martin Browne, take you, Harper Míng Huà Eve, to be my lawfully wedded wife.'

Louis cleared his throat and turned to face the guests. 'First of all, I would also like to thank everyone for coming on this special day.'

'Louis,' Harper whispered, 'you have to stick to what the lady says.'

'Ah, yes, sorry.' He kissed her on the hand and cleared his throat again. 'I, Louis Martin Browne...' He looked at the celebrant for help but a friend of his seated nearby got there first.

'Take you, Harper Míng Huà Eve! Come on, Louis!'

'Thank you, Max.' Louis waved at him from the pagoda. 'I would just like to tell everyone that sometimes I forget things.' He turned back to face Harper. 'You see, my brain is not as good as yours, my love.'

Harper put her palm to his cheek and stroked the side of his face. 'It's okay.'

The celebrant spoke more slowly this time. Louis followed her words.

'To have and to hold, from this day forward, for better or worse, for richer or poorer, in sickness and in health, until death do us part.'

Louis bowed his head. His chin was trembling.

'In sickness and in health...' the celebrant prompted.

'I can't do that bit. I can't say that word.'

Harper was barely moving. I was close enough to see a single tear trickle down the side of her face.

'Louis,' the celebrant whispered, 'is there something you would like to say instead?'

He nodded and looked up at Harper. 'I know that the heart inside your chest is sick. I know you are scared. I wish I could make you better but everyone tells me I can't fix your heart, and I am sorry about this. I am so sorry. I wish my brain was different so that I could become a doctor and learn how to fix you, just so that I could have longer with you. But even though I can't do this, I can stand by you and I can love you with all that is inside my heart. My watch

343

cannot tell me how much time is left for you, but no matter what, I will be by your side, as your man, for the rest of my life and yours.'

My chest ached, but I decided not to fight it. I followed the emotion as it rose to my eyes and I let it consume my thoughts. As I watched my sister deliver her vows, I gave myself up to the harsh reality that soon I would no longer hear the scratch of her fountain pen, held the wrong way against paper. I would never see her spinning in the garden or in the snow. I would never again annoy her, never tell her she was being too loud, never feel embarrassed by her, burdened by her, never again tell her to do things my way. I would never hold her, touch her, never smell her, never hear her singing in the kitchen as she helped Wài Pó cook. I would no longer have her as my constant reminder that there is so much on this earth we will never understand with our minds, and that is okay.

Maxine and Ronnie filled the garden with my mother's music as Harper and Louis shared their first kiss as husband and wife. I looked at Olly, who was seated in the front row. He smiled at me and nodded.

As we followed Harper and Louis out of the pagoda, Olly met me and entwined his arm in mine. At that moment, a lemon emigrant butterfly landed on Louis's shoulder in front of us. I held my breath until I could hold it no longer. In my exhale, the butterfly vanished.

Acknowledgments

This book has had a long gestation period, and there are many people to whom I owe my thanks and appreciation.

To Gaby Naher at Left Bank Literary, the very best agent. You have believed in this novel from the start and I am continually thankful our paths crossed all those years ago.

Alex Craig. I am so grateful for the wonderful synchronicities that brought this manuscript to your table. Your deep understanding, guidance and vision for 'the hum' has been such a gift and it has been a great joy and privilege to work with you.

To James Kellow, Robert Watkins, Brigid Mullane and everyone at Ultimo Press. I thank my lucky stars that I have had the chance to be a part of your exciting vision for Australian publishing. Thank you for giving me this amazing opportunity.

Thank you to all at Hardie Grant, especially Sandy Grant, Julie Pinkham and Julia Kumschick and the entire Hardie Grant sales team.

To Ali Lavau for your insightful edits and comments.

To Alissa Dinallo for the stunning cover.

I have had wonderful mentors that have empowered me as a writer. From the very beginning, Mary Lacey Vittachi – in my youth you incited in me a deep passion for storytelling. Anna Maria Dell'oso, you believed in me, and gave me confidence to write. It goes without saying that same applies for Xu Xi, Amanda Hampson, those at The Faber Academy, in particular Kathryn Heyman and the Australian Writers Mentoring Program. Kathryn, I am especially grateful for the way you allowed me a safe space to find my voice.

To those at UTS, especially Delia Falconer and Debra Adelaide. The Australian Society of Authors and the Ray Koppe Young Writers Award, Varuna Writers' House. The Sydney Writers' Room for providing a wonderful sanctuary to write.

There have been so many individuals who have generously given me their time, shared valued expertise and were instrumental in my research and learning. First and foremost I would like to thank Robert Blackburn and the school of Biological Sciences at the University of Sydney. I have loved every minute learning about bugs and butterflies. Rob, watching you work in the lab has been one of the highlights of this writing process for me and I am forever grateful for your patience and time. Thanks to the Society for Insect Studies.

To all the medical professionals who have given me their time and extensive knowledge: Professor David Celermajer, Dr David Stirling, Professor Jeremy Chapman, Professor Liza Thomas, Dr Shravan Varanasi and most of all Dr Matthew Puliyel. You have been beyond generous with your time and knowledge. I have enjoyed pestering you with my many questions and learning so much from your feedback.

To Marge Lo, Fay Wong, Helen Chen, Catherine Platt, everyone at District-15, especially Li Xu and Venkatraman for your time, translation and knowledge.

Last but never least, to my friends and family who have at different stages supported me and my work. To dearest Ana Vanovac. All these years I have been writing, we have been talking. Our conversations about love, life and grief have deepened me, nourished me and have forever changed me.

Simon Westcott for your support and guidance. Anjali Nihalchaand. Witnessing your resilience, grace and wisdom have over the years changed me as a woman and a writer.

Ileana, there is so much I could say. You and I both know how your guidance has deepened me and helped me find my home again and again.

To my fellow talented writers, especially Zoe Knowles for your continual encouragement, support and passion, Jack Stanton-Cameron, Jonas Kubitscheck and Harry Goddard. Thank you all for journeying with me as Harper and Marlowe came to life and supporting me in this very long birthing process.

Jeneffa Soldatic and my fellow actors in particular: Sian Ewers and Daniel Monks for being a large part of my exploration of both Marlowe and Harper.

And to my family: Mathew and Shoba, for always encouraging me. Alisha for enthusiastically reading my work, supporting me and for always talking about books, books and more books. You are the best sister-in-law a girl could have.

Amy Gaspar for your fierce and loyal tiger heart.

To Fulvia and Edward Bent, for your support, advice and knowledge on all things botanical and horticultural.

Leigh Tong, for all your introductions and support.

Alexander. You have been a constant source of strength that has kept me going. You know in a way that few others will, what this journey with Camilla has been like and I'm so lucky to have you as my brother and friend.

To my mother, Marjory Bent. The way you read and write inspires me. Your intelligence, strength and grace has fuelled me. You have always given me every opportunity in the world to blossom.

To my father, John Bent. Your enchantment has been contagious. The magic I found while in nature with you all those years ago, holding tightly to your steady hand, has found its place in my work and will remain in my heart.

To my darling Nihal. Your unwavering faith in me has been my protection, strength and sustenance. As Harper and Louis might say: You are all of my sunrises and all of my sunsets. I find such joy in our love.

Camilla. The pulse of your gentle soul is behind every word on these pages. Without you, 'the hum' would never have found its way into these words and given my life such meaning and grace. You are my muse and one of my greatest loves.